Joseph Glackin hails from Motherwell in the West of Scotland, a former steel town where the common experience he says, a good preparation for his w years in the West African country of war where, as a priest, he worked d and other victims of a disintegrating

CW00740089

He has also worked in child protecti South Sudan, Sierra Leone, South Africa, Rwanda and Eritrea. He presently works as Head of Programme Development for Hope and Homes for Children, a charity working to end institutional care of children worldwide.

By the same author:

A Lone Star Weeps, Thirsty Books (2013)

In Freedom's Shadow

An Inspector Gloria Mystery

JOSEPH GLACKIN

THIRSTY NOIR

First published 2015 by Thirsty Books, Edinburgh
thirstybooks.com

ISBN: 978-0-9932828-0-5

The paper used in this book is recyclable. It is made from low chlorine pulps produced in
a low energy, low emission manner from renewable forests.

Printed and bound by Bell & Bain Ltd., Glasgow

Typeset by Main Point Books, Edinburgh

In memory of John Dayen, Kollie Zinnah and Konah Flomo who, like many of Liberia's children, faced suffering and deprivation with deep courage and unquenchable humour.

Chapter One

What a depressing way to begin a new week, Gloria thought. The rainy season had started with a vengeance and outside, and in some places inside, the rain was pounding down. Years of neglect, and some recent botched repair jobs, meant that her office in the National Police headquarters was damp and uncomfortable. But the report she had in front of her was the real cause of her gloomy thoughts. Gloria's job was to investigate crimes against children and the worst of these still haunted her sleep. This case was not nearly as brutal as some she had come across but somehow the ordinariness of the setting and the casual violence it described just added to its pathos.

She read it again. Prepared by Izena, the report was typically thorough and detached. On Friday of last week a certain Richard Varley, aged 13, had ordered the family houseboy to climb into an empty water barrel 'for a joke', screwed the lid of the barrel back on and gone to school never giving it another thought. Several hours later the cook had opened the barrel to store something and found the houseboy dead inside, suffocated. The dead boy, Titus Moore, aged 15, was Richard's distant relative brought down from his village in northern Liberia to work for the family in return for his board and lodging and having his school fees paid.

It was all the more tragic because she realised she had known the boy herself. He was a quiet polite boy who had played on her nephew Abu's football team. The Varleys lived in an opulent mansion not far from her apartment and were famous, or infamous, 'business people' which here in Liberia could mean almost anything. They were reputed to be, and certainly lived as if they were extremely wealthy, but were also known to be very mean, and had a reputation for treating each other quite badly, never mind those who worked for them. Richard had been sent to America during the war and had been attending school there until his behaviour had become so bad that the family had brought him back to Liberia to 'discipline' him, clearly without much success. Titus on the other hand, the son of a distant relative, had been with the family for eight months and, despite the promises, hadn't seen the inside of a school. He had become a full-time family servant instead.

Although it was nine in the morning it was so dark in her office that Gloria had to light a kerosene lantern to be able to read. The power had just gone off again, and the smoke and heat from the lantern were doing nothing for her temper. Part of her frustration came from the fact that, as far as she could see, her role in this case would only be to steer Richard Varley through the judicial proceedings and ensure he received a fair trial when really she would have preferred to challenge the tradition which allowed this practice of exploiting poor relatives to take place. This was the new Liberia supposedly, so how was it that poor children were still being sent to the city in the hope of an education and were then often abused, and in this case, killed?

She left her office and made her way down the dark corridor to the large room that served as the communal office for the rest of her team. She had been told it was only temporary until their new offices could be decorated but that had been four months and several murders ago and there was still no sign of any new offices. Gloria was even more annoyed because she knew that the Family and Child Protection Unit had only been set up under pressure from several of the bigger NGOs. They had been happy enough, insistent in fact, in having their names and logos attached to everything in the beginning but when they realised that she and the team were capable of running the Unit on their own, without the outside expert help agencies loved to give, they promptly lost interest. Gloria had even been criticised by some of the agencies at their last meeting for being too political and high-profile. What was needed, they said, was more grassroots work in schools and communities. Gloria had pointed out they were a police unit. Their job was to follow wherever the investigation took them. She knew that education and awareness-raising were important but, she had insisted, they had to take second place to real life investigations. Anyway, she thought to herself as she walked towards the office, surely the case of Richard Varley, sad though it was, would not involve too much politics or publicity.

The office was a hive of activity, but more in the manner of a noisy classroom than a police station. She knew they were still on a high after their success in uncovering a network of child exploitation. They still had many painful memories from that investigation but the fact that their novice unit had managed to expose a major trafficking network was a triumph. Unfortunately they had made a lot of enemies as well and Gloria knew when the publicity had died down there would be recriminations. She didn't bother trying to pass any of this on to the team. Let them enjoy their victory.

Another cause of the noise – and, she had to admit, her gloom – was that her deputy Moses Anderson and his wife had gone on a long holiday. She couldn't blame them. He had nearly died and his wife had been close to being put in prison on trumped up charges, but she still missed Moses a lot. Sometimes he had seemed like the only other adult on the team. She really hoped he was enjoying North Carolina where they were visiting Hawa's sister. The fact that he called every other day to ask how things were going suggested that he was already finding the enforced rest and endless family reunions difficult to stomach. Well, he had another five weeks of it to get through. As long as he remembered to bring back those detective novels she had asked for it would be a worthwhile trip for her. She was tired of borrowing tatty novels from her friends at the convent.

'Right guys, let's get the meeting started, we still have work to do. Quick round up on what's happening, what everyone is working on. As far as I know, Izena, you Ambrose and Christian are still working on tracing and reunifying the children from the diamond mine. I thought we agreed all that would be handed over to Global Vision to finish. I know you all feel strongly about this but it's not our job.'

Izena gave her usual slightly disapproving look. She had got used to and in fact had even warmed to the children she had previously not liked very much and she didn't mind Ambrose. Working with Christian, an unreconstructed former fighter from the civil war, she found difficult but she was still unwilling to give up the work.

'We have only seven children left to trace families for, Inspector. Two of them are still in hospital and we are having a real problem finding any relatives for the others. In fact I'm not sure their families even want them back.'

There had been so much publicity about these children that it was unlikely people hadn't heard about them, even in the most remote parts of the country, so unfortunately that might be the case.

'Ambrose, how are you getting on?' Ambrose had been given the grisly task of working with volunteers to dig up the remains of children who had died, partly to identify them but also to include them in the charges against those behind the whole trafficking ring.

'It's a real cemetery there. So far we think we have found fourteen bodies. They all seemed to have been buried in old sheets in shallow graves on the edge of the mine. Identification is almost impossible. We don't have the first thing to work with, just lots of small bones.'

It was an impossibly sad job but Ambrose, former seminarian, fighter and now trainee police officer, seemed not just to be coping but to get enormous satisfaction from it. Each set of bones was treated with the greatest of respect and given they were only a year or two out of the civil war where death had been all too common and many bodies had been buried in unidentified graves, that was a significant improvement.

'And remember,' said Ambrose, 'any remains which are not identified and claimed will be re-buried in the new Memorial Garden.'

The President had announced the setting up of the President's Children's Fund from the proceeds of the sale of the large diamond which had been such a prominent part of the last case. She had also decreed that the first project of the Fund would be the construction of a Memorial Garden for all the children who had been killed in the war with a special section for the victims of the trafficking network. Unfortunately the President had also decided to build the Memorial Garden on the site of another memorial, the one dedicated to the Unknown Soldier, which had been blown up during the war. Her many enemies in government were using this to attack her as 'unpatriotic' and 'ignorant of the sacrifices of the men and women who had fought to protect the country.' Even a Memorial Garden was political dynamite here, Gloria thought. There had been open fighting among Representatives and Senators which represented the fierce struggle for power that continued to plague the country.

Gloria wasn't too concerned with that. She had persuaded the president that as well as a memorial they needed to do something practical and she had agreed to fund the Missing and Abused Children Helpline Organisation, a series of free and confidential phone lines to be set up across Monrovia where any child could call with a worry or complaint and would be guaranteed a response. Despite the unfortunate acronym, MACHO had proved a popular idea across the political and social spectrum and should be up and running by the end of the year.

'Good, let us know if you need any more help. We also have the Varley case which you may have read about, the child accused of killing the houseboy. Of course the CID are keen to keep us away from murder investigations now but we have the job of making sure that Richard

Varley gets a fair hearing. The Chief says this is a test case to make sure the new juvenile justice system is actually working and that will be our role.'

The Chief had forgotten to say that the Varleys were one of the richest families in the country and very well connected.

'For your information the Varleys are very generous contributors to the President's 'Each One Teach One' education campaign and even more importantly her impending election campaign. But, as I said, that's just for your information.' She raised an eyebrow and the younger members of her team, with the exception of Izena, laughed.

Old Alfred slumped in the corner looked up and frowned. He was a true believer in the present government and especially in President Helen Sirleaf. He did not like any criticism of her or her government and was always ready to boast about them having Africa's first female Head of State. It was all a bit galling for Gloria as the same Alfred found it very difficult to take orders from 'this young girl' as he referred to her. He was always ready to explain his theory about how women should not serve in the police except as secretaries or lowly officers because they were not able to think logically about things and were not strong enough for the job. Liberian men and their thoughts and theories never ceased to amaze Gloria – and rarely in a good way!

'They've got Richard Varley in a cell downstairs so I will interview him now before he goes to the hearing at noon. Paul, you come with me and Alfred.' 'Young' Alfred, although they had stopped calling him that at his request. 'I want you and Lamine to make sure all the reports are up to date. Yes I know it's not the most exciting work but we need to keep a written record of everything we do and keep it up to date. At some time in the future we will have to defend the things we are doing today, you can be sure of that.' There was subdued muttering as they went off to their various tasks and Gloria and Paul went to talk to Richard Varley.

Richard was a skinny boy with bad skin and a bad attitude, but the splayed legs and deep frown couldn't disguise the fact that he was very frightened. Gloria had to remind herself that his thoughtless bad-boy behaviour had apparently caused the death of someone else, and all just for a humiliating joke. But on the other hand, from what she had read, his family background wasn't exactly supportive. Lots of money and little or no attention, shunted off to America and then brought back when his behaviour became embarrassing and dumped in the family home with a succession of strangers who could look after him but couldn't help him with discipline or guidance. There certainly didn't seem to be a whole lot of people stepping forward to testify that he wasn't bad, just misunderstood. The preliminary report said the cook had found the body and called the police before telling the family elders because, in her own words, 'those people will just keep everything secret.' It was no coincidence that the old lady, who had been with the family for many years, was retiring that week and had told other staff in the house how mean the family had been to her after all her years of service. All of this added up to an unlucky set of circumstances for this boy who would probably otherwise just have been punished by his grandfather without any investigation by the police while poor cousin Titus would have disappeared without a mention.

'Hello Richard, my name is Inspector Sirleaf.' She had decided to go for the more formal approach estimating that his would work better with someone like him. 'I want you to just tell me what happened yesterday morning, in your own words.'

'What are you people goin to do to me?' He spoke with an American drawl learned from movies and practiced in his posh boarding school in New York. But his one sprawled leg tapping up and down in a very distracting way let Gloria and Paul see how nervous he was.

'Let me repeat the question for you Richard, I think it is easy enough to understand. You are going to tell us in your own words what happened yesterday and then we will explain to you the next stage of this process. If you tell us the truth it will be better for you in the long run. Whatever you do you will be going to court in two hours time. If we understand what happened, it will be much easier for us to help you.'

For all his nervousness Richard's stubborn reflex refusal to give in to authority was stronger. She could see him struggling with himself, desperately wanting to accept the offer of help but at the same time defying them to force the story out of him. If this is what he's like when he's scared and in real trouble, Gloria thought, he must be a nightmare under normal circumstances. But both Gloria and Paul left Richard to his own internal fight. After some moments he started speaking in a tight-lipped monotone which was never going to endear him to whichever magistrate he was going to appear before. Magistrates in Liberia preferred a deferential tone and in the absence of that might settle for faltering, hesitant or even incoherent but not this defiant, reluctant one.

'I were ready for go to school' – Richard now seemed to have settled on Liberian English as his preferred mode of communication – 'but that boy, that boy is too lazy. He not fix no breakfast for me, nuttin, and I were gapping too much. So I got mad and I punished him. That's all, eh this is Liberia, anything can happen.'

'You didn't punish him Richard. You locked him in a barrel and he suffocated. You know what that means don't you? It means he couldn't breathe, and when all the air ran out he died. All because you were hungry and he hadn't made any breakfast for you. Is that it?'

She stopped. It was strange, she had really wanted to feel some sympathy for him and he was doing all he could to prevent that.

'Is there anything else you want to say?' The boy was silent. 'Because now you will go to court and the magistrate will decide what happens next. As you are only thirteen you can't go to prison – well, you shouldn't go to prison but if he decides to ignore the new rules, the magistrate may send you to prison anyway, they're full of twelve and thirteen year olds already.'

Richard had stopped tapping his foot and straightened up. 'Prison? You can't send me to prison, I'm only a child.'

'Well, maybe in New York but you are back home now and, although your family is rich, there are a lot of people who want to see you punished severely. As you say, anything can happen here.'

That had the desired effect and Richard's swagger reduced considerably.

'But it was an accident, I didn't mean to hurt him, he was my cousin and my only friend in that house.'

'Right, and who else was around while you were doing it?'

He hesitated. 'Nobody, there was no-one else around at the time.'

Gloria leaned back and let Paul jump in. 'So you did this for a joke or a punishment Richard and there was no-one around to see you doing it. I thought that would be the fun of a joke or even a punishment, that other people can see you doing these things? When I was your age that was how it went.'

'Well, I'm not sure, it was early and it was dark down there, I don't really remember.' He looked as if he had been cornered. 'I really don't remember.'

They were obviously not getting the whole story but it looked as if Richard had said all he was going to say. Gloria remembered they were supposed to be helping him through the judicial process as part of their child protection remit so she stopped the questioning.

'Ok Richard, when you go before the magistrate I think you should just talk the way you have been talking now, never mind the different accents, just speak quietly and respectfully.'

'Are you going to be there?' he asked.

Gloria looked at Paul. She wasn't sure, none of this had been tried before and really shouldn't he be accompanied by a social worker and a lawyer? She didn't really know.

'It's not really our job Paul but ask Izena to see if she can get a social worker from one of those children's organisations to come with us to the court. Better get him some food as well, he's obviously dangerous when he's hungry.'

Ouch, she thought, that had slipped out and not everyone appreciated her sense of humour. Paul appeared not to notice and left. Gloria looked at Richard who seemed to be drained of all energy now and was sitting slumped but in a tired not a defiant way.

'Your family have brought some clothes for you to wear so eat something and then you can wash and change your clothes.'

'I really didn't mean to kill him, really Titus was my friend but I sometimes I just act very bad, it's like I can't help it. Maybe I should go to prison, maybe that would help me.'

This child changed so much, so very quickly.

'Just get ready for court, answer the questions you are asked truthfully, and no slouching or slurring.'

Chapter Two

This was Gloria's first sight of the new juvenile court and she wasn't impressed. It was a perfect miniature of the adult courts. Whichever agency had funded this, she thought, had really not been thinking about children at all. The main court room was smaller than the adult court but no less imposing. She took in the wood panelling, gilt handrails around the raised witness stand, and the presiding judge or magistrate's throne-like chair on a high platform. So whatever the intention had been, the effect on children was going to be just as daunting as the adult court. Whether victims or accused, children were not going to feel any more comfortable in this environment. Gloria was starting to get annoyed. This was so typical, lots of money wasted on decoration and a nice finish for something that was not going to work. She smiled though when she saw the statue of Justice which had been placed behind the judge's chair. It was beautifully carved with the scales and the sword in a dramatic pose but some joker had removed the blindfold from the eyes and tied it around the mouth instead. She pointed it out to Paul and told him to fix it as discreetly as he could.

The court had been officially opened by the Chief Justice two weeks earlier. He had hailed it as a sign of the new Liberia's commitment to 'reforming the justice system to strengthen the rule of law', whatever that meant. Unfortunately, more serious than the fixtures and fittings was the reality that they had no system for dealing with juveniles. There was still only the Central Prison in Monrovia so if a child was convicted of a serious crime they were going to end up in an adult prison, and the community courts which were supposed to deal with less serious issues had not even been set up yet. Gloria had attended a very interesting workshop on restorative justice led by a former Ugandan judge who had explained it had taken years to set up a very successful system in her country. It had all sounded so positive but so very different from their situation.

Like anything new in town, the court and this, its first official case, had attracted a great deal of attention. The media led by Rufus Sarpoh

– self-styled investigative reporter – were interviewing anyone they could find and there seemed to be no shortage of volunteers. Several prominent politicians and the new head of the CID, as well as numerous well-meaning aid workers, were all admiring their handiwork and giving their opinion on Liberian justice. After only five minutes Gloria realised she would have to speak to the judge or this case was going to turn into a circus. She went through to the back of the court, flashed her ID card and knocked on the door of the small preparation room.

On opening the door, she recognised the judge as Dorothy Weah. She didn't know whether that was good or bad. Dorothy was one of Liberia's great political survivors. She had been a minor government official before the war, had escaped from the city before the fighting had reached the capital and returned in time to have a number of positions in the transitional governments without upsetting any of the real power players. She had then joined Taylor's elected government, resigned before it fell and was now apparently back under the patronage of the current President, Helen Sirleaf. Most other appointees had been in office just long enough to steal whatever they could before being re-shuffled, or arrested.

Dorothy Weah was preening herself – there was no other word for it – in front of a long mirror.

'Good afternoon your honour, could I have a word. I'm Inspector Sirleaf from the…'

'Oh I know who you are Inspector, everyone does, so no false modesty. Why are you here, surely you haven't started arresting judges along with government ministers and businessmen now?'

Gloria could feel her hackles rising. She had intended to be polite and reasonable, had even wondered if she could gain an ally here at the juvenile court but it didn't look as if that was going to happen. She knew she had upset a lot of people in the establishment, not because they feared she would come after them but because she had shown the patronage system could be beaten, and that worried them.

'Not yet your honour. I've been assigned to work with the accused in this case until everyone is familiar with the way the new system is going to operate. And that's what I wanted to talk to you about. There are a lot of people out there who are not connected with the case directly. In fact the court room looks more like a film set.'

Judge Dorothy Weah stopped fiddling with her clothes and her hair and looked at Gloria.

'A film set? That would be your expert opinion would it? And how would that be a problem for you? Maybe it's because you don't have the starring role, is that it?'

'It's not my opinion your honour, it's all explained in the new Juvenile Justice Guidelines which were published last month.' She suspected Judge Weah had not even read them. 'The only thing I'm concerned about is that the accused, this child, gets a fair hearing under the new system we have worked so hard to put in place and I don't think that can happen if we have everyone crowding in looking for some entertainment.'

The judge paused and then turned to face Gloria.

'Inspector, let's be honest here. This country is sick and tired of children who are out of control and violent. What people want to see is that children who kill and steal are punished and locked up, that's what's going to bring back some security. And that is what the government wants this court to do. So no, we are not going to sit around and consult some set of guidelines and ask them how they feel and is there something in their past that made them behave or act in the way they did. If they act like adults they will be treated as adults. This Juvenile Court will help us to do that more quickly, more effectively and more visibly.'

Gloria was well aware that the flexibility in the new Guidelines as to how trials involving children should be conducted might be used against the children rather than to support them, but hadn't expected this. What a mess! If only all those well meaning people from around the world who had spent so long working with them to develop the Guidelines could hear this.

But she should have seen something like this coming. Since the end of the war the analysis of who was responsible for the violence and destruction had changed. So while the warlords who had led the fighting and profited from it had gone on to pursue careers in government or business and even in the church – there were several former warlords who were now pastors in their own churches – the children who had fought, or rather been manipulated or threatened into fighting, were now being portrayed as the main offenders, even the cause of the violence and breakdown.

'You can go Inspector, this is my court and you will keep to the rules.'

Fuming, Gloria left and went back into the main court room which was now packed with people. *Richard Varley will be lucky if he isn't* lynched on the spot, she thought.

She spotted Peter Dennis, the new Minister of Social Welfare, hovering at the back and trying not to give interviews. He had just been appointed after his boss decided to resign to 'spend more time with her family' when the Ministry had become implicated in a wide scale trafficking scandal. It was good for the Ministry that Dennis was less politician and more technocrat but he was still nervous, knowing the political establishment were furious about what had happened. She went over to him but before she could explain how worried she was about her conversation with the judge, all the police radios in the room, of which there seemed to be a great many, crackled into life and people started moving around, listening in or responding. The CID officer came over to speak to them.

'Sorry for interrupting Minister but there's been a riot at one of the schools in town, GW Horton on Carey Street.' They both looked surprised, it wasn't one of the roughest schools by any means.

'A riot? What do you mean?' The Minister looked wary – although this was a police matter and not a Ministry of Education matter, he knew it would somehow end up on his desk.

'The children were protesting about the food in the canteen and then set fire to the administration buildings and assaulted the principal when he tried to talk to them. The police called for back-up and the riot police went in. Unfortunately the rioting has spread and students from Haybrook Mission, and Holy Redeemer have joined in. There is complete chaos in the centre of town. We are all being recalled now. Probably you too Inspector.'

Gloria nodded, she didn't carry a radio herself but she could see Paul waving frantically at her across the room.

'You're right, I think I have to go.'

The court room was rapidly emptying as the news of the riots spread with police and reporters heading towards the trouble and everyone else heading off to collect children from school or buy emergency provisions – people's reactions in an emergency were automatic now. There was soon no-one left in the court except Richard Varley standing forgotten with Clementine, one of the social workers from the St Luke's project. Judge Dorothy Weah chose that moment to come through the court and for a few awkward moments there were just four of them crowded in the exit.

'Can I take it you've adjourned the hearing then your honour?'

Gloria couldn't help herself. 'It's just that no-one bothered to inform us, and you're the last to leave. Well, apart from us of course.'

'Of course I've adjourned Inspector. Just take the boy back to police headquarters and I will inform you of the new date for the hearing.'

'Well actually your honour, that will be a problem. We are all on standby for the riots plus we are not allowed to detain children in the cells for longer than forty eight hours and that's already past. We were going to ask you to allow him to go home under supervision from his family.'

'His grandfather is waiting in the car,' Clementine added helpfully. 'He's willing to post any amount as bail.'

'Well, there's no need for bail in the case of a juvenile, as I'm sure your honour knows, but you need a sworn affidavit from his guardian that he will observe the bail conditions and return to court when called. Your honour could do that right now, even a written version could be witnessed by us.'

Dorothy was stuck. She was desperate to get out of the court but she was responsible.

'Go bring the grandfather,' she barked at no-one in particular while pulling out a sheet of paper from her Gucci briefcase. She was writing as Gloria went out to the waiting jeep and rapped the window. The driver's side window rolled down so she had to crane her neck to speak into the back seat.

'The hearing has been postponed. If you come and sign an affidavit you can take Richard home until a new hearing date is fixed.'

There was silence and then the back door opened and Africanus Varley got out. He was a huge man dressed in a chief's gown with a beautifully carved walking stick and a huge pair of dark glasses. He didn't speak, just walked into the lobby where he towered over everyone. Richard shrunk back at the sight of his grandfather. There was clearly one person at least he was afraid of – and even Dorothy lost some of her hauteur. She started to explain what the paper signified but Gloria took it out of her hand saying.

'The rioting is getting closer, there are mobs out at Bye-Pass now, we better let these people go.'

With the paper signed, Richard was handed over with the agreement that Clementine would check on him every day. It was only as the jeep sped off Gloria realised she had never heard Africanus Varley's voice, he had not spoken a word in the ten minutes it had taken to sign Richard over. He was probably too important to speak to them she thought.

Now there was only Clementine and herself on the steps. 'Thanks Clementine,' she said. 'I'm heading back to headquarters first. Do you need a lift anywhere?'

'But I thought you said the riots were already at Bye-Pass. If you go down there on your own you could be in trouble.'

'I don't really know where the riots are, but then neither did Judge Dorothy and it helped her to make up her mind.'

Clementine laughed, said she was going back to her offices in Congo Town and disappeared.

As if on cue Paul appeared from the side of the building. Gloria was sure he didn't look so officious on purpose but she had the distinct impression that he and Ambrose were vying to replace Moses as her trusted sidekick and confidante which was never going to happen. Apart from their newness on the job, they were only half adults as far as she was concerned, they were getting there but there was a long way to go.

'What's the news from town then, are things under control yet?'

'No, ma'am, the opposite in fact,' Paul was hurrying her to the car, 'there's complete chaos in town by the sounds of it, hundreds of children have left their schools and others are moving towards the town.' He gestured to the growing crowds of schoolchildren on the road in front of them who were chanting and singing as they headed to the town centre.

'Haven't they closed the town centre off? That should have been the first priority.'

'Apparently the riot squad were anxious to deal with it themselves but according to Alfred they just made it worse. There's already reports that they invaded GW Horton where the students were occupying the canteen and attacked them, using tear gas and batons. The sight of students being dragged out the school by their friends with blood and torn clothes caused both panic and anger and within minutes students from Haybrook and Holy Redeemer were pouring down there. Doesn't Abu attend Holy Redeemer?'

Gloria just nodded. She really hoped he wasn't involved in this but the familiar sinking feeling in her stomach told a different story.

'So another brilliant intervention by us, for all the training we've had it feels like we only know one way to respond and that's with batons and boots. Of course talking to these kids would have been seen as weakness.' She remembered what Judge Weah had just said about people being tired of seeing children who were out of control and violent.

Chapter Three

The road down to police headquarters was normally bustling with traffic and people but was now absolutely empty except for the cars heading in the opposite direction.

Headquarters was similarly empty and from the top floors it was possible to see smoke rising from the centre of town. There were scores of police vehicles in the streets around the town centre but judging by the noise the police hadn't yet regained control. Chief Inspector Kamara, now acting Police Director, had called her to his office. The acting head of CID, Inspector Barnyou and her friend Lawrence Boakai, the Head of the Traffic division, were also there. An odd collection of departments to deal with a riot but the constant upheavals within the police force meant that responsibility was allocated on the basis of whether the Chief Inspector trusted you and not on whether you had the correct title or uniform.

'Gloria, we have a problem.' As that was the only time she was ever invited to this office, she guessed as much. 'The riots are spreading and at the moment we have lost control of the city centre. I don't think the riot squad handled it very well.' Lawrence gave her a quick grin and made one of those hand signs he picked up from the American TV shows he loved. She had no idea what it meant and gave him a half wave in return.

'I agree, I don't think gassing and beating up school children is going to do us any good.'

Barnyou didn't even give Kamara time to respond. 'Come on Inspector, by all accounts those children were out of control. And you know as well as I do that many of them are not really children. The schools are full of ex-fighters who are angry, bored and used to violence.'

'Well, even more reason not to take them on with force, they would just see that as a challenge. Why didn't somebody talk to them?'

'And have you seen the streams of children heading into the town? My officers are reporting crowds of them on Bye-Pass and most of them are certainly children.' This from Lawrence whose Traffic department had the best equipment and most up to date vehicles, as if traffic control was Liberia's most urgent post-war challenge.

'Look, it's too late for 'should haves' and too early for post mortems, right now we have to get this under control before anyone else gets hurt or there's any more damage.' The Chief liked simple solutions and direct action. 'There have been some scuffles with market traders down near the barracks and a few attempts to break into the supermarkets on Randall Street but no real damage yet.'

I'll bet, thought Gloria. The mostly Lebanese shop owners in town had survived years of threats and looting during the war, they were hardly going to allow school children, however big and tough, to break into their premises.

'I would suggest sir that the first thing you have to do is stop any more children from getting into town. Set up some police roadblocks on the main streets and start turning them back but without any fuss.' She looked at Lawrence. 'Maybe Inspector Boakai could do that as his people know the streets so well.'

'Good idea. Boakai get on to that right now. Put the roadblock at Bye-Pass as they all have to come in that way, I presume they won't try to crawl through the swamp. But handle them gently, we don't need another angry mob heading back up into Sinkor. The army are putting a small contingent of soldiers out to guard the banks and other buildings but they have been told not to engage with the children. The President was asked to leave the Executive Mansion but she refused of course so there is some extra security around the Mansion but it is up to us to sort it out. The Defence Minister' –'acting' Minister, thought Gloria – 'has said if it is not dispersed by nightfall he will put the army on the streets. He says that people are nervous and angry and the children will be in danger if they don't go home.'

Lawrence got up to leave but Gloria stopped him. 'I think we also need to get the parents to go into town and take their children out of this. These are schoolchildren not rebel fighters. They are now over excited and dangerous but they are still children. I think the sight of their mothers and fathers will stop most of them. Maybe Lawrence can give us some of his escort vehicles, the ones with the speakers on them and we will start going around informing people and maybe you can issue a statement on the radio and TV telling people to go for their children especially parents with children at those three schools. Let them know they shouldn't be afraid.'

The Chief looked at her and smiled. 'Another good idea Gloria, right get on with it. Barnyou, get me an update and make sure your officers have stopped beating up those children. There will be repercussions you know.'

Barnyou looked gloomy rather than angry. He hated this job.

'I will do my best sir but they may have to use force on some of those older ones. It's not as easy as Inspector Sirleaf says, and I think encouraging more people to head into town is a very high risk strategy. But if those are the orders I will get on with them. I'll get you that report as soon as possible.'

On their way out Lawrence pulled her over. 'Gloria, I don't think you know how serious this is, there is real fighting going on down there.'

'I know Lawrence but they are still children or young people. There seems to be this growing opinion that they are all out of control, that they were responsible for the war, and that now we are going to take out on them all the things we couldn't do to the leaders and the politicians.'

She told him about Judge Weah and her comments.

'If we're not careful we are going to end up giving these children more cause to fight. Most of them had nothing to do with the war and the ones who did were forced or manipulated into taking part. But now, instead of looking at the ones who were really responsible, we are going to punish the children. It doesn't make sense.'

Lawrence recognised the truth of what Gloria was saying. Recently the newspapers, politicians, and the 'public' had all started to talk about getting the children back in line, of getting back to their traditions and the respect there used to be for adults. It had all made perfect sense to him until he listened to Gloria.

'Lord, you know me Gloria, I just hear it and pass it on.'

Gloria stopped and looked at him. 'Well, maybe it's time you did a bit more than that then. You are one of the smartest people I know but you never seem to have an opinion of your own. Do you have any opinions or is "dey say" – the local name for the rumour mill which never slept – 'enough for you?'

There wasn't time for any further discussion and they went downstairs in an awkward silence. They had been close friends since their days at the Police Academy but the last few moments was the nearest they had ever come to a disagreement. Lawrence was the most reliable source for gossip, or 'local information' as he called it, in the entire force. He knew just about everyone from street kids and market traders to politicians and senior officials.

Gloria wondered why Lawrence's lack of opinions was annoying her so much today. He had always been like this and it had never been an issue before.

It was only a few moments until they reached the garage and Lawrence handed her and Paul the keys to two of the Presidential motorcade vehicles. Equipped with loudspeakers, they were usually used to warn vehicles and people to clear the road when the President was travelling anywhere. Today, thought Gloria, they could do something more useful. She briefed Paul on what they were going to do. He would drive through Sinkor, Old Road and Congo Town and she would try and get across the bridge to New Kru Town. If they could reach at least some of the parents and persuade them to come for the children it might help. It was also a risk but the only other option seemed to be to turn the troops on them. The last time the army had invaded an educational establishment was their attack on the university in the 1980s and scores of people were killed or injured. No-one wanted a repeat of that.

They would have to cover most of the city if they were going to reach all the parents because both Holy Redeemer and Haybrook were private schools with very good reputations and students came from all over the city to attend them. Her nephew Abu had transferred to Holy Redeemer just this year because she thought he would get a better education. She hoped he had been sensible and gone home but he wasn't answering his mobile phone.

Gloria took Alfred with her and allocated Ambrose to go with Paul, ordering Izena to stay in the office and keep them updated. She turned the vehicle out of headquarters and down the road into town determining to stay on Bye-Pass and hopefully reach the bridge without encountering marauding children. The street was empty of traffic and they sailed through the checkpoint which Lawrence had already put in place. As they came down the hill to Broad Street it was a different story, there were children everywhere chanting and singing. It was strange because it could have been a scene from the war when the rebels arrived in town except that almost all the children were still in their school uniforms or some version of the uniforms. T-shirts tied around their heads, shirts open, trousers rolled up and high on the excitement and the danger.

The thrill and the excitement were part of the problem, Gloria thought not for the first time. Most of them were bored. There was so little for them to enjoy and it was only the daily grind of looking for food and medicine or the hours spent in hot overcrowded classrooms in the hope of a 'better future' that kept these children under control at the best of times. They saw too much in the movies and from their friends who had left the country. Colourful pictures from abroad of a life where young people seemed to spend most of their time enjoying themselves and the comparisons with their existence must be painful. Here we expect them to act like adults: earn money, look after their brothers and sisters, go to school and at the same time we treat them like children, never listening to them or letting them speak.

Her thoughts were interrupted just before they reached the turn-off for the bridge. The car was suddenly surrounded by a mob of dancing children, sweat pouring off them, who were chanting the latest street hit 'Who Are You'. The tune was familiar to Gloria through Abu and the words had become the latest war cry for the city's youth.

> You say you are my parents but I must buy my own food;
> who are you?
> You say you are my teacher but I have to give you money;
> who are you?'

And so on. It had sounded like just another song but in these angry mouths now it sounded more like a threat. But the children were not really intent on confrontation, they banged on the car doors and the roof but let it go through. Some of them even started waving in when they recognised Gloria who had become an unlikely role model for many of the girls. Others, boys and girls, were shouting at Alfred who as well as being a police officer also played semi-professional football. His winning goal two weeks ago against the Chad national team had turned him into a local celebrity.

Gloria had discovered that being a local celebrity had only increased the jealousy among her fellow officers and was a real hindrance when investigating a case but today it was proving useful. Although, to be fair, the mob, if such it was, was ignoring most passersby and nearby shops and houses, intent only on the demonstration. Since they were so close she told Alfred to drive up Ashmun Street first, in the hope she might see Abu outside Holy Redeemer.

The top of Ashmun Street was dominated by the Holy Redeemer

cathedral and school. The crowds outside here were all adults who seemed to be milling around without much purpose. She told Alfred to let her out and go on up the hill at the back and talk to any parents he could find. She crossed the road, waved at the crowd of priests and nuns who were standing around outside the cathedral but kept walking over to the teachers and, she presumed, parents who were on the road outside the school. She went straight over to Francis Bryant who was standing alone a few yards from the others.

Francis was a tall slightly stooped man with the air of a college professor. Few people knew that only a matter of months ago he had been the leader of a gang of 'socially aware' criminals living in the rocks down by the American Embassy. He had helped her before with useful information but impressed her more with his ability to teach and communicate. Gloria had persuaded him and then helped him get back to his original profession of teaching. The dire shortage of trained teachers meant that his talent and experience had been welcomed and he was a big success with the students.

'Hello Francis, classes suspended are they?'

Francis gave his small smile. 'The children decided to leave early Inspector. I think some of your colleagues inspired them to some direct action.' He paused. 'Are you looking for Abu? I'm afraid he went off with his classmates, they were pretty fired up.'

'What actually happened? Couldn't you stop them?'

'Some of the children from GW Horton came up here running away from your officers. They were in a pretty bad state, torn clothes, blood running down their faces and quite hysterical. The word spread in minutes that children were being attacked by the police and the older children just streamed out. No-one could have stopped them. We just made sure the smaller ones stayed in the classrooms. I don't blame them but it's not a good situation.'

Gloria explained her idea of getting parents to go down and collect their children as a way of diffusing the situation. Even hardened veteran Bryant looked shocked.

'Inspector you're not seriously encouraging people to go down there. It will only increase the chaos and then someone will definitely get hurt. We've got parents here and there is no way they are going any further down the street. There is real fighting going on around GW Horton and Haybrook and the only reason it hasn't reached here is because we've got the 'men in white'' he indicated back to the crowd of priests in their white cassocks. 'The sight of them deterred your riot squad and then the archbishop started blasting them and they turned away. Instead of sending parents down I think you should take your people out, they have so over-reacted and it's only going to get worse.'

A voice calling her name distracted her before she could answer and she turned round to face Archbishop Francis Gray. He looked grim and anxious.

'Inspector Sirleaf isn't it? What is going on?' Archbishop Gray was famous for his fiery temper, his loud laugh and his deep commitment to social justice although there was no sign of the famous laugh today. 'Can you tell me what is happening and is there any way we can help?'

'I only know as much as you do bishop, I came here to try and mobilise parents to go down and fetch their children but I think I have underestimated the seriousness of the situation.'

'Well, probably not the seriousness Inspector but I would say you are targeting the wrong people. Army, security personnel, police – we never seem to get it right in this country. You have armed riot police attacking schoolchildren in their schools! That is an international crime you know.'

'Until we know what is really going on bishop I don't know what to say but your people could go home if they wanted. The children on Bye-Pass are not stopping traffic.'

'Well, we have decided to stay. If we hadn't been here those thugs' – she took that to mean the riot squad – 'would have been all over this school as well. We can't afford to keep on rebuilding and renovating.' The school and other buildings had been badly damaged twice during the war.

'What might be helpful would be for you to go on the radio and start reassuring people, everyone will have their radios on by now looking for information.'

There were four or five popular radio stations in town and one of them was Radio Caritas, the Catholic station which was on the same property as the cathedral.

'Not a rant now bishop, just try and calm things down.'

'I heard from your Chief Inspector how fond you were of giving orders to your superior officers Inspector, I hadn't realised you had extended that to the church as well, but thanks for your wise counsel.'

Gloria was sure she caught the beginnings of a smile on his face as he spoke but squirmed all the same. This was the man who had broadcast to the capital for eight hours as rebel groups had advanced on the city two years ago, urging people to be calm, to help their neighbours, telling them where the shelters were and calling on all armed groups to respect the 'civilians'. He had only stopped when the power was cut off and the radio station surrounded. The station had been burnt to the ground and the archbishop had been taken prisoner. He never talked about what he went through on the days that followed but his eyes had the haunted look of many of those who had survived violence and torture during the war.

Delighted to be active, the archbishop was already over talking to his people and organising them. Gloria turned back to Francis but he had disappeared. She got on the phone and tried calling the Chief Inspector. When there was no answer she rang through to Lawrence who answered on the first ring.

'Lawrence, how are the checkpoints?'

'It's quiet here, most of the children have turned back and the President has very cleverly opened the Executive Mansion grounds so for that crowd it's like a big party. She came out and spoke to them and they are now playing football and kickball on the grass.'

'She always gets it right, doesn't she? But Lawrence, I was wrong,' she paused and waited for his funny comment but there was none. 'This is much more serious than I realised. Why didn't Barnyou speak up at the meeting and tell me what was really going on?'

'Well, maybe he didn't know everything and besides,' he paused, 'sometimes Gloria it's really hard to tell you anything.' His tone was serious. 'And you forget how dangerous this town still is. If you want to be Miss Apple…'

'It's *Marple*, Lawrence.'

'Huh?' She had stopped him in mid flow again.

'I think the lady you are talking about is Miss Marple. She's the old lady who solves crimes and helps…'

'Yes, whatever. I'm just saying that if you want to be Miss Mappo' – Gloria bit her tongue – 'you will need to go and live in a different country, it aint goin to work here.'

Gloria decided this wasn't the best time for a discussion on the relative merits of fictional detectives and their crime-solving methods. Nor was it the time to explain that she didn't read those books for ideas on how to be a good detective. She just liked a good story. Lawrence was clearly very stressed so she moved the conversation on.

'I've told Paul to stop urging people to go for their children. The town centre is very tense right now. The Chief needs to get down here and see this for himself. I just spoke to Archbishop Gray, he and a lot of other people are saying we should pull out the riot squad altogether, that they caused the trouble and they are keeping it going. Barnyou won't like that idea though.'

'Well, the number of children being taken to hospital is increasing. There are pick-ups going through here with children in the back with all kinds of injuries. It will be a miracle if no-one is killed.'

She told him what she had asked the archbishop to do and that she and Alfred were coming back to try and meet the Chief.

'Are you ok there?'

'Come on Gloria, we are Traffic police. Everyone knows we have shiny vehicles, nice uniforms and that we sometimes harass innocent motorists for small money but they also know we don't throw people in jail or beat up children. They are not angry with us. Get back over here.'

'I will but I am going to go down town first and see for myself what's going on.'

'Is that wise Gloria? What have I just been telling you? Even a national hero like you won't be safe in the middle of a riot.'

'You really need to read those books Lawrence. Miss Marple does her best work from behind the curtains not on the edges of an angry crowd. This is all my own work. But I will be careful.'

'Please, watch yourself.' He signed off.

Chapter Four

Alfred was delighted at the thought of having a look at the town centre before they headed back. Gloria knew he relished a bit of adventure and suspected he was hoping for some dramatic stories he could share with his colleagues back in the office. She could do without the adventure but hoped she might get some first hand information about what was really happening. She also had a vague hope she might see Abu – concern for his safety was a niggling worry at the back of her mind.

The change as they drove slowly down Broad Street towards Carey Street was very noticeable. As they moved towards the town the crowds of children increased in age and in size. There was a very different atmosphere and before they had even turned into Carey Street, Gloria could feel the tension in the air. Added to that, the children had been out in the sun for hours now and were clearly dehydrated and she knew it could go very wrong very quickly. At the bottom of Carey Street GW Horton school was still the focus of the trouble. There was a lot of debris strewn across the road and children were sitting and lying at the side of the road, some tired and some wounded, but the shops and supermarkets, all their steel shutters closed, had not been damaged. In fact some of the Lebanese and Indian business people were standing outside their shops chatting to each other and to the children. Some were drinking the strong aromatic coffee they loved and it looked as if all of them had been handing out water and food to the children. Gloria stopped when she saw Hassan standing outside his jewellery shop. He looked very relaxed and when he saw Gloria he sent his assistant to bring her a cup of coffee. Gloria was delighted, just what she needed.

'You don't look worried Hassan considering you have only a few steel bars between all that gold and silver and these rioters.'

Hassan just raised a perfectly groomed eyebrow. 'I survived the war Inspector. These are just children and, by the way, most of them have been very well behaved. Unlike your colleagues. Hello Alfred, keeping the Inspector safe are you?'

Alfred played on Abu's football team, Struggle United Sports Association, and Hassan was one of their main sponsors.

'Mr Hassan, is everything safe with you? Have you seen Abu?'

Hassan shook his head, handing Gloria her coffee. 'I haven't seen him Alfred but I hope he isn't down there in that school. All this is just playacting,' he indicated the children on the street in front of them, 'but I hear a group of children have barricaded themselves into the school. And that will definitely be more serious. Is there nothing you can do to call those people off?' He looked at Gloria and pointed to the heavily armed and helmeted riot police in their black gear who were striding about grabbing and hitting anyone within their range. 'I am definitely more scared of them and if I lose any stock today it won't be to the children, that's for sure.'

Gloria's heart sank. It was a lot worse that she had thought and it was immediately obvious that everyone she had spoken to was right. These thugs in their uniforms were going to do a lot of damage to their already fragile reputation. She thought back to the Peace Corps volunteer who had encouraged her through school in Westpoint. On more than one occasion he had said: 'In Liberia you are all too fond of uniforms, all form and no substance. That must be why all these perfectly nice people turn into monsters when they dress up as police or army.'

Admittedly he had been sick at the time and a bit disillusioned but Gloria knew what he meant. She had seen it herself with polite friendly neighbours turning into arrogant bullies when they were able to exercise some power. She knew it was not only a Liberian phenomenon but here where there was so little else to give people status it was quite marked.

She tried again to get through to the Chief but without success and similarly with Barnyou. Alfred went off to look for Barnyou and Gloria called Lawrence and told him what was going on. As always in a crisis, Lawrence leapt into action.

'These checkpoints are fine, I'm coming down to you.'

As soon as Lawrence rang off, her phone went again.

It was Moses on a crackly line from North Carolina. 'Hi boss, how's it going?'

Normally she would have given him a very bland answer but the noise and shouting had already alerted his instincts and when he asked again, sharper now, 'What is it, where are you?' She decided to tell him the story so far.

'And you're in the middle of it of course.' It was a statement not a question. 'Boss don't do this, get the Chief to make a decision on this one.'

'You know it's not that easy Moses – and not just to get him to make a decision. Barnyou is new and nervous and not even sure how much authority he has over the riot squad. They only merged all those different units last week into the Public Order Division so that it now includes CID, fraud, anti-corruption, riot police etc. No-one is sure yet how it should work but the riot squad seem to be operating independently and Barnyou isn't confident enough to rein them in.'

Moses hadn't heard about the changes and was quite indignant. 'Why did no-one tell me?'

'Because you're on holiday. And before you ask, our name hasn't changed but our remit has been expanded to include human trafficking, customary law, traditional justice etc. And no, I don't know what it all means yet.'

Lawrence's jeep came skidding up at that moment and Gloria finished the call promising to keep Moses up to date with everything.

'I spoke to the Chief,' were his first words, 'and he is trying to contact Barnyou to reduce their presence on the streets. He wanted to know if you would be willing to go down and try and speak to the students in the school.'

Gloria didn't know if that was a good idea. 'Why don't they get someone from the Justice and Peace commission or one of those groups? It's more their kind of work isn't it?'

'You know what I'm going to say Gloria. He doesn't want to lose control of the situation. If we all withdraw it will be a failure for the police. If we pull out the riot squad and you go and negotiate with them instead it will be just good policing strategy.'

She decided quickly. 'All right, let's do it before things get any worse.'

Even as she spoke they could hear the buzz of the crowd getting louder and angrier and there was a surge down through the riot police towards GW Horton.

'But we better hurry.'

They jumped into Lawrence's jeep as it was the only chance they had of getting through the crowd and started to inch forward. Alfred used the loudspeaker to announce them as the Mediation Commission, politely asking the crowd to make a way for them. The students obligingly made room for them to pass through and they soon caught up with another jeep which was trying to force its way through.

Gloria could see Barnyou inside, the windows all tightly rolled up as opposed to theirs which were open so that they could have a friendly word as they passed. As well as that, Barnyou had a phalanx of riot squad surrounding his jeep and pushing the children out of the way. She drew alongside and signalled to him to open the window which he did very reluctantly and without slowing down.

'Inspector, the plans have changed. Have you heard from the Chief?' Barnyou looked grim, in fact Gloria thought he looked quite ill. 'The Chief wants the riot police out and has asked me to try and start some negotiations with the students.'

'You? Negotiate? That is not only crazy but it's way too late. I gave the orders for my officers to charge the building and regain control. They are in place now and ready to go. We want this finished and spoiling these children with sweet talk and promises is not going to help us.'

Gloria was once again dumbfounded by this relentless stupidity.

'It's a school Barnyou. And they are schoolchildren. If you do this we will certainly be back on the front page of the international news. The archbishop is already saying that what we are doing here is criminal, we can't make it worse. If you charge and someone gets hurt or killed we will be finished. Let me try and talk to them, it will only take a few minutes.'

She saw him waver and then with a nod he started speaking on the radio. He signalled her car to follow and forced a way through the last hundred yards to the gates of the school. There was a line of riot police at the gates and then a very empty yard all the way up to the school buildings. It was quiet here. The police were standing in a grim line and the students in the school had barricaded the windows and doors with desks and chairs with the Liberian flag draped over the main doors. The sight of the flag gave her a pang of worry: hanging the flag over the barricades was the kind of dramatic gesture Abu would enjoy.

Taking the loudspeaker Gloria opened the gates and started walking slowly across the yard. There was an immediate stir behind the barricades and she started talking, introducing herself and explaining she had only come to talk to them. A lone voice asked her to stop where she was until they could decide and after a few moments the noise of scraping told her they were moving the heaviest pieces away from the front door; they were going to let her in. She could see a group of them manhandling a huge wooden platform away from the entrance and start waving to her to come forward but she had barely taken three steps when she heard a noise behind her. Turning round Gloria saw Lawrence running towards her shouting something and behind him a wave of riot police, shields up and batons out surging forward. She turned back to the school and tried to signal to the students that she didn't know what was happening and then Lawrence had grabbed her around the waist and with surprising strength was dragging her to the side. She stumbled, losing a shoe and then felt herself being half dragged, half carried to a small kitchen building at the side of the school.

The wave of police rolled past and headed to the main entrance where, with Gloria's help, the most serious barricade had been moved. In seconds they were smashing their way in and the screams of frightened students could be heard above the noise of breaking furniture and the thunder of boots.

She realised she and Lawrence were lying together on the small kitchen floor where large pots of rice and soup were still bubbling away on the fire.

'Are you okay Gloria?'

'I am fine, nothing broken or damaged, but they…'

'They used you to get the students to open the doors, that's all, otherwise it would have taken them ages to break through. They damned well used you and then were quite ready to trample over you to get in. They had no intention of talking to these kids.'

The noise of breaking furniture had subsided but the screams were higher and louder. 'We have to get in there, they will kill them.'

She hadn't finished saying this before Lawrence was on his feet and pulling her up.

'Let's go then. And call the Chief.'

They were round the corner heading to the main doors but they were not the first. The crowd had moved in and there was a mob in front of the doors already. Picking up the loudhailer Gloria started shouting for people to move back and Alfred and the others who had arrived started pushing people back just as the first students began running out the doors. Girls and boys with blood running down their faces, clothes torn and terror on their faces and behind them officers with batons raised, obviously caught up in the hysteria. The crowd started dispersing as quickly as it had formed, people shouting and pushing their way back.

Gloria could see that there was no way anyone could negotiate with these men in masks and shields but pulling Lawrence behind her, they slipped in the door as the riot police rushed by.

The main entrance was empty of people, just the smashed remains of the barricades, some trampled posters and the Liberian flag crumpled in the corner.

'Gloria, let's go to the canteen, that's where they will have been hiding. It's down here.'

Lawrence was pulling her down a corridor to the right. The noise was hideous, children screaming and the unrelenting thwack of batons from the classrooms on either side where groups of students were still being beaten by officers. Gloria stepped into the first room and there was a pause. She didn't bother trying to speak. She and Lawrence both pulled out their phones and started taking photos. The officers moved towards them leaving the students in a heap on the floor but Gloria and Lawrence were already on their way down the corridor, taking photos as they went. In between, Gloria spoke to the Chief – well, shouted at him – explaining what was going on. Beside herself with anger, she wasn't being coherent but she thought the message was getting through.

The corridor seemed endless but Lawrence was now pulling her to the right.

'I can't see Abu, but I know he's here.'

'Well, you don't know that Gloria. Come on, Abu is smart, he might well be outside worrying about you. Keep going, the canteen is just at the end.'

'How do you know the place so well?' Gloria was out of breath now but the ragtail conversation was helping to keep her going.

'I went to a government school just like this one, they were all built to the same specifications. We didn't all go to private schools you know.'

She had no breath left to snort at him but she gave him a raised eyebrow. 'Gosh there are so many interesting things I don't know about you Lawrence.'

Their arrival at the canteen stopped any further conversation. It was a large plain room which obviously doubled as the assembly room and exam hall. It had a cement floor and open brickwork instead of windows so there was much less to smash here. A few broken chairs and tables was the only evidence of the disturbance. That and the large group of students sitting on the floor squeezed into a corner surrounded by riot police. Many of them looked in a bad way, covered in blood and at least two of them appeared to be unconscious. But the beatings had obviously stopped for now. As they entered, two of the officers turned and came straight over to them. Covered in dirt and with only one shoe

Gloria felt at a disadvantage initially but clearly both she and Lawrence were still recognisable as Inspectors and the officers gave an awkward salute.

The momentary madness was gone then, thought Gloria, so now we will go back to being upholders of law and order eh?

'What is going on here? Who is in charge?'

'Inspector Barnyou is in charge ma'am.'

'Really, well I think that needs some investigating. What are you doing with these children? Some of them need to go to hospital and you better allow the medics in here.'

'They are under arrest ma'am.'

'Can't you take those helmets off? I don't think you are in any danger now.' She pointed at the silent children cowering on the floor. 'Or don't you want to show your faces?' The officers looked at each other but made no attempt to remove their headgear. Gloria shrugged, bent down, took off her remaining shoe and then flipped it at the nearest officer who instinctively raised his riot shield to protect himself. His fellow officers laughed but Gloria sucked her teeth in contempt and went back to her phone. She was clearly not going to get any sense out of these people.

Alfred, Paul and Ambrose, along with Lawrence's Traffic officers, were already going through every classroom taking the names and details of the students and then standing guard over them. Izena had ambulances on the way from Catholic Hospital and two private clinics and teams of medics from JFK Hospital had already arrived and were giving first aid.

'No child is moved unless it is to hospital,' she barked at them. 'Make sure you get the children's names and if you have cameras take photos of *everything* you can.' She glared at the police officers in their riot gear.

Three medics wearing the JFK logo came in just then and the riot squad stood back without a word and let them attend to the children on the floor. The medics took four of the children away but after Gloria had talked to the remaining children, who ranged in ages from nine or ten to nineteen, the riot squad officers insisted on taking them into custody. Apparently, under the new juvenile justice laws children could indeed be detained if the charges were serious. The officers had charged the children with inciting a riot, destruction of public property and endangering public order.

There was nothing Gloria or the others could do except follow them back to the station after making sure the crowd dispersed, which it did quite quickly as soon as it began to get dark.

Back at the station Gloria did not get the reaction she had expected. When she eventually got to see the Chief she could tell he wanted this presented as a success story.

'It got out of hand Gloria, that's clear but we are still putting our new force together and all the events of the past months interrupted the training and restructuring. All of this has made it difficult for people. I know it was badly handled but at least no-one was killed. Barnyou's deputy has been to the hospital and they say all the children will be released tomorrow – well, most of them, there are some broken bones and eh, a few fractured skulls.'

Gloria stared at him in disbelief. 'Tomorrow there will be pictures in the papers of police dressed in boots and helmets beating nine and ten year old children, how are you going to make that a success story? A few fractured skulls… ay ay ay! We, the police,' she was speaking slowly and loudly now, like some foreigners did when they wanted information, 'deliberately brutalised children. With respect Chief, it wasn't 'badly handled', it was a disaster. There was a serious breakdown in the chain of command down there at best. At worst, the riot squad was acting outside the chain of command which is very dangerous. We really don't need any more independent groups and not ones who are armed and aggressive. Barnyou allowed me to go in to negotiate and then the riot squad came in behind me.'

'I know, I know, I heard about that…' The Chief tried to head her off but Gloria was in full flight.

'If it hadn't been for Inspector Boakai I would have been injured or killed. Now I am not paranoid but I know there are a lot of people in the force who think I went too far in my last investigation and I'm sure there are some who would be glad to see the end of me. I don't want to be doing my job while looking over my shoulder all the time.'

The Chief nodded and held up his hands. 'There will be an investigation Gloria and, I promise you, it will be thorough, but at the moment we are clinging to our reputation here as you know. The President has even considered abolishing the entire police force and putting the army on the streets while a new force is trained from scratch. I know no-one really believes she would do that but if we have any more large scale disasters she might be forced into it. So let's try and get this one sorted. We acknowledge it could have been handled better but we must emphasise that we restored order and that we will not tolerate these outbursts of violence.'

'What about the children who have been arrested, there must be at least a dozen of them in the cells downstairs and more in the hospital. We need to get their details and then let them go. Surely we are not going to put them all through the court system.'

The Chief looked worried. 'That's the other side of this. We can't go through all this disorder today and then simply release everyone. That will send the wrong message too. You know that a lot of people are calling for tougher action on children, anyone who does wrong.' He held up his hands. 'I don't need a debate on this now. You and your team go down and see them tonight and make sure they are okay. Tomorrow we will call their parents and probably release most of them with a warning. The ringleaders will have to face some punishment though, we can't avoid that.'

Gloria got up. She respected the Chief but he did not like dealing with the politics behind policing. She remembered what Ron, the British policeman who had been training them before he was murdered, had said on one occasion. 'For every complex problem there is always an answer that is simple, clear – and wrong.' He had stressed that easy answers and quick solutions were almost always the wrong thing in situations like theirs which were so complicated. Few people seemed to have remembered that part of their training.

Chapter Five

There was a strange atmosphere in the building. She could feel it as she went downstairs. The day's events had split the force again. She came across Lawrence on the way and was surprised how good it felt to see him again.

'Thanks for saving me from injury or death Lawrence. I will have to return the favour some day.'

Lawrence looked more than tired, he looked defeated. 'Have you found Abu yet?'

She shook her head. 'I am going to check on those children and then I am going home. He wasn't in the school and he is not in hospital so I think he must have gone home or gone down to Westpoint to my mother. He still goes to his grandma when he's scared.'

Lawrence smiled. 'We all need our grandma. But in the absence of my grandma I am going to find comfort in food. I am starving.'

'You look it. Me too.'

'Well, why don't I wait until you have checked on the children, tracked Abu down, found a pair of shoes to wear and *then* we can go for something to eat.'

Gloria looked at her feet. She had forgotten she was shoeless.

'No wonder the Chief didn't take me too seriously. Ok, I'll meet you out front, but I can't guarantee I'll have shoes by then.'

The check on the children did not take too long. There were fourteen of them in the cells. They had all been bandaged, allowed to wash and then fed and they were sitting around chatting when Gloria went down with Ambrose. Ambrose had volunteered to stay the night 'just in case' and Gloria was happy with that. Apart from one of the youngest who was curled up on a cell floor the others seemed to be relaxed and perhaps even enjoying telling the stories of the day. The one on the floor was tired, the others told her and he didn't respond to Gloria at all. It was as comfortable as a set of holding cells could be and probably better than some of their own homes but Gloria still felt very uneasy about leaving children locked up like this. She told them Ambrose was going to be around but they didn't pay him too much attention.

She and Lawrence drove to her house together. Gloria couldn't face driving tonight and besides it was much faster in an escort car. She had called her various relatives and friends and no-one had seen Abu but the noise from the apartment told her he was inside.

The sound of 'Who Are You?' was blasting out of the speakers and Gloria's relief at seeing Abu sprawled out on the chairs watching TV with a loud musical background quickly gave way to irritation at the overturned glass and the dirty plates on the floor beside him. He had eaten and was apparently waiting for someone to come and clear up. She switched the music off and was heading for the TV as Abu sprang up.

'Auntie Glo, where have you been?'

'Where have I been? What about you? I have just been worrying about you all day and I come in and find you so relaxed with nothing to worry about. Couldn't you even phone and tell me you were alright? Honestly Abu you are getting worse, if you keep this up you'll soon be so like your cousin Flomo I won't be able to tell you apart. And get this mess cleared up.'

It had been a difficult few months since her last case which had almost been fatal for Abu. He had enjoyed being a hero and loved the attention but was finding it difficult to get his feet back on the ground. He was still good natured and could be very funny but he had found the change to Holy Redeemer school quite unsettling. No-one knew him there and he found he was no longer the centre of attention.

Abu had already collected the plates and in a way which had become too familiar over the last weeks, had shuffled off to the kitchen where she knew from experience there would be a lot of noise but no further communication. She put her head around the door and bit her tongue at the mess. Was he doing this on purpose? Only Abu's clearing up seemed to leave the place dirtier than when he started.

'I am going out for something to eat. I'll see you in the morning.' She took the grunt as acknowledgement of what she had said and left him to it.

A quick change of clothes and she joined Lawrence downstairs. He had managed to clean himself up a bit but had refused her offer to come up to the apartment. He was talking to Rohit her neighbour as she came downstairs.

'Another hard day Inspector ma'am.' Rohit was always formal but he had been a good friend in the past.

'Well it's never quiet Rohit, you know how it is here, every day some new wahala!'

'Yes, Abu was saying they had trouble in the schools. I was joking with him asking why he wasn't in the frontline but he said you wouldn't like it so he just came home.'

Gloria just nodded. At least he was talking with someone.

They left Rohit and drove up the hill. The China Garden was almost empty but with the usual full complement of staff. They found a table on the veranda where there was a slight breeze and Lawrence ordered for both of them as usual. They had been eating out together for years and knew each other's preferences.

'So is Abu still being crabby then?'

'And some! He just needs something else to focus on, all that energy. School, football training and now he's taken up the guitar as well. But he still seems to have more energy than he knows what to do with. I thought teenagers were supposed to be tired all the time!'

'You did remember that his friend was killed yesterday didn't you?' Gloria stopped short. In all the excitement of the afternoon's events she had completely forgotten how well Abu had known Titus Moore.

'Oh no, it totally slipped my mind Lawrence. No wonder he was acting like that, that football team is like his extended family and he takes his duties very seriously.'

Lawrence was quick to reassure her but Gloria wasn't going to be consoled so easily. How could she have forgotten something so important and then written Abu off as just being sullen. She started going through her mental checklist again. Spend more time with him, treat him more like an adult, take him more seriously – and then she stopped. If she could just keep him safe and make sure he wasn't dragged into another of her cases that would be enough. Lawrence brought her back down to earth.

'He understands Gloria, you know how proud he is that his auntie is the big policewoman – in rank, not in size,' he added quickly and she smiled, jokes about her size still made her laugh, 'and anyway it's not good thinking about these things when you are hungry.' They agreed on that just as the food arrived. They both stopped talking while they concentrated on eating. It had been a long day. She told Lawrence about the morning's events at the juvenile court.

'Have you ever met Dorothy Weah?'

'Met her? She was under the impression that being a judge entitled her to an escort vehicle to get her to and from work every day. She came to my office every day for a week after she was appointed, demanding one.'

'That sounds like her. So what happened, she didn't have an escort car when she rushed off this afternoon?'

'Of course not, do you know how many of them think they are entitled to escort cars and other trappings? It would be mayhem.'

'So you couldn't get rid of her then?'

'Oh no, that would have been easy, but I just kept her coming along every day so I could find out more about her. Thought it would be useful. In the end I told her that we could get her an escort car but it would have to be one that wasn't used for the President or the vice-President and I showed her a selection of confiscated vehicles she could have. She decided that it was better if she just drove her own vehicle. There's not much dignity in having a battered pick up or one of those old sedans trawling down the road in front of you.'

They both had a good laugh at that. Gloria decided that was an image she would keep in her head the next time she had to deal with the judge, which might be very soon.

It was late by the time Lawrence dropped her back at the apartment and she noticed that he waited for her to get through the front doors before he drove off. She also noticed that instead of annoying her as it would have done in the past, she was enjoying the attention and the care. Must be the beer after a long day, she thought.

The apartment was quiet and dark when she got in. It was now tidy and peaceful and that always made her stomach knot a little because in her recent experience that's when some bolt of bad news generally struck. But as she slipped off to sleep she thought that maybe it wasn't like that and the day's events, confusing and disturbing as they were, were just the kind of incidents they would have to deal with. At least no-one had died, well no-one except Titus Moore, she reminded herself.

Her phone started ringing at five o'clock and as she fumbled for it in the dark she felt the familiar knot in her stomach tighten. By the time she pressed the 'answer' button she was out of bed and pulling on her clothes. It was Ambrose.

'Inspector, you have to come down immediately, I don't know what's gone wrong or what happened. And they won't let me back in but the noise is terrible down there but I don't…'

'Ambrose, slow down. In fact, stop talking.' Ambrose stopped abruptly.

'Now just answer my questions. Where are you right now?'

'I am in our office upstairs but…'

'Just my questions Ambrose. Where is this terrible noise coming from?'

'Sorry ma'am, the noise is from the holding cells. I have been going down checking every hour but there was nothing happening until I heard some shouting and went down at four. There were more police in there and there was a lot of shouting. I asked…'

'Wait Ambrose, what do you mean there were more police?'

'I mean different police, not the usual custody ones, you know Gaye, Thompson and the rest of them. These were ones I hadn't seen before and they were in riot gear. When I tried to go in they wouldn't let me, told me they were questioning suspects, that they had taken over the investigation.'

Gloria could feel the hairs on her neck beginning to stand up. This didn't sound good at all.

'Ambrose I'm going to come down right now. At this time of the morning I should be there in ten minutes. If you feel safe enough go and stand where you can see what's happening and don't let them take any of those children away.'

By the time she ended the call Gloria had struggled into her wrinkled uniform and was heading for the door when Abu came in with the crumpled look of someone who has jumped out of bed.

'What's happening aunt Glo? Where you going time like this?'

Gloria stopped, caught between the guilt of what she was putting her nephew through and her urgent need to get to the station.

'It's ok Abu, I just need to go to the office. There's a bit of confusion, nothing to worry about.'

She knew he didn't believe that, and the sight of him looking anxious about her and so vulnerable himself really pulled at her. But there was trouble and she had to go.

'Go back to bed and I'll see you tonight. Keep your phone on and I'll give you a call. In fact, better not go to school until it's clear the riots are finished. Just stay home and study. And Abu I'm sorry about Titus, that was terrible. I'm ashamed I forgot about it with all the riots going on.' She could feel the words 'we'll talk about it later' on her lips but stopped herself from saying them – we're not in some American movie she reminded herself. Abu said nothing but as she went out the door he draped one arm around her shoulders. 'You're really getting small aunt Glo, are you not worried about that?'

'Enough, I had Lawrence making remarks about my size last night, I don't need you joining in.' She gave him a quick half hug back and then was out the door.

She saw him at the apartment window as she drove off, gave him a quick wave and then settled down to try and make herself look respectable. It was still dark but as she drove along the beach in the first glow of the dawn she could see a group of Aladura church members in their white robes and red sashes singing and praying, some of them rolling in the sand. Further along were the early morning joggers, driven out she suspected as much by the heat of the tiny tin roofed huts, as by the desire for exercise. Exactly ten minutes later she was back at police headquarters.

Police headquarters was a huge building badly damaged in the war and equally badly patched up since the war had ended. In the wake of their relatively peaceful elections, funders of all kinds and NGOs had rapidly lost interest in Liberia. Many had started to leave and look for a fresh war to feed on. Stories of peace unfortunately didn't bring in the money and without money how could they support the huge aid caravan. The young experts at the front, supported by an array of consultants and logistics people, and at the back the media who fed off the misery, some would say even magnified it. Some of Gloria's friends were convinced that the biggest benefit of international rescue operations was the money that was spent in supporting all of these people, the hotels, the restaurants and the bars. They were the biggest winners in this game. With their withdrawal they were leaving behind a lot of unfinished projects, like children bored with their toys and rushing off to play somewhere else.

She gave herself a shake, too much thinking while negotiating the gloomy stairs was not a good start to the day. As she rounded the last flight she almost tripped over Ambrose who was sprawled on the landing. He tried to sit up but fell back again groaning.

'Ambrose what happened?' She bent down to help him up after checking there was no blood or open wounds.

'They've taken the children, as soon as we finished speaking they came up from the cells with a group of them.'

'What did they do to you? Did they attack you?' Gloria could feel her anger getting up again. There was a slight pause and the Ambrose looked up at her.

'Not really, well not at all ma'am, they didn't even see me. I was watching them come up the stairs and I was trying to count how many of the children they had when something landed on my shoulder, a rat, a really big rat,' he added quickly, 'and when I jumped I slipped on something and fell backwards. The next thing I remember is you shaking me.'

Gloria was moving even as Ambrose was finishing his explanation. 'Go to the clinic and get a check up, it must have been a bad fall if you were out for a while but see if you can get hold of Paul or Alfred and tell them to get down here as quickly as possible.' Ambrose started to say something but she brushed him off. 'Just do it Ambrose, now.'

She picked her way carefully down the stairs. They were covered in all kinds of debris and were so badly lit that it would be very easy to trip over something. When she got to the holding cells there was complete silence. The gate was lying open and there were no officers around. Gloria went in cautiously. The holding cells were just a broad corridor with barred cells on either side facing each other. Moving forward in the dark and the silence Gloria had the eerie sensation of being watched. As her eyes adjusted she could see shapes in the two cells she had been in the previous night and as she approached them she heard the rustle of cloth, but it was a nervous sound to her, like someone covering up, hiding.

'Who's there? It's me guys, Inspector Gloria, you met me last night. I just want to know you are ok. Come on out of there and let me see you.'

There was silence then, a wary stillness and she knew they were deciding if they could trust her. Before she could say anything else there was a movement from the cell beside her and the unlocked gate swung open. Gloria turned and started walking back to the stairs.

'Come on let's get out of this dark.'

Her decisive movement seemed to finally break the spell and as she walked out she heard a shuffling behind her and knew they were following. Out the door and up the stairs she kept going, knowing if she stopped or turned they might run back into the dark. She finally stopped in the empty reception hall at the top and turned round. Her shock was like a physical blow, and she felt herself take a step backward. These didn't even look like the same children she had spoken to last night – bruised, ashen and totally terrified. Where were those lively frisky pekins she spoke to yesterday? She did a mental head count and could see there were five children missing. She looked to the biggest boy in the group.

'What's your name?'

'Who me?'

The traditional response irritated her today. 'Yes, you.'

'Emmanuel, ma.' He just stared at his bare feet. She noticed none of them had anything on their feet.

'Emmanuel, can you tell me where the other children are. I can see something bad happened here but if you tell me what you know I can sort it.'

'The soldiers took them, they came and beat us, calling us rebels and rogues. They just kept beating us, asking who the leaders were. Then they asked for our names divided us into two groups and left with one of the groups. They told us we should stay there and not make any noise or they would come back for us.'

'Alright, I need you all to go upstairs now. You'll be safe, I promise.'

The children didn't look convinced. But with Gloria in front they trailed behind up the stairs and into the office. The office was empty, Gloria remembered it was still very early and pictured the others rushing to get in first to meet her early morning call. The two ladies who were responsible for cleaning – or what passed for cleaning in this shell of a building – were loudly discussing the news outside her office and Gloria asked the younger one to go down and see if Auntie Fata was around. Auntie was a huge old lady who sold food most days in the reception area while dispensing her words of wisdom to anyone who cared to listen – or not listen in Gloria's case, which made Auntie more intent on giving it.

'Go ask Auntie if she has some breakfast for these children and tea with plenty of sugar.' On reflection the request for plenty of sugar was a bit unnecessary but it should help them recover from the shock. She looked at them again, huddled together and afraid, not sure if these adults were different from the ones who had taken their friends away.

'Emmanuel, come and sit with me here,' she pointed to the chair beside her desk. 'I know you are afraid but I also know you want to help your friends. Do you know their names? If you give me the names I can try and find them and make sure they are safe.'

Emmanuel just stared at her. Gloria could imagine the calculations going on in his head. Authority was an uncertain thing, especially for children. Adults who showed an interest in you were usually looking for something, and then might either ignore you or turn nasty on you. And it was especially true if that authority was wearing a uniform.

After five minutes Gloria gave up and concentrated on getting something for them to eat. Auntie Fata's food was always good and the children were soon eating with great concentration. She heard Paul and Ambrose before she saw them and turned to see them both stuck in the entrance like some comedy sequence, their eagerness to be the first in the office clearly winning over good sense. She just stared at them as they wriggled to get out of the jam they were in. Before she could say anything however she heard laughing behind her and turned around to see the children holding onto each other and pointing at her officers! There was nothing quite like someone else's misfortune or humiliation to give everyone else a good laugh, she thought, but in this case it was worth it. By the time Ambrose and Paul had extricated themselves the children were talking to each other again.

'Did you get your head seen to Ambrose?' She knew he hadn't.

'I can't go all the way to the hospital for this small thing ma'am. It's nothing.' Especially if Paul found out how you got it, she thought.

'Okay, but you will have to go anyway. I want these children taken for examination. They say they were beaten up and some of them have very bad bruising. You need to get some photos and a statement from the doctor. See if you can get Dr Brown to do it.' Dr Brown was a kindly man as well as being a good doctor and had a lot of patience with children who had suffered trauma. 'And get him to look at you as well.'

But Ambrose clearly wasn't listening. She saw him looking at the children.

'What is it?'

'It's the missing ones ma'am. They're all the small ones. If I remember rightly it's the five smallest ones who are missing. How could they say they were rounding up the ringleaders and then take away those and leave the older ones?'

It was true. The five who were missing were all the small children including the one who had been sleeping when she went down to the cells the first time. Now that was worrying.

'Paul, you go and talk to them. Since you made them laugh they might be willing to tell you what happened. In fact both of you can go with them to the hospital but see if you can get the names of the other children first. I am going to find out who took them and why, and I'm going to get them back.'

'It should be easy ma'am,' Ambrose piped up again, 'I took all their names and details last night so I have all the information. There are five missing and they are all sixth graders from GW Horton as far as I can remember.'

'Don't *remember* Ambrose, get the paper out and we'll check right here and now.'

She was tapping her hand loudly on the desk by the time he had found the paper.

She called Emmanuel over and explained what was going to happen. 'I need you to tell the rest of the group what we're going to do, if you are happy then they will be happy as well. You do want us to find the others don't you?'

Emmanuel nodded. 'What school are you from anyway?'

'I attend Holy Redeemer. I'm in the same class as your son Abu. I've seen you in the school before.'

But not enough to trust me, thought Gloria. Well, as far as they were concerned it was the police who beat them, arrested them and put them in the cells and then scared them last night and took their friends away. They were not going to differentiate between one kind of police and another.

In a few minutes they had the names of the children who were missing. They were all sixth graders from GW Horton as Ambrose had said and all of them were ten or eleven years old. The last name on the list hit her like a bucket of cold water: Prince Sirleaf. No relation to her but she knew him. He was the President's grandson. That's why the little boy who had been sleeping when she went to the cells had looked familiar to her. She cursed herself. Why had she not recognised him. But it had been dark and besides you didn't really expect to find the President's ten-year old grandson in a cell.

The president had made the very public gesture, with a lot of media coverage, of bringing all her family back from the States to live in Liberia and had been insistent they attend government schools rather than the private ones. She remembered the fanfare there had been when Prince had started at GW Horton. By all accounts he was smart, funny and over-indulged and his grandmother's favourite. But how on earth had no-one from the Mansion been down to insist they release him. What kind of security were they operating?

'Ambrose, change of plan, you and Izena' – she had just walked in with Alfred – 'go to the hospital. Paul will come with me and Alfred you take Lamine and Christian – where are they by the way?'

'They usually come in a bit later ma'am,' was Alfred's polite way of saying that standards were slipping. Without Moses around some of the newest recruits, former fighters in the war, had obviously decided to make up their own rules.

'Right, when they come in go back to GW Horton and interview the principal and other teachers and the students and see if you can get a coherent story about yesterday's events. You can send Christian to Haybrook to do the same, and Lamine can go and talk to Francis Bryant at Holy Redeemer.'

Lamine had been the unlikely connection between Francis Bryant and herself and she knew that Francis would not just give him the information but make sure he really understood it.

'And then tell them I want to talk to them in my office this afternoon.'

In a matter of minutes the office was empty again and she looked at Paul. 'Right, so where do we start. By the sounds of the description the guys who came last night are the same riot squad goons from yesterday but what possessed them to come back and take those children away? We'll start with their boss. Barnyou already owes me an explanation about his men's behaviour yesterday.'

'Did you not get the messages ma'am? Judge Weah has reconvened Richard Varley's trial for this morning. And the Director wants to see you at two o'clock in his office, so we don't have a lot of time.'

Gloria frowned, not more meetings and that awful woman again. If it had been Moses he would have known what the meeting with the Director was all about. It didn't do to go unprepared to these things. Maybe Lawrence…

'Thanks Paul. We'll go in fifteen minutes. Go and see if you can find out the exact time the court case is scheduled for. It should still give us a few hours. And ask old Alfred to get in touch with St Luke's and tell them to be on stand by.'

She went back to her office and found Lawrence waiting for her with a cup of coffee. The man was turning into a mind reader! Or was she really so very predictable? She was glad to see him but couldn't help resenting his immaculate uniform compared to her crumpled outfit of the day before which, with the way the day was shaping up, she wasn't going to get a chance to change.

'Thanks Lawrence this is just what I needed, but shouldn't you be on motorcade duty?'

'No it's all cancelled today, no sirens on the streets until we are sure everything has gone back to normal.'

'What's the news out there then? Have the schools re-opened?'

'Gosh Gloria, where do you hide? It's all over the news about children being taken from the holding cells and there's fear of more student disruptions.'

'Well that's why I don't know what's going on out there, and why I look such a mess,' she added. 'I've been here since early morning because of those children.'

Lawrence gave her a sympathetic smile. 'I know that, I was just joking you. It's bad huh?'

'It was always going to be bad – police involved in the disappearance of sixth graders – but, even worse,' she paused, 'one of them is Helen's grandson.'

Lawrence frowned as if he didn't understand what she had just said.

'They took the President's grandson? And how come the President's grandson spent the night in the holding cells, didn't anyone realise or try and do anything?' He shook his head. 'Eh, if he has been kidnapped deliberately, then this case is much bigger than we thought.'

'I think it's bigger already. More missing children and one of them is related to the President. I need to go and talk to Barnyou before the Chief gets to hear and wants a meeting. By the way, what's the meeting about this afternoon? Are you invited?'

'Of course I'm invited. And I know what it's about. You're going to love this. There's an independent group of observers coming to monitor the local elections, the theory being that if they go well it's a good indication the Presidential elections will also go well. The Chief wants to make sure they get access to wherever they need. I think you, as the poster girl of the new modern Liberian police force, will be showing them round. The Chief wants to discuss logistics, which means telling us what we can and can't say to them – especially you. And especially with this new case. Unless of course you manage to recover all of the children by two o'clock.'

'Very funny. Do you not have some buttons to polish or something?' She got up from the seat. 'Thanks for the coffee, I better get moving. See you at two.'

She found Paul waiting and they headed two floors up to the CID, or the Public Order Division as it was now although no-one had bothered to change any of the signs. Maybe no-one believed these changes were going to last very long. The area was surprisingly calm and clean unlike her own offices, and the receptionist told them Inspector Barnyou was in a meeting but she was sure he would see them immediately. Which he did. They had hardly sat down when Barnyou himself appeared and took them into his office. Despite the seriousness of their enquiries Gloria couldn't help noticing how smart his office was. It wasn't just clean with proper furniture but there were even pictures on the walls and books in the bookcase that looked as if they were read.

Barnyou looked embarrassed. 'Inspector I was going to come and discuss what happened yesterday, to explain.'

Gloria interrupted him. 'I'll wait for that with interest but right now we have a much more serious case on our hands. The children who were detained were in the holding cells last night. In the early hours of the morning some police – from the descriptions it sounds as if they were riot police – entered the cells, harassed and tortured the children and took the five youngest ones away. That's what I want to talk about at the moment. I just want you to tell whoever has them to bring them back. One of them is the President's favourite grandson by the way.'

Barnyou had gone from looking tired and embarrassed to looking ill. He nodded. 'I know. I have just had a phone conversation with the President.' He put his head in his hands and groaned. 'I have no idea who these people are or what they are up to. Even at the school yesterday I gave the order for the officers to stand back and then instead of that a small group of them rushed the building and the others joined in. Apparently someone heard something different! This incident last night is even worse. Most of the riot police were rebel fighters in a previous life, and all were members of the Independent Fighters for the Liberty of Liberia, and you know who their boss was.'

Indeed she did, Prince Julu, former rebel leader, lately Minister of Defence and now in prison, thanks to Gloria, for his involvement in the exploitation and death of a large group of children. This didn't sound good at all.

'Julu filled the riot squad with his former fighters, they were like his personal security. But still that doesn't explain what happened yesterday.'

'So what are you saying, that you have no control over them, that they act independently? There must be someone giving the orders. Have you any idea who it is? Surely you could discipline them or re-structure them so they are not all in the same unit?'

'I discussed this with the Chief but he is worried they could cause serious problems for us. He feels we should be grateful they didn't run amok when Julu was jailed and says they need careful handling for a few months before we move on them. Plus he says we have no evidence against them. A command misheard at the school yesterday and then some people dressed similarly to them last night is not going to convince the Chief.'

'But we know it's them, we're sure.'

'We know its people dressed *like* them, that's what we know. There were officers there yesterday that no-one can account for. The squad commander says there were at least five officers he can't account for but with their visors down and in all the confusion there was no way to identify them.'

'Well that's not good Barnyou. You've got people out there in proper riot squad uniforms causing this kind of trouble.'

Barnyou just looked at her. 'I know Inspector. It is very frustrating but that's the way it works around here, you should know that. It's why I never wanted this job in the first place. It's like having an arsonist as part of your Fire and Rescue Service, it's just not going to work is it?'

She knew what he meant but the Fire and Rescue Service wasn't perhaps the best example he could have used. Last week's newspapers had all featured pictures of Monrovia's one working fire engine parked outside a burning hotel in central Monrovia with the crew watching helplessly while it burned to the ground. Crew members were quoted as saying they had arrived promptly but had been unable to access any water, and as their ladders had all been stolen last month and not replaced, they were unable to rescue anyone from the higher floors. All they could do was join the chain of local people trying to dampen the fire down with buckets of water. So they didn't really need an arsonist in their team to stop them doing their job.

'That is very tough but the immediate thing is to find out who they were and get those children back.' Gloria looked at Paul who had been silent the whole time. She had a feeling Paul had aspirations to join the CID probably thinking that it was more man's work than their unit.

'Well you heard the Inspector, off you go round the bars and clubs and see if anyone is talking about these rogue officers. Someone will know something.'

'On my own ma'am?'

'I think you'll be safe enough Paul. It's broad daylight out there.'

'No I didn't mean that, I'll be fine on my own.' He looked at Barnyou. 'It's just that you usually send us out in pairs. Do you want me back for the court case later?'

'No, I'll be fine on my own as well. Just keep in touch and get some information. We need something today.' She turned to Barnyou. ' And Inspector, there are some very basic questions the press is going to want answered like why, for example, did we have ten and eleven year old children locked up in a holding cell? And even more importantly, why, having locked them up, we were not able to protect them right here at Police Headquarters? And why did no-one notice the president's grandson was missing? I'm sure Rufus Sarpoh is sharpening his pencil even as we speak.'

Barnyou looked over at the bookcase as if there might be an answer to the questions there but none was forthcoming. 'My own son is ten years old, I could never imagine locking him in a cell. Yesterday was just madness but what are we supposed to do? No matter how bright and shiny the police force, we are still dealing with a society that is traumatised and angry. Until someone knows how to fix that the best we can do is hold it at bay for a while. Oh, and it turns out that Prince's mother sent him a message to say she would not collect him and he would go to his grandmother after school. Apparently that was quite common. She would drop him at school in the morning and collect him afterwards, or he would just make his way home. They had no security, they wanted to keep his life as normal as possible. So she was in the hospital with the baby all night, his grandmother had hundreds of children camped on the Mansion grounds until late, and nobody noticed he was missing.'

Gloria felt a pang of sympathy for him but she knew that hand-wringing wasn't going to solve anything, they had to make the best of what they had. They took their leave of Barnyou who seemed sunk in misery. He really hates that job, she thought. He should move to Traffic where things were a lot more straightforward.

Chapter Six

Gloria found the expected summons to see the Chief waiting for her on her desk. She decided the best thing would be to go and see him now otherwise he would be tracking her all day, but she warned herself to keep her temper. She had a lot of respect for the Chief and genuine understanding of the delicate line he had to walk between justice and politics, but he seemed to be weighing in heavily on the side of politics these days and forgetting about justice. Well, with the President's grandson missing he would be tying himself in knots trying to solve the crime but without upsetting any of the 'dark forces' at work. She, on the other hand, had no line to walk. She would just keep investigating, but the familiar knot in her stomach wasn't a good sign.

The Chief was not sitting down when she went in, he was pacing. The building seemed full of agitation, she thought. Gloria didn't sit down either as she didn't want a long drawn out discussion.

'Ah Gloria, right, well…'

'The President's grandson has been taken, I know sir, along with four other children. That is my priority and I presume that's why you wanted to see me.'

The Chief seemed relieved to get all that out of the way. 'I won't go over all the political implications Gloria, I'm sure you can work those out for yourself but we need some action and quickly.'

'Good, well get the riot squad in here and let's find out which of them took the children and get them back. We have a crime, we know who did it and we know where to find them. Shouldn't be too difficult then.' She was pushing him and she knew it.

'Alright Gloria you win, but there are wider considerations here. We have no real proof it was the riot squad. We need to be careful about antagonising them but on the other hand we need to get the President's grandson back, and find out what this was all about. We –'

'Pardon me sir but we need to get *all* the children back. They are all our responsibility.'

'Of course Gloria, that's what I meant, don't be so prickly. Our other problem is the visiting election monitors. I was going to discuss them this afternoon but maybe we can think about it now. I know you'll have heard about them already from your friend Lawrence and I know you hate this kind of thing, but I need you to do this Gloria. These people are very influential and they need to be convinced that Liberia – despite one or two problems – is on the right track. If not, then the money stops coming and it all collapses again.'

Gloria hated this kind of pressure. Suddenly it sounded as if she was responsible for the country's economic and social well-being.

'Couldn't they just meet the President? They all still love the idea of Africa's first female head of state. Surely that would be enough?'

'No, they want to see the rule of law in action, a basic principle of democracy, and they are required to talk to people other than the President. They'll be just as interested in you as they will be in the President.'

'Ok, ok I know what you are saying sir and I understand but we need to prioritise this case and I need to know you will support me if we come up against opposition from inside the force.' The Chief just raised an eyebrow but he had at least stopped pacing.

'Get on with the case Gloria, but on this one keep me up to date with everything, no exceptions. And be back here this afternoon for the official briefing. Now you better get off to court I think.'

Gloria saw it was almost midday and went back to the office. It was empty. She called Paul 'Did you find out the time of the case?'

'I left a note on your desk ma'am, she's starting again at 12.30. I got the impression that Judge Weah would be happy if you were not around.'

'I bet she would, but unfortunately I am on my way now so she's going to be disappointed.'

It took Gloria only fifteen minutes to reach the courtroom, five minutes to spare before the case was due to start. It was a different scene from yesterday, no press, no crowds, no ministers. Obviously news of the riots and the subsequent abduction of the children was the big story now.

Inside, the court was very quiet. She saw Clementine at the far side talking with Richard Varley who once again seemed to be in court alone except for his lawyer and social worker. You would think he was an orphan instead of a member of one of Liberia's leading families. Her thoughts were interrupted by the entrance of Judge Weah and the court standing. Her honour didn't spare a glance for anyone else in the room and instead glared at Richard as if she had not expected him to turn up.

'As you will be aware' – she was now addressing a mostly empty court room – 'this is the first sitting of the juvenile court under our new legislation. One of the options in the new legislation is for us to change the format of the court hearing to allow a more child-friendly approach.' Gloria sat up, maybe the judge had been listening after all.

'But as a society we have suffered at the hands of these out-of-control youth. I myself have seen and suffered from their violence as I'm sure you have also.' Gloria could feel her temper rising. She looked around the court room wondering who Judge Weah thought she was talking to. Richard Varley had been out of the country during the war so could hardly be blamed and she knew one of the lawyers and the court clerk had both been in the States while the war was on. So that left her and Clementine, the social worker, neither of whom were inclined to blame children for the war.

'So I want to tell you to take this case seriously. We are not a 'concerned community' coming together to work out what is best for everyone. This is a court of law and this young man is on trial for the death of another more vulnerable person. Neither his age nor his social background has any bearing on what happens here. Is he guilty is the only question, and if so, what is a fitting punishment?'

Gloria almost choked. This was a homicide case, that was true, and not some minor theft or assault. The new juvenile legislation did not allow murder cases to be heard as some kind of community meeting anyway but Judge Weah's little introduction was so biased and so political that it could very likely discredit the new system. But Gloria knew there was no way she could interrupt now and also if she left the court the judge would notice, so she was stuck in this charade.

She was also distracted by the thought of the children who had been abducted. No matter how hard she tried to concentrate on the proceedings her mind kept returning to them and the feeling that time was running out. She had told Ambrose to take the children straight home when they were finished at the hospital, she didn't want them going back to the police headquarters. But apart from that there was no more movement.

She pulled her mind back to the case at hand where the Judge was still talking. Was she not going to allow anyone else to have a say? Her phone rang loudly in the quiet of the court and Judge Weah paused long enough to glare at her. Gloria saw it was Inspector Barnyou calling and made a vague gesture of apology in the judge's direction and went outside.

'Inspector, you need to come down here at once. I am at GW Horton School. Two of those children have turned up here. They are terrified but seem to be unharmed. Before you ask, neither of them is *the* grandson.'

Gloria thanked him and found herself entertaining the thought that she might have to change her opinion of Inspector Barnyou. She called Izena to ask where she and Ambrose were.

'We have dropped off the last of the children ma'am and are heading back to the station.'

'Good, well you'll have to leave the rest of your food' – the noise of glasses and the hum of happy diners was a dead giveaway.

Izena laughed. 'You caught us ma'am, we were just having lunch.'

They were probably at Musu's Spot, the new eating place she had heard Izena talk about. Good food, good music, good prices, although she didn't know if that was their motto or just Izena's opinion.

'That's not a problem except if you are still waiting for your food to arrive.'

'No, almost finished. We'll be on our way if Ambrose can just squeeze the last piece of fried fish in without choking. But not too fast I hope, because there'll be no kiss of life from me.'

'You come straight to the court and observe the rest of the case against young Varley, and I have to warn you it is a mess. Tell Ambrose to wait for me at the office and then we are going back to GW Horton. Two of the missing children have turned up.'

She rang off leaving Gloria wondering if there was something going on between them. She couldn't remember hearing Izena quite so light-hearted but she wouldn't have thought Ambrose was Izena's type – any relationship with Izena would definitely mean suiting her – but then she missed a lot these days with Moses away.

Braving the glare again Gloria had a quick word with Clementine, explaining she was leaving and Izena would join her soon. Clementine didn't look overjoyed. The combination of a mad judge and the haughty Izena wasn't a happy prospect.

'Don't worry about Izena. Look, this case is already off the rails anyway. I can think of five different grounds for appeal without even trying too hard. So it doesn't matter what the verdict is. But Izena needs to sit through it to make sure Judge Weah knows we are taking it seriously. I don't think you'll have to talk to either of them.'

Clementine looked relieved. 'They're probably related, or at least go to the same parties, so it might help.'

Convent-educated Izena came from the wealthy Cooper family and her precise English and sharp tone gave a lot of people the impression that she thought she was better than everyone else.

'Well, let me know what happens Clementine. I presume the boy will go back to his family again today.'

Clementine nodded. 'I hope he will although they are not showing a lot of interest in what happens to him.'

Chapter Seven

GW Horton was quiet as Gloria and Ambrose approached. The entrance was still a jagged carpet of rubble and debris from yesterday and there were no signs of any clear-up operation in progress. They went straight to join Barnyou in the Principal's office.

Mr Sawyer, a short fat man, was sitting on a stool where his desk should have been. His office had been completely trashed and he looked as if he had suffered a similar fate. With his head bandaged, a swollen eye and his left arm in a sling it was clear yesterday had not been easy for him. Despite his appearance and the chaotic surroundings, Mr Sawyer only wanted to talk about the children. He was genuinely relieved that two of the children had been found and kept asking more questions about the fate of the others, none of which they could answer. Barnyou was silent with his head hanging down again. He had looked up when she came in and offered her the stool he was sitting on, the only other one in the room.

He now interrupted to explain that the school caretaker had been told to come in this morning and try and secure the building to prevent any further damage. He had worked his way around from class to class leaving the cafeteria to the last. It had not been so badly damaged and there was nothing left to steal and as it had no windows, only small openings in the blocks, there was no way for anyone to get in.

'He said it was the strangest thing Inspector,' Mr Sawyer took up the story. 'The cafeteria is quite dark anyway and on a cloudy day like today it is even worse. He just went for a quick look, planning to come back tomorrow. He had been in there for maybe three or four minutes and his eyes were adjusting to the gloom when he saw two small figures sitting on top of the store cupboard. It's built out of bricks with wooden doors so it survived the riots. He went closer and saw two children he recognised from the sixth grade just sitting absolutely still with their eyes closed. It took him a while to get them to come down and he sent someone to call me. I knew immediately they were two of the boys abducted yesterday so I called Inspector Barnyou. We can't get them to say anything although physically they seem to be unharmed.'

'Where are they now?' She knew that would be Ambrose's first question.

Mr Sawyer looked back at Gloria. 'They are in one of the classrooms. We thought you could try and speak to them.'

Gloria shook her head. 'No, the best person to get them talking at the moment would be my officer here.' She gestured to Ambrose. 'He dealt with the children yesterday and I have to say they talked to him a lot more freely than they did to me.'

She could feel Ambrose's delight at the praise without even looking at him. 'You go with the caretaker, but be very gentle. Obviously they are in shock.' She turned back to the school principal. 'I must say Mr Sawyer you are too calm today. After everything that happened yesterday I thought you might be glad to see some of the children being punished.'

Sawyer paused for a moment and then with a look at Barnyou explained to Gloria that in his opinion the trouble yesterday, including his own injuries, had not been caused by his students.

'The students were angry yesterday, that is true. We have had problems with the management of the cafeteria, complaints from the students about the quality and the quantity of the food, the prices and even the hygiene. So I called some of the senior students to a meeting to discuss how we could improve things. The meeting was going well but I found out this morning that somehow the story spread that the students were holding me against my will which was absolutely not true. The first I knew of it was when some of that riot squad burst in here with batons and shields and helmets and started beating the students. It was terrifying. They didn't ask any questions, in fact they didn't speak. It was the strangest thing.' This sounded like the principal's catchphrase.

'Naturally I tried to intervene, to tell them they were making a mistake and then they turned on me in the same way and beat me mercilessly. The shouting and screaming attracted other students – the police officers made no attempt to hide what they were doing – and some of them tried to stop the beating and the whole thing escalated.'

Gloria could guess the rest. The sight of uniformed officers, wounded and hysterical students and a bleeding principal would have been enough to cause panic which, in a town always on a knife edge of tension, grew into a full riot in a matter of hours.

'But even then the police could have calmed things down' – Gloria was thinking out loud now – 'if they had wanted to.'

'Well that's it Inspector,' said Barnyou, 'this was a plan of sorts but to what end it's difficult to know. Why go to these lengths to stir up school students? To kidnap the President's grandson? They would better have done that in secret.'

They sat in silence for a few moments until eventually Gloria stood up. 'I'm going to see if Ambrose has found out anything from the children. What will you do with them Mr Sawyer?'

'I will take them back to their families. They live in the same neighbourhood but we need to make sure they get proper support and protection.'

Gloria nodded. 'I will get my officer to do that, you need to rest and besides the sight of you bandaged and bleeding will not do much to calm people down. He can stay with them until we have got to the bottom of all of this.'

Sawyer shrugged. 'Inspector I know that one of the missing children is Prince Sirleaf but I didn't hear it reported anywhere on the news this morning so I presume you're keeping it quiet. What are you doing to get him back?'

'How do you know he is missing Mr Sawyer? We only discovered it ourselves this morning.'

'It's my job to know Inspector. I'm the principal here, people tell me everything. It is very strange.'

Gloria and Barnyou exchanged looks. The man was clearly still in shock.

'Gloria,' said Barnyou, 'I will meet you at the Chief's office and then I am heading over to St Monica's school and then down to Gray T Wolloson. I've got reports of students gathering in both those places even though all the schools are closed. The children are too vexed over this police business and I can't blame them.' He shrugged. 'We really make our own trouble in this town.'

St Monica's was always a flashpoint for trouble situated as it was in the busy market, but Gray T Wolloson was the school inside the army barracks. Students rioting inside the barracks would not be good.

'Well it was to be expected I suppose, but please don't…'

'Don't worry there will be no riot police, not even any armed police. I myself will go and talk to them. But I was wondering if you could spare your officer' – he nodded in the direction Ambrose had gone – 'he seems very good at this.'

'No way Barnyou, sorry. Ambrose is good but he's just a new recruit, he hasn't even had his first assessment yet. But I will let you have Alfred and Paul. They are both good, as long as you are sure there will be no weapons.'

Barnyou nodded. 'Thank you.'

Gloria found Ambrose sitting with the two boys on a bench outside the makeshift kitchen at the back of the school. The boys looked up warily as she approached and she saw them stiffen and stop talking.

'How is it going then?' she asked generally, knowing the children were not going to respond but not wanting to exclude them.

Ambrose just stood up and said they should get the children back home as they had been up all night.

'We can talk later ma'am?'

'We can't really Ambrose. You are going to stay and keep an eye on the children until everything is sorted out – and try to keep the newspapers away as well.' She added this in a half whisper but without much hope. As soon as the news leaked that the President's grandson had been abducted there was going to be an explosion of speculation, and the Monrovia rumour mill would go into overdrive, but short of keeping the children locked up there was no way to prevent that.

Gloria persuaded Barnyou to take the children in his car while she and Ambrose followed behind.

'Okay Ambrose what did they tell you?'

'About the place they were taken to, nothing. They say they were thrown into a pickup and driven for a long long time over some kind of bumpy road and then when the car stopped they were told to get out but the people were shining flashlights in their eyes so they couldn't see anyone, not even each other. They had to climb a lot of steps and they could hear each other crying and screaming and then the same voice, the leader of the group, the one who did all the threatening and shouting started slapping them and hitting them with a leather strap until they were all lying down on the floor trying to shield themselves. The voice then said they were going to be burned, that some of them were going to be put in the water and drowned. Then these two were dragged down the stairs again. They thought something terrible was going to happen to them but instead they were put into a different car and driven along a road until they were kicked out. When they opened their eyes they were near the school and they ran inside and climbed onto the cupboard to hide.'

'So having their eyes closed was their way of hiding? I think it's something very young children do – you know, if I can't see you then you can't see me.' Gloria stopped. 'But how did they go from literal blind terror to telling you all of this in that short time.'

'Well ma'am, the one thing they both remember is that the leader of this group, the 'voice' as they call it, was a woman. They don't remember anything about the others but they know the one who scared them, who threatened them and beat them, was a woman. That's why they were so scared of you I think but not of us men.'

'Ah so that's why they wouldn't even look at me but were happy to get in a car with Barnyou, I mean I don't think I am more scary than Barnyou! But a woman? I didn't think they had any women in the riot squad, I'm sure we would have heard about it. We can ask Barnyou when we get back. So they were terrorised and then released so we would hear about them. Were they hurt in any way?'

'They are very scared obviously and they have some bruises and scratches, but no actual wounds. The noise and the use of the leather belt was really just to terrify them, which it did, or maybe more importantly terrify the other children. So what's the message then?'

'I don't know yet. It doesn't sound as if they will be in much danger but you better stay with them just to be sure. Look, there's no need for me to stay,' they had reached the road leading into Bassa Community, 'although I would love to stop for a coffee.' Gloria's not-so-secret favourite coffee shop run by Ma Mary was in Bassa Community but there just wasn't time. She was already late for the Chief's official briefing, she knew the President would be expecting a report and more importantly she had to pass on the information about the mysterious woman to Barnyou.

Ambrose jumped out of the car and promised to be in the office the next day. Gloria drove back and made her way up to the Chief's office calling Paul who had very little to report and telling him that he and Alfred should meet Inspector Barnyou at headquarters and go with him to the schools. Izena said the court case had ended in confusion again after Richard's grandfather had turned up with another lawyer who had protested about the legality of the proceedings and had then just removed Richard from the court.

'The legality… and the morality. That judge…' she remembered who she was talking to and stopped. Izena made a face. 'It's ok ma'am, I have met Judge Weah a few times socially and what I saw today confirmed my opinion of her, a silly, vain woman.'

Gloria grinned.

The Chief was sitting behind his desk this time but got up as soon as Gloria was shown in. Barnyou arrived soon after saying he couldn't stay long as there were more reports of students gathering further out of the city. Lawrence was already sitting down doing something with his phone. As soon as Gloria was in the door the Chief started speaking.

'I've just spoken to the President. She is, naturally, very worried about her grandson. Any progress on this?' He paused and looked at Barnyou and then back to Gloria as if he wasn't sure to whom he was addressing his question. Gloria had already decided she was not going to report on this but Barnyou indicated with his head that Gloria should answer.

'Two of the children have turned up, although not the President's grandson. They have identified a woman as being the leader of the group which took them.' She saw Barnyou look up at this piece of information. 'They weren't physically harmed but they were terrorised and threatened, mostly by the woman. We are thinking that their 'disappearance' from the group is to make the remaining children, specifically Prince, even more scared so it might be that this really is targeted at the President. Clearly this woman is not at all scared of being found out though, or else she really thought she had scared the children into silence.' She paused and looked at Barnyou – really, suspicions that these were renegade members of the riot squad would be better coming from him – but he said nothing.

'Barnyou and I are working closely together to identify who these people are.' There was another silence. Barnyou remained silent, Lawrence wasn't in a position to comment and the Chief looked disappointed.

'I was hoping you would have made more progress than that,' the Chief looked at Gloria and Barnyou but their expressions were enough to stop whatever else he had been going to say. There was an awkward pause and then he decided it was best to move on. 'Ok, what are our next moves?'

For the next ten minutes they tried to plan what each of them would do. There was so much happening that it almost fell to Lawrence to report to the President about the state of the investigation but, personable as Lawrence was, the Chief realised that having the Head of Traffic talk the President through the investigation into her grandson's kidnapping was not a good idea.

'You'll have to do it Gloria. I'll arrange for you to meet her immediately. Realistically, we won't be able to keep this out of the news, in fact I'm surprised they haven't been tipped off already so we need the other parents informed as well.' Gloria stopped listening at this point, the lack of sleep and the events of the last few days beginning to take their toll. She looked up at the noise of scraping chairs to see Barnyou leaving.

Barnyou wasn't waiting for the official briefing on the visit of the election monitors. His radio had been crackling on and off for the whole meeting and an anxious-faced deputy had been in twice to give him updates on student movements across the city. As far as Gloria could gather from the briefing that followed, she was going to spend a lot of time with the election monitors and she was to be open and honest with them while at the same time making sure they didn't hear too much about corruption and mismanagement. She rolled her eyes but said nothing more, after all the Chief had put Lawrence in charge of all the transportation for the visit which would be a big help, and it meant they would be working together. That thought cheered her up.

Chapter Eight

The Executive Mansion was full of people of every shape and size but Gloria was met by Sammy, the President's private secretary. Sammy was a tall man of few words who resisted all Gloria's attempts at conversation. He took her in a private lift straight to the fifth floor where the Presidential offices were. The long corridor and the antechambers were all busy with people hunched over computers, but it was very quiet. Sammy took her through a large room full of supplicants who had managed to get this close to the president with their requests for help. Mothers with babies, old men in badly-fitting suits, students clutching sheaves of paper and a group of market women. They were all sitting in silence staring straight ahead or down at their feet as if engaging with other petitioners might somehow reduce their chances of being helped. The smell of poverty and desperation was strong in the room.

'How do these people get in here?'

'Oh, one afternoon a week anyone can come to the gates and try to meet the president. I don't know how they decide who to allow in but it's all about the president being accessible and being in touch with ordinary people.'

Gloria wasn't required to sit and wait and, with a nod at the impassive security guards on the door, Sammy took her straight in. The presidential office was a huge room with floor to ceiling windows which looked over the ocean. Even with the curtains pulled, the light was startlingly bright and Gloria had to squint to see where she was going. President Helen Sirleaf was sitting behind an ornate wooden desk working on a pile of papers stacked high against the wall.

'This is how they keep the President busy,' she indicated the papers, 'pile on the reports, draft bills and fancy administration and hope I don't notice what's really going on. Look at this,' she held up a thick folder, 'this is a four hundred page report on recommended changes to staffing rotas here at the Mansion. While in there,' she pointed to a thin green file sticking out from the middle of the enormous pile, 'is the report certain people don't want me to see, the independent assessment and recommendations for changes to the civil service which involves reducing the payroll by half.'

Sammy looked as if he was going to protest but she waved him away. 'Ok Sammy you can go now. Inspector Sirleaf can see herself out when we've finished.' Sammy bowed and silently left the room. The president smiled at her. 'I just like to keep him on his toes. Sit down Inspector and tell me what is going on with my grandson and those other children.'

Although she was dressed for an official reception later that afternoon in a vivid green, gold and red outfit and head tie to match, the President looked tired and worried. She looked like any grandmother would whose grandson had been kidnapped, except that this grandmother was also responsible for running a country. She could not allow her worries to interfere with her job. Liberia was still a fragile democracy where only a delicate balance of power and vested interests was stopping its return to chaos. There was no shortage of people waiting for her to make a mistake which they could then exploit for their own ends.

'We are doing everything we can, your Excellency. Two of the children turned up today,' the President nodded, 'and despite their ordeal they were able to give us some information. The children were taken by people dressed as members of the riot squad.'

'Dressed as?'

'Yes ma'am, we are still checking but as far as we can be sure they are not actual police officers. They were led by a woman and the children were very clear that this woman was the one in charge, she gave all the orders and she was the one threatening them.' Gloria paused.

'Go on Inspector, don't try and spare my feelings, I just need to know the situation.'

'Well, this woman was very rough with the two children but she did not harm them physically. It seems to have been more of a device to scare the three remaining children, and we can't avoid the fact that your grandson is probably the main target, perhaps to bring pressure on you. But there have been no attempts to contact us or make any demands, so at the moment we are in the dark about what their motives are.'

'Money and power Inspector, what else? And of course this is aimed at me. Sooner or later they will be in touch with some impossible demands.' She paused again. 'I really love that boy Inspector but we both know there is nothing I can do to save him if they ask for a ransom. I am not rich and the treasury is empty, as usual. Not that we could have used treasury funds anyway,' she added quickly, 'and I don't know what political demands they might make.' She sighed heavily. 'My daughter didn't want to come back you know. The family were settled in the States and the children were happy. But I insisted that we show solidarity – and give my many critics less ammunition. And this is what happens.'

'As soon as we know any more we will let you know ma'am and as I said we are doing everything we can.'

'I'm sure you are.' She handed Gloria a slip of paper. 'That's my personal mobile number. Call me at any time but don't give the number to anyone else. Are there any resources you need that I could help with? We have had offers of help from the Americans and the Russians but I am reluctant to accept.'

'No ma'am I think we have all we need to follow up all the leads. We are trying to keep the investigations discreet at the moment to avoid putting any more pressure on the government.'

The president looked Gloria in the eyes. 'I have heard great things about you Inspector which I know is sometimes a great pressure. Believe me, I know what it's like to have everyone pin their hopes on you, but I am also realistic and I know one person can't change the whole system. All I am asking is that you please do everything you can to get the children back.' The shake in her voice was unmistakeable. Then she straightened up and the mask was back in place. 'I have to attend a reception for these election monitors now. I believe you are also showing them around.'

'Yes, about that ma'am…' The president held up her hand and laughed.

'No, sorry Inspector, don't ask me to get you out of this one. You will have to do it. I can't have any of those other guys doing it, not when I want these people to believe Liberia is moving forward. Which it is, of course,' she added quickly, 'just not quite at the pace they will expect. Just do your best with them, we need these people's support.'

There was a knock at the door and a tall young woman came in. She ignored Gloria and addressed the president.

'Your Excellency, we need to leave now.'

It didn't sound like advice, more like a command, and she had disappeared before the president could reply. Gloria raised an eyebrow and the president smiled.

'You've just met Matilda Wesley Inspector, my Head of Protocol, a role she takes very seriously.'

'I can see that ma'am. She does know she works *for* you doesn't she?'

The president actually laughed out loud. 'Well let's just say I didn't actually choose her. She comes from the influential branch of the Wesley family who were some of my biggest opponents during the election. But to keep this coalition government together I need their support so,' she indicated the open door where Matilda had been standing, 'one of the smaller concessions I've had to make in the cause of national unity.'

She had stood up and was moving to the door as she was speaking. 'Although, in fairness to Matilda, she is very efficient.'

They shook hands and Gloria found herself in the lift heading back down to the ground floor. The President was famous for her abrupt conclusions to meetings. Well, she did have a country to run, thought Gloria as she stepped out the lift into the main reception area. The place was even busier than when she had arrived. There were photographers already flashing their cameras, security officials ranged around the room, assistants with clipboards and files and drivers. All the paraphernalia needed to transport a President five minutes up the road to the City Hall.

As she headed for the main doors Gloria saw Matilda heading towards her. She was dressed in a smart business suit, white blouse, tiny gold earrings and a thin gold chain with a cross on it. Discreet, understated, business like. She's like a designer nun, Gloria thought, but without any of the warmth or common sense. Unfortunately, the smart appearance was spoiled as soon as Matilda opened her mouth. She had a harsh voice and a very abrupt manner. She took Presidential protocol very seriously and spent her whole life trying to organise and control the President's public and private calendar which in Liberia was like scooping water out of a leaky boat with a teaspoon. The vice-president had remarked that at least with Matilda they were safe from final annihilation because if the four horsemen of the apocalypse turned up at the Mansion there was no way she would allow them to enter until they had been properly registered and the seating plan re-ordered. No wonder she always looked so tense.

'Inspector Sirleaf, I don't have you on my list.'

'What list would that be Matilda?'

'My Order of Exit list.'

Gloria raised an eyebrow. 'I have no idea what one of those is Matilda.'

'It's the official protocol for the President's departure from the

Mansion this afternoon to the reception at City Hall. It details who will be here, where they will stand etc. And you're not on the list.'

'You have a protocol for the President's walk from the lift to her car?'

Despite the long day and all her worries Gloria could feel herself beginning to smile. Life really was absurd. Maybe that really was the answer to the question about the meaning of life.

'Don't worry Matilda, I won't upset your plans. I am leaving now.'

'You can't leave yet. The President will be down in exactly forty five seconds. No-one can leave or enter during the two minute protocol zone. I'll find you a place to stand until she has gone.'

Gloria knew it was easier just to give in and found herself standing behind a group of photographers wondering if the 'two minute protocol zone' was something invented by Matilda. Her unique contribution to the world perhaps.

As she had suspected the President swept through the lobby in a five second blur and was gone before anyone could take any pictures, much less engage her in conversation. Gloria left by the main doors as the Presidential motorcade, outriders, sirens, medical car and two pick-up loads of soldiers all disappeared up the road. The first cars would be arriving at City Hall before the last had even left the Mansion grounds, she thought. But for now all she wanted to do was go home. What a day it had been.

As she couldn't remember if there was any food in the house, Gloria stopped at Park N Shop, the newly reopened supermarket on Center Street. It was still a novelty to wander around the air-conditioned aisles and look at the shelves full of imported chocolate, champagne and caviar. Gloria bought bread, butter and coffee and was putting them in her car when she saw a familiar face grinning at her. Pascal was a boy who had lived on the street and, with his friend Boyes, had adopted Gloria as their friend and confidant. Unfortunately Boyes had been a victim of a trafficking ring and had been taken to Sierra Leone. He had not been among the children Gloria and her team had rescued from the mine where they were being forced to dig for diamonds and although they had searched for him he had never been found. It had been a while since Gloria had seen Pascal and he had changed enormously. Although he was still small he had lost the rough look of the street and had a well-fed glow about him.

'Auntie Glo,' he had adopted Abu's name for her, 'how are things? Any news about Boyes?' He asked this every time they met and had never given up his belief that Boyes was out there somewhere and would come back.

'You don't know him,' he had said when they tried to prepare him for the worst, 'Boyes was quiet but he was much smarter than me even,' which was the highest praise from Pascal. 'There's no way those people would be able to do anything to him.'

'Sorry Pascal, no news yet. You know we will look for you as soon as we hear anything.'

'I know. You know Alex old ma,' he pointed to the small angelic faced child next to him. Gloria knew many of the street kids and it broke her heart especially to see the young ones on the street. Alex barely lifted his head and just mumbled a greeting. 'He is not feeling fine so I am taking him to the clinic.'

Gloria had been trying for months to get Alex and his friends to get off the street and go into one of the projects. She felt his forehead, he was burning up. They were walking to the Chinese clinic a few doors up.

'He really needs treatment Pascal. Have you got enough money?'

'I have auntie, thank you.'

'How is school anyway? I suppose it must be easy for you.'

Pascal didn't smile. 'The school is ok, but the children are too small and…'

Gloria knew that the transition from street to family was always difficult and had worried that Pascal might not make it. He had lived on the street for years and had become used to being in charge of his life, even if it was a difficult one.

'But old ma Anderson is too nice to me.' He had brightened up again and spent a few minutes describing how he now had his own room, new clothes, food every day but also that the Andersons had told him he was the big brother to their two young children and allowed him to take the children to town, and sometimes to collect them from school if he was home early. The Andersons were a nice couple, Gloria had known them for years and they obviously knew that making Pascal feel part of the family and trusted was as important as giving him food and sending him to school. The stigma of being a street boy ran very deep in Liberia and entrusting your children to a boy you had taken in off the street was something many people would consider madness. But the effect on Pascal had clearly been enormous.

'So what cases are you working on now auntie?'

Pascal also fancied himself now as a kind of volunteer consultant to the police. Gloria was constantly having to find ways to encourage his interest without giving away important information. But with Pascal, who seemed to have retained all of his street networks, that was more difficult than she had imagined.

'I hear you have Richard Varley in jail.'

'You know Richard is not in jail Pascal, and you also know what he did so stop fishing for information.'

'But that boy is sad not bad. He shouldn't be in jail. The grandfather should be. Now, he is bad.'

When she first got to know Pascal and Boyes they had explained to her the importance of being able to 'read' people if you were going to survive on the street. For them there were three categories of people you would likely meet, the mad, the bad and the sad – or a combination thereof. They had explained to her in great detail their complicated system for awarding points to adults depending on how they spoke, dressed, acted, walked etc. and this was how they decided if they could trust them or not. Gloria hadn't understood the points system but the two boys had proved themselves capable of summing people up very accurately so she hadn't dismissed it out of hand. Some academic would probably write a learned paper on it one day.

'Ok Pascal, never mind the Varleys, there is something useful you could do for me. I'm sure you've heard some children were taken from the police headquarters last night. Some of them have come back but we need to find the others. Can you ask your people if they have heard anything that could help us?'

Pascal was nodding wisely. 'The old ma's grandson, that is very bad.'

'I'm not even going to ask you how you know about the President's grandson. That is secret information.'

Pascal just grinned. 'Secret eh? In Liberia? And with your police people? I beg you ma, that one can never be a secret.'

'Well alright, but just see if you can get me some information, and don't tell anyone else.' Pascal nodded. They were at the clinic now and Alex looked as if he would find it hard to walk much farther.

'Tell Abu hi auntie. I will see him at practice on Saturday.'

Gloria just nodded. Half the people she knew seemed to belong to Abu's football team. She slipped some money into his hand. 'Make sure Alex gets good treatment and let me know how he is. Alex, I will look for you soon, ok? Don't be giving the doctor a hard time, you hear.'

'Ok ma.' He managed a feeble grin.

Gloria was home ten minutes later and found the apartment tidy and quiet. When she sat down she suddenly felt exhausted and wanted nothing more than a cup of coffee. Abu popped his head around the kitchen door.

'The food's nearly ready – potato greens tonight.'

It was one of her favourite dishes and not the easiest to prepare so she appreciated the effort Abu was making. They sat down ten minutes later and the food was as good as she had anticipated. There was something deeply satisfying about Liberian food.

'I met Pascal just now, he said to tell you hi. I didn't know he was in your football team.'

'Well, he's not too serious, he comes only one one time that's all but I think he's a bit confused. He can't spend all his time on the street with the boys but he's not used to the rest of us yet. He can't play anyway, too slow and he hates to train. But I think he will be good for the junior team.'

Junior team? Gloria didn't ask for any details. If it kept Abu busy it was probably a good thing.

'Do you know Richard Varley? The boy who killed Titus.'

'Mmmm,' his mouth filled with rice, Abu could only nod. 'Of course I do. He's a foolish child.'

'Bit of an understatement, he seems to have been responsible for Titus's death.'

'No, it's not possible. I know he likes to act like some kind of gangster from the ghetto but he's not bad. It's all an act with him. We all knew it. If he ever met a real gangster or one of those rebel boys he would run a mile. Richard Varley is just, I don't know, just a small boy. He would come with Titus to the practice ground but not do anything and then he would try and buy us all drinks or food and he always ended up getting vexed about something and running off. He smokes and he was drunk a few times too, so he's not ok. But Titus always defended him, saying he wasn't so bad, we should give him a chance, that there were funny things happening in the house.'

Abu got up and started clearing dishes off the table so that he had his back to her although he was still talking. This was what Abu had always done if there was something he found hard to talk about.

'Why you always put the blame on the children Aunt Glo? Eh, you don't see big people in your job.'

'I see what I see Abu, that's police work. It's not about what I feel or whatever.'

'I see what I see too and I saw that pekin.' Abu was now over at the window fiddling with the glasses. 'He came on the beach to train with us one day and this particular day he joined in everything but when we all got in the water at the end he took off his shirt and we saw his back. Aunt Glo, someone had been beating that boy with iron, the marks all down his back were red and deep. When he saw us looking he just went crazy, told us he had been in a fight in New York with some gangs, that we were all 'country' children who knew nothing and then he ran off. But they were new marks not old ones. He must have been suffering. So, he's a bit crazy but he's not bad and Titus was his hero although he didn't like to show it. Anything Titus said, Richard would do. No, he's not bad but someone in that house is.' Abu finished his speech and disappeared into the kitchen, the sign that there would be no discussion.

Gloria thought her instincts had been right about Richard Varley. Beating children was still very common in Liberia she knew, and many people believed it was the only way to properly discipline their children – and sometimes their wives too – but inflicting wounds with an iron bar was something most Liberians would find utterly wrong. She shifted in her chair trying to get her thoughts straight. There had been so much drama today already but the thought of Richard Varley back in a family which was abusing him she found really disturbing.

It was almost seven when she decided to give Clementine a call. Abu had brought her coffee in and she went onto the small porch. Her view of the beach and the sea never failed to soothe her a little. There was no reply from Clementine and she decided that calling Ambrose or any of the others would be a waste of time tonight. First thing tomorrow it would be then – along with everything else.

'Hey Abu, thank you for cooking. Are you ready for school tomorrow?'

Abu, when he appeared, didn't look as if returning to school had been uppermost in his mind. But he didn't argue.

'Aunt Glo we want to have a service for Titus. Can you help us with that?'

'It's a nice idea but I'm not sure how I can help.'

'I could get one of the nuns to come and say some prayers if...' She tailed off when she saw the look on his face. Obviously the last thing he had been thinking of was getting some nun in especially since he was convinced Sr Angie, a voluble American, was still trying to get him to join a youth group, a thought which filled him with horror.

'No, our chaplain will say the prayers but we need to borrow a vehicle to go to the cemetery afterwards.'

'You won't have the body Abu so there will be no trip to the cemetery, that's the family responsibility. Not that you were going to get a vehicle anyway – and don't even think of asking Lawrence for a car!'

'Ok, but can you help us with something for the refreshments afterwards?'

She had fallen into the trap again. He asks for something big, you say no, he asks for the thing he was really after, you say yes. It happened every time and she always fell for it. He was smiling, he knew he had won. But Gloria was relieved to see him looking happy again, big grin, his eyes clear, and it was in a good cause as it often was with Abu.

'Ok you win, but I want a list this time and keep it simple. How many people?'

'It's just for the club.' Gloria looked up suspiciously.

'I'll need some more detail than that Abu. Your club?'

'SUSA, Aunt Glo. Struggle United Sports Association, you still don't know our name after all this time?' He rolled his eyes in an exaggerated fashion until he caught her glaring at him and stopped. 'Anyway, it will be about sixty people.'

'Sixty!' Gloria had been thinking in terms of fifteen or twenty. 'Sounds more like your own rebel group than a football team.'

Abu sighed. 'There's the senior team, the junior team and the academy team, the training staff, club officials and our supporters. Actually it might be nearer to ninety.'

Gloria, sensing defeat creeping up on her again, got up quickly.

'Let's just agree on sixty then. And no rice and no soft drinks. Popcorn, kool-aid and candy should be enough.'

Abu didn't argue. He was an excellent tactician. 'I'll go work on the list and get it to you by tomorrow. Thanks aunt Glo. And we need you to be there as well to talk to the whole group.'

The other thing Gloria hated doing was addressing groups about vague matters to do with crime or anything else.

'But Alfred is in the club. Surely he can talk to you all.'

'No Aunt Glo, we need a big person to do it, and you are famous.'

'Ok, enough of the flattery Abu. Go get some sleep before you think up any more things for me to do.'

He bounced back inside and seconds later she heard him on the phone discussing everything with Morris. Clearly her willingness to pay for refreshments was something they had factored in earlier. She wasn't entirely sure whether she liked their ability to predict her reactions.

Chapter Nine

She heard the news first on the radio. Swift FM, the newest station in town, described itself as the 'first with the news' and they had lived up to their description.

'The badly mutilated body of a young boy was discovered early this morning on the steps of Holy Redeemer cathedral on Ashmun Street. Our reporter who was first at the scene interviewed parishioners who found the body as they made their way for the early morning service. The body is that of a boy aged between nine and eleven years but our reporter says his injuries are so horrific that it will be hard to identify him. As we wait for the police to give more details, this station is asking if this is the beginning of a new wave of ritual killings especially as the local elections approach and, if so, what is the government doing about it? Promises to stamp out this evil practice sound very empty this morning and parents must be asking themselves if it is safe to let their children go to school. In a related issue, rumours from the Executive Mansion are saying that the President's grandson is one of the children who was taken from police headquarters and is still missing. Opposition Senator Miles Gwedu has asked for assurances that the personal pressures on the President will not in any way compromise national security especially at this delicate time. There has been no statement from either the Executive Mansion or the police so far.'

Gloria knew it must be the body of one of the missing children and her heart sank. If they had doubted the ruthlessness of these people then that doubt was banished. As far as she knew no demands had been made but they were still prepared to kill to make sure their demands met a receptive ear when they were made.

By the time she reached the office the gaggle of reporters at the front doors had turned into a small crowd. She bypassed them and got up to her office where she found the Chief waiting for her.

'It's grim Gloria, really grim but let Barnyou focus on this one.' She nodded. 'It's one of the missing children but it's not the President's grandson. She has been informed and they are getting ready to issue a statement this morning. We need to find those other children alive Gloria. That is your task, so don't get distracted. These child murders are always terrible for you but you have to get your people working even harder on tracing the other ones. Make sure you liaise with Barnyou so you are sharing information. Now unfortunately, you still have to get on and meet the election observers. If they start discussing the murder please reassure them that this is not an outbreak of ritual killings as the radio suggested.'

'I will try my best sir. But are we really sure this is not a ritual killing? With the elections so near it wouldn't be surprising.'

Liberia had an unfortunate but well documented history of ritual killings and it was all too common for children to disappear and be found mutilated in the run up to elections. There was still a strong belief in some quarters that eating or using certain body parts gave you power or access to power and might be the crucial decider in an election. A city mayor from down the coast had been accused of being involved in the ritual killing of two children the previous year and he had implicated a local businessman and a well known pastor. All three had been tried and found guilty of murder.

'Obviously we will know more once the child's body has been examined but for the moment the story is that this is the work of criminals. And keep me informed.'

He had taken to ending almost every conversation with that particular exhortation as if he suspected Gloria was somehow operating independently of him. He left to speak to the press and Gloria went into the main office where the atmosphere was heavy. Although she was sickened by the murder herself she knew she had to get them all moving and quickly.

'Some clarifications first. Inspector Barnyou's team, or teams, will be handling the murder case as it is now.' She held up her hand as soon as the protests started.

'Just listen. There is no time for a discussion here. Inspector Barnyou is in charge of the murder case, end of story. Our job remains to find the remaining two children. It is likely, having murdered one of the boys, they will make some demands today on the President. They are ruthless and they are determined. It doesn't seem there will be much room for negotiation so we have to get the children first.' She paused.

'I have to be with the election monitors today so this is how it's going to be. I know you people are vying for position but forget all that today. Alfred, you will coordinate the search for the children and Izena and Lamine – nice to have you back with us by the way – will work with you. Yes Izena, that means you will be taking orders from Alfred today.'

Instead of the protests she had expected Izena looked surprisingly happy to be with Alfred.

'Paul you need to liaise between us and Inspector Barnyou to make sure all information is shared, leads are followed up on and…'

'And because we don't trust them ma'am.'

She had no time to argue and it was too late for pretences. She just nodded.

'How did you get on at the schools yesterday by the way?'

She had already heard from Barnyou that Alfred and Paul had enjoyed themselves immensely being the centre of attention and showing their colleagues in CID how these things should be done. But they had done a good job. They had asked for the student leaders and had spent time discussing with them, listening to them and a combination of Alfred's footballing fame and Paul's ability to talk and listen had defused the situations at both schools.

'Oh we managed fine ma'am. I don't think there will be any more problems there but we promised to go back and visit them, and also we suggested that they have a representative on the investigation committee into what happened at GW Horton. They liked the idea but Inspector Barnyou wasn't sure.'

'Sounds like a good idea to me, well done. And the amount of time they will have to spend finding a representative who is agreeable to all the school student bodies should keep them off the streets for a while. Ambrose, I need to see you in my office. And Christian, the good news is that you will be with me and the election monitors today. You have precisely five minutes to sort your uniform and then meet me at the car. Old Alfred will manage our communications here. You all keep in touch at all times. If there is a breath of a lead, the slightest hint of anything, I want to know about it. Right, off you go.'

Ambrose followed her into the office. Although he was a new recruit she had seen him in action enough to know that she could trust him to investigate the family background of Richard Varley. The Varleys were powerful and if they thought they were being accused of abuse they would close ranks, or call in some favours, or maybe just hire a hit man. She explained the situation to Ambrose and his frown cleared. This was work he was good at and felt strongly about.

'You go and talk to Clementine at St Luke's, see if she has any suspicions and then between the two of you get in and talk to Richard. You know it's delicate but if the boy is being abused we have to get him out of there. It might also have a bearing on the death of his cousin.'

'Ok ma'am. And what about the children we took home yesterday? They could be in danger from these people.'

'I had almost forgotten them. You are right, they could be in danger. Go and warn the community leaders there to keep an eye on them and call round there during the day. It's on your way to the Varley mansion anyway. And call me and let me know what's happening.'

It was eight-thirty now and Gloria had to be at the Mamba Point Hotel at nine thirty. She was headed for the door when she saw Barnyou heading for her office. The man was haunting her. She stopped and let him in while explaining she had to be on her way. Barnyou opened an envelope and threw some photos onto her desk. They were large glossy shots all showing the dead boy from different angles.

'I just thought you should see these, to see what we are up against. This is ten-year-old Anthony Keimouth.'

Gloria didn't really want to look at the pictures. She wasn't squeamish but she had never got used to the sight of death and she suspected these pictures would be bad. And they were.

'They cut out his tongue, his left eye, his genitals and his right ear. And he was alive while they did it, or at least when they started.' Gloria looked at the pictures and even in the lifeless stills she could hear the screams of this child as he was tortured. Her stomach heaved and for a moment she thought she might throw up. When she looked up Barnyou was looking at her and he was clearly very angry. Then he collected the pictures and without another word walked out of the office.

Gloria went down to the car where Christian was waiting for her.

'You drive, and our first stop is Bassa community.' She reckoned she had time for one of Ma Mary's coffees, and she really needed it. As usual there were no other customers. She didn't know how Ma Mary survived in business but it suited her fine not to have to wait or, worse still, make conversation with other people. Ma Mary started brewing the coffee as soon as she saw her but looked a bit surprised when Christian asked for one as well. They sat in silence and drank the strong bitter drink and for a few moments Gloria could forget the pictures she had just seen of Anthony and the terror that seized her when she thought they might not find the other children in time. There just never seemed to be an end to the evil and it seemed to be children who suffered over and over again. And she had to spend the day with a group of election monitors. How could that be a good use of her time?

The Mamba Point Hotel was quiet these days. A favourite refuge and haunt of reporters and journalists during the war where even in the darkest days Maria, the flamboyant owner manager and general overseer, had been able to rustle up pizza and cold beer, it was now filled with consultants, writers and even the occasional tourist. The last time Gloria had been in the hotel was a few months ago when one of her colleagues had been murdered in his room. That she couldn't forget.

She had been told the election observers were a group of four: Lex A'kimbo from South Africa, Lorretta Howsing from Texas, Patrick Feelan from Ireland and Magda Larsson from Denmark. They turned out to be four of the most annoying people Gloria had ever met, and that was saying something. It wasn't that they were abrasive or intrusive, it was the very opposite. In the course of their introductions they each made it clear they didn't want to interfere with her police work, that they understood Liberia was still in transition and needed support, all of which would have been fine if they had left it at that. But each one also wanted to let her know that they had a special interest or a connection or an insight into Liberia which she could not do without.

Lex, a journalist by profession, kept talking about African solidarity and trying to compare the experience of apartheid with Liberia's colonial relationship with the USA which had kept them 'in slavery to US foreign policy'. Gloria didn't enlighten him that many Liberians before the war had considered themselves American and would have been insulted to be called African. Lorretta, clearly from the Bible belt, couldn't stop talking about how 'spiritual' everyone was here. She was really hoping they would be able to meet some of these warlords who had converted and were now 'ministering to the broken'. Gloria on the other hand was really hoping they wouldn't meet any of them given her strong urge to slap them whenever she came across them. Patrick Feelan, an Irish politician, also tried to make parallels between their experiences of oppression and war, and worse, for an Irishman, he seemed utterly devoid of any humour. Magda was the one Gloria came closest to liking and that was because she seemed to know nothing of politics but a great deal about Danish crime fiction of which Gloria was a big fan.

She sat back and looked at them all. With the ice broken, they were now all talking at the same time. She had no idea how people like these were judged to be qualified as election observers or monitors. They all seemed to be living in a fictional or historical version of their own country which Gloria didn't recognise. As far as she knew South Africa was struggling with rampant corruption, rising violence and disillusionment with the ANC, Ireland and the USA were broke and Denmark was famous only for pickled herring and crime dramas. None of them knew anything about Liberia pre-1990 and only one of them, Magda, had any previous experience of election monitoring. Still, she hoped this meant they would allow her to do her job and not make too many demands on her.

'So Gloria, tell us about this story in the paper this morning,' said Patrick. Her heart sank, she had hoped to avoid talking about the murder of Anthony Keimouth until she could talk about the progress they were making. 'It's quite a funny one really,' she heard him continue.

Funny? She leaned over and saw he was talking about a story which had been doing the rounds for days now. He didn't seem to have noticed the gruesome photo of Anthony Kheimouth right next to it. No, Patrick was focused on a story about a British man, a pilot, who had been arrested for not pulling over quickly enough to allow the Presidential motorcade to pass. He claimed to have shared a cell with a Nigerian accused of murder and a chicken accused of stealing $500. It was a long story with eyewitnesses telling how they had seen the chicken leaving a neighbour's house with the money 'tucked under its wing' and how it was due to appear before the magistrate to answer questions. They were all laughing by now. She knew they had all heard some version of this story in other countries. Oh, dear old Liberia, so quaint and cute.

'Well, here's Inspector Boakai now, he's in charge of the motorcade amongst other things I'm sure he can give you the background.'

Lawrence was, she thought, looking very smart this morning but he was also very serious. After the introductions he took one look at the paper and the story of the chicken and explained coldly that the pilot's arrest was not quite as he had described it. The man had been found drunk in his car, parked on a closed road outside the Executive Mansion. He had not shared a cell with anyone, never mind a chicken, and had been released at the request of the British High Commission as he turned out to be a minor official from the embassy in Ghana. No explanation as to why he was in Liberia was given.

'You will have to be careful what kind of stories you listen to here and on what evidence you make any judgements.'

She had never seen Lawrence quite so cool with people. He looked positively offended at their mockery. And they got the message with Patrick blurting out apologies and explanations as they filed out to the vehicle while the others glared at him. As they were climbing into the minibus Lawrence leaned over and whispered to Gloria. 'That should keep them under control for a few hours at least.' Gloria giggled. Never underestimate a Liberian!

That was the only laugh they had all day. The round of meetings with election officials and trips to look at the registration process was only broken up by Gloria's frequent calls to her team. They kept to their word and phoned frequently with updates which were more and more discouraging. No-one had any idea who the female leader of the group could be, Alfred and his team had come up with nothing at all and Ambrose had reported only a sullen silence from Richard Varley. Gloria hated days when nothing seemed to be happening, especially with the feeling that time was running out for the other children and the pressure of the political fallout from the kidnappings. And all the time she was having to explain to the monitors how the country was working now, what the main challenges were, how she saw the future. She was finally able to drop them back at the hotel at four in the afternoon. She had been told that Senator Miles Gwedu would be entertaining them for dinner but found him in the hotel lobby as they arrived.

Senator Gwedu looked like a cuddly toy, his round face, short round body, big smile and loud laugh had endeared him to many a foreign delegation. He had not taken part in the civil war, had not been involved in any corruption scandals while in office, drove a modest car and lived in his family home in Duport Road and had refused all attempts by the President to get him to join the cabinet. Instead, he had continued to speak out on all kinds of issues and challenge the government on everything from civil service reform and fiscal controls to their relations with neighbouring Sierra Leone which was just recovering from war, Cote d'Ivoire where war was in full swing, and Guinea which was sliding into conflict. He appeared to be untouchable, but right now he looked very uncomfortable.

He greeted the delegation with his usual charm but after enquiring how their day had been he told them he would not be able to join them for dinner that night. He had been called to an urgent meeting at the Executive Mansion that evening but he was sure Inspector Sirleaf would make sure they were properly looked after. Gloria was both furious and intrigued. What was going on at the Mansion that needed his presence, and how dare he casually volunteer her to entertain them in his absence?

Patrick, who had been especially accommodating all day as if to make up for his blunder in the morning, spoke up for the group. 'It's been a long day and I'm sure Inspector Sirleaf has to get home, we will be fine.' But Gwedu wasn't letting go.

'Absolutely not, it's part of our...' Oh no, thought Gloria, he's actually going to say it. '...African tradition of hospitality and welcome.' Gloria caught Lawrence's eye and they both felt like giggling again, what was wrong with them today? But really that old 'African tradition' thing, what few traditions had remained after the settlers had replaced all the chiefs with their own people a hundred years ago had been thoroughly wrung out of them by ten years of civil war, but here was Gwedu spouting it again.

It was Lawrence who saved the situation. 'It's not a problem. If Inspector Gloria can make it, we will both join you for supper this evening so the Senator shouldn't worry.'

Gwedu then just nodded at them and left. For all his uprightness and forthrightness, his easy smile and his laugh there was something cold about Gwedu. He may look like a cuddly toy but I bet if you made the mistake of crossing him, thought Gloria, he wouldn't forgive easily.

It turned out that Lawrence, who still lived at home with his widowed mother and young sister, was supposed to be babysitting Fatu that night.

'It's my mother's evening for her book club.'

Gloria was astounded. 'Her book club. I never knew there was such a thing in Monrovia and especially not – '

'Not for poor widows?'

'No, I didn't mean that Lawrence but I just never associated Edith and book clubs, it sounds so foreign, I suppose.'

'She was a teacher remember, and she loves reading. They started it during the war when she and some of her friends, mostly retired teachers, decided they had to do something other than sit around frightened all day waiting for another rebel attack. They didn't actually have any books so they just chose one they all remembered and one of them led the discussion on it. They started with *Red Dust on Green Leaves* because they had all read that at school, and went on from there. I think tonight it's *Far From The Madding Crowd*. Don't look so surprised Gloria, there are a lot of well educated people in this town.'

'Yes I do know that, I must be spending too much time with mad politicians, criminals and crafty teenagers. It does sound interesting though.'

'Well, I don't know that it's that interesting. Mum says you sort of know what everyone is going to say before they even start. Her best friend Mrs Kromah always disapproves of the book, Mrs Kamara only comments on the food that's mentioned in it and Mrs Gray, the bishop's mother, always tries to –' Gloria's phone rang and she signalled to Lawrence that it was the Chief.

'How did today go Gloria?'

'I don't think they will be too much trouble sir.'

'Good, and any news on the boys?'

Reluctantly Gloria had to admit there had been nothing. 'Did the President receive any demands?'

'No, it's been quiet. Ok well, have a rest this evening then. '

Gloria explained what had happened with Senator Gwedu. 'Lawrence and I will join them for supper.'

'Meeting at the Mansion eh. I hadn't heard about that one. Ok, thanks Gloria.' He rang off and she joined Lawrence at the care.

'So are you coming tonight or not?'

'I'll come but I will have to bring Fatu. Are you bringing Abu?'

'Oh I don't know if he'll want to come. And your sister is only thirteen so it's not as if they'll have much to talk about. I'll ask him.'

Lawrence dropped her off at the apartment promising to come back for her at six thirty. She went inside wondering when it had started that Lawrence dropped her home and collected her. She decided it was going to stop – from tomorrow. She had been driving herself around all her life and she wasn't going to end up like so many women she knew, reliant on a man to get around.

Abu was on the stairs in front of her talking with Rohit. He had just finished his football practice, judging by the sweaty t-shirt and sand everywhere, and he and Rohit were having an animated discussion. He better not be asking for one of Rohit's vehicles she thought. Rohit ran a large hardware store across the bridge and, contrary to many people's ideas of Indian businessmen, was one of the kindest, most generous people she knew. He was very fond of Abu too. His own sons were grown up and working in India and the States, and his wife had moved back to India when the war had started and seemed to be in no hurry to return.

'Thank you Mr Rohit, that is too nice of you. The team will be really happy.'

Rohit was smiling. 'Good evening Inspector ma'am. How was your day?'

'Hi aunt Glo, see you upstairs.'

Gloria waited until Abu had gone in before, feeling a bit sneaky she had to admit to herself, she asked Rohit what Abu had wanted.

'No Inspector. My nephew is coming to stay with me next week and I was asking Abu if he could join his football team. He's only sixteen and I want him to make some friends. I don't want him sitting in the house all day after school playing on a computer. Abu is a nice boy, he says Rahul will be very welcome. I told him we had some footballs and some practice bibs which arrived by mistake at the store and that he could have them.' Gloria grinned. Rohit had been in business for more than forty years, it was unlikely the balls and bibs had arrived by mistake.

'Thanks Rohit. You will come and eat with us when Rahul comes. Abu will cook.' It was no secret in the apartment block that Abu was a far better cook than Gloria and she always felt obliged to let people know he would be cooking when she invited people to come and eat with them.

She continued upstairs and went in to find Abu showered and dressed and poring over a sheaf of papers. She explained what had happened and asked him if he wanted to come out for supper that evening.

His immediate and enthusiastic response gave her a bad feeling about the list he was working on. Simple refreshments for sixty people it was not going to be, she was convinced of that. She declined the offer to look over the list saying she needed to make some calls before they went out.

Before she could start, her phone rang again. It was Ambrose.

'Ma'am, it's Richard Varley. He spoke to Clementine this afternoon when they were on their own. He has changed his story. He says he was beaten very badly, but claims it was his cousin Titus who beat him with an iron bar and that's the reason he turned on him and managed to get him in the barrel and put the lid on. He was scared of him. Then he was too scared to let him out and that's why he left him in.'

'So now he's saying Titus beat him and he killed him by accident because he was afraid. Why is he only telling us this now?'

'He couldn't answer that. He says he was in shock.' Gloria realised that Abu had overheard the conversation and she could see how angry he had become. She signalled him to sit down again as Ambrose went on talking.

'The story doesn't make sense anyway ma'am. When he wouldn't talk to us this morning I left Clementine there and went to the hospital. I asked Dr Brown just to take a look at the body which he did. He said immediately that Titus hadn't suffocated in the barrel, he had obviously been tied up and something put in his mouth and then put in the barrel. He was dead before even going in. They don't have the equipment to prove it but Dr Brown says he would stake his professional reputation on it. There's no way Richard Varley could have done that on his own.'

'And it's very unlikely that Titus would ever beat his cousin with an iron bar. Everyone says he was Richard's protector. So more lies, but just different ones now. In the morning we have to reopen the investigation. I will ask the Attorney General to halt the court case until we have investigated thoroughly. She will be glad I suspect, after the mess Judge Weah is making of it. Is Richard safe there though?'

'We could take him in for questioning right away in the light of his new statements.'

'Let me call the Chief and Clementine. If the Chief authorises it we take him and put him in one of the St Luke's homes. It's the quickest way. If we try to get the department of social welfare to do it it will take days.' She rang off and looked at Abu who was literally shaking with rage.

'If they try and spread that story about Titus we will do something Aunt Glo, I'm not joking. They took that boy and used him as a servant, did nothing for him or his family back in the village and now they're going to spoil his name. No way!'

'I know Abu. Don't worry, it's not going to happen, we won't let it happen. There's no evidence to support it at all.'

'Come on aunt Glo, who needs evidence in this town when you have money?'

'Well, more people than you might think. We are going to get Richard Varley out of there and we will get the real story.' She was already pushing the buttons and got through to the Chief on the second ring. She explained briefly what was going on. The Chief was uneasy when he heard it was the Varley family but in the face of the evidence he had little choice. 'Go on then. Take him out but try not to upset the grandfather.' Gloria snorted quietly to herself and called Ambrose back.

'Go and get him Ambrose. If they ask for papers say they will get them in the morning but permissions have been given. Take Alfred with you if he's still there.'

'No ma'am he's still out but Christian is here.'

'Ok, take Christian then. Call me as soon as you have him or if there is any problem.'

Abu had calmed down a little by the end of the conversation and Gloria explained what they were going to do. He didn't say very much, but when she offered to go through the famous list of refreshments needed for the memorial service, he shook his head and said it could wait.

'Go on Abu, let it out, otherwise you will be in a bad mood all evening.' He didn't need any more encouragement.

'This country is crazy. Every day people telling us that we are the problem, that we are rude and out of control, and threatening to put us in jail or in the army, but look now, who are the ones beating and kidnapping school students, the police. Titus is murdered and his so-called family invent a whole story to put the blame on their own son instead of finding out the truth. Adults –' He stopped and looked at her. 'Well, not all of them but most of them are useless. No wonder none of us want to grow up, we are scared we will turn into you people. Well, not you aunt Glo.'

'And not Alfred, or Moses or Mr Rohit...'

'That's true, but the rest of them.' He made a face but she could see he was calming down. Abu's temper was short and sharp.

'Look, why don't you get ready and we will go eat with these people. You can give me your professional opinion on them when we get back. And Fatu's coming as well.'

Abu didn't react to this news. He knew Fatu well but she was a child as far as he was concerned, not someone of much interest to him.

Chapter Ten

The Mamba Point Hotel was busy and the air conditioning was a welcome relief. It hadn't rained all day which was unusual for the season but the air was still and humid. Gloria declined the offer of a table on the terrace, she knew from experience that the beautiful night view of the moon hanging over the ocean would inevitably be offset by the clinging heat and the noise from the neighbouring apartment block. Everyone there had a generator by the sounds of it, and those who didn't would be sitting outside talking louder than usual. They found a table close to the bar and waited for the guests to come down.

'Are we early Lawrence? We will get ourselves a bad name if we keep this up.' Lawrence looking relaxed in a white linen African shirt just nodded at the other end of the table. Abu and Fatu had ensconced themselves away from the adults and, contrary to expectations, were deep in conversation. Fatu, who was quick to point out she was fourteen and a half and not thirteen, was very pretty and looked quite grown-up.

'Your small sister is growing up fast Lawrence.'

'Yes, and I think Abu has noticed!' It was true that Abu's original pose of casual indifference had been replaced by a look of real interest. As far as they could make out, the subject of conversation was football.

'Fatu is captain for her school's kickball and football teams. She is tall for her age and loves sport, but mum says it's not proper and she should be concentrating on her studies. But she is not winning that particular battle.'

They broke off as the visitors arrived together. Gloria wondered if they had all met beforehand or if it was just chance that brought them down at the same time. Introductions made, they ordered their food and then listened as Lawrence told a detailed and very funny story of the President's last trip up country. Muddy roads, illegal checkpoints and her car full of chickens and goats received as gifts as she went through. The visitors loved all that and of course it was good for the President's reputation as a sensible down-to-earth woman, which seemed to be something westerners really liked to hear. She had to admit that Lex and Magda made a special effort to include Abu and Fatu in the conversations. Lex and Abu discussed the relative merits of African football players while Magda got a detailed description of the various hair styles, of knotting and braiding that were currently popular in Monrovia. Lorretta was noticeably quiet. After her exuberant outpourings of the morning, she had very little to say, ate very little and seemed almost anxious to finish her food and get back to her room. A few discreet enquiries from Gloria revealed that despite being very careful about drinking only bottled water, and not eating uncooked vegetables, Lorretta was suffering from what was known in Liberia as 'runny tummy' – diarrhoea not quite bad enough to confine you to your room but enough to make you very uncomfortable. Gloria told her to go and lie down, drink black tea and just get some rest. She explained that sometimes it was just the climate or the change in pace that made people ill and she was sure it would pass. Lorretta gratefully left just as Gloria's phone started ringing. It was Ambrose again. She excused herself and went on to the terrace to take the call.

'Hi Ambrose, have you got him?'

'We have ma'am, it was very easy because there was no-one else in the house apart from the staff. I explained to someone who told me he was the steward of the house – whatever that means – that we had to take Richard in for more questioning, and he should tell his father and grandfather when they got home to call Clementine, but that Richard would not be in jail but in a secure facility. He's in St Luke's hostel over in Vai Town so I doubt they will find him there. Clementine assures me it is a decent place and as many of the boys there are waiting to go home they are quite responsible. I think Richard will be alright.'

'Thanks Ambrose, good job. We will interview him there tomorrow so make sure Clementine comes along.'

'Any news about the missing children ma'am?'

'Nothing yet. Ok Ambrose, good night, see you tomorrow.'

Back at the table she felt that familiar impatience creeping up on her. She wanted to get away and take some quiet time to think through what had happened before tomorrow. Patrick had left soon after Lorretta but Lex and Magda were still deep in conversation which meant she was able to explain to Lawrence what had happened, and then they drew the supper to a close after reminding the monitors that Senator Gwedu would call for them in the morning. He was going to take them round some of the party offices so they could meet a few of the numerous opposition parties. What a delight that would be for them, she thought. It also meant that Lawrence was going to be free as well and he volunteered to come to Vai Town.

They were all in the office early the next morning and a glum-looking Alfred reported that they had followed up all the leads on the kidnapped children without success. They had even tried to work out what direction the children had been taken in and where the two released children had come from but there were still too many options. Apparently no-one had seen anything and, even more unusually, there were still no rumours in the bars and markets. Everything was drawing a blank which was, in itself, very suspicious. She set them back at their investigations and then made her way over to Vai Town with Ambrose and Lawrence. Duala market was mobbed with vehicles, people and animals as always. It didn't seem to make any difference what time of day or night you tried to get through, it was always the same. They crawled along after Lawrence refused to switch on the siren and force a way through.

'Two reasons Gloria, there is no physical space to overtake anything here even if these cars were going to pull over and secondly, these are market traders and these Kru old ma's are dangerous. A police siren is only going to make them vexed and then you might not get through at all.'

Gloria snorted quietly.

'And that snorting thing you've started doing, it's really not good for your image.'

'I'm just saying we should be able to get by them, what if it was an emergency? And as a Kru woman myself I don't think I'm afraid of these women.'

Lawrence just rolled his eyes. He knew she was impatient to get some movement on the cases, it was going to be a long day. By this time Gloria was on her phone and Lawrence and Ambrose looked at each other as they heard her ask.

'How are things ma'am? I'm sorry we have nothing more to report but I wondered if anyone had contacted you?'

So now Gloria was talking to the President directly. That was going to upset about a hundred of Matilda Wesley's protocol rules. It was a short call and when she rang off she looked at Ambrose and then at Lawrence and muttered something about just catching up. Lawrence recognised the signs and decided to take a chance. He put on the siren and started to inch his way forward. Nothing happened until he gently bumped the taxi in front and it reluctantly pulled over an inch or two. By some miracle they squeezed past with Gloria leaning out her window shouting encouragement to the market women. Whatever she was saying was working as the women, instead of getting angry, were all roaring with laughter and pulling their market tables back a little to make some more space. Lawrence decided not to ask what Gloria was telling them. That level of laughter could only mean it was a joke at someone's expense and, judging by the way the women were looking at him, Lawrence had a feeling he was the butt of it. Gloria caught his eye and just shrugged.

'It's working isn't it?'

They slowly inched forward but as they had to keep the windows open to placate sellers and drivers, the car quickly filled up with a humid heat which was almost unbearable. Combined with the smells of the meat being cooked at the side of the road, the sting of the pepper which was everywhere in the air, the smoke from the burning piles of rubbish at the side of the road and the flies, it made Lawrence seriously contemplate abandoning the car and walking the rest of the way.

'God, Ambrose you must be in agony in the back, it's bad enough in the front.'

Ambrose just smiled and went on reading *The Famished Road*, a book he had produced from his bag. Gloria, head out of the window, on the other hand, was now in the swing of things and clearly enjoying the noise, the banter and the joking. Lawrence thought longingly of his usual air conditioned, obstacle free ride to and from work as part of the Presidential motorcade. He had forgotten what ordinary drivers had to suffer. Gloria poked him in the side and pointed to the taxi they were currently trying to get past.

'Look at the sticker.'

It was an old game they had played for years when they were training together, to collect as many different bumper stickers as they could without any repeats. The taxis and minibuses were famous for their pithy words of wisdom, wit or wickedness but Lawrence hadn't noticed bumper stickers for years now. Gloria was pointing at the taxi in front and he saw what at first glance was a very familiar quote from psalm 23. Unfortunately a combination of dropped and wrong letters had changed 'shepherd' into the legend 'The Lord is my Sheephead' which was proudly displayed on the bumper. They both laughed and went on laughing until they finally broke free of the traffic and turned left on Ambrose's directions, down a muddy track which led to the hostel.

Unlike most of the other women Lawrence knew, Gloria never seemed to need time to re-adjust her hair or her uniform. She was straight out of the car and up onto the porch of the hostel while he was still getting out. Clementine was already there and they disappeared inside as he was locking the car.

'Hey my man, no need to lock the car, tha not rogues living here.'

Lawrence looked around into the face of a small child who had the eyes of an adult.

'Is that so pekin, so I should just leave my car so?'

'I will watch it for you.' Lawrence straightened and left the door unlocked. 'My name is Oldman, big brother, try and look for something for me. I beg you.'

'I will try, just be here when I get back is all.'

Ambrose followed him inside and Lawrence remarked that sometimes all these children needed was for someone to trust them, to let them know that not everyone thought they were bad.

Ambrose kept walking and with a glance behind at the boy said. 'Personally I wouldn't leave dry rice out here without locking it up but good for you sir for trusting him.' He paused. 'I just hope we have something to get back to the station in when we finish.' Lawrence glared at his back as they went in but there was no time for further comment.

The large living area was empty except for Gloria, Clementine, Richard Varley and a large man who was introduced as Robert, the caretaker for the hostel. Lawrence thought that the caretaker could easily have passed for a night club bouncer which probably said a lot about what it was like working with these children. They sat down and Gloria addressed herself to the boy.

'Richard, we need to talk to you again about what happened in the house that morning. There are some things about your story that just don't seem to be true.' Gloria paused. 'It sometimes happens that adults blame children for things because they think the courts will not deal so severely with children. Unfortunately, being the cause of someone else's death is serious whether you are a child or an adult. I think you heard the way the judge was talking about you in court.'

Unprompted, Richard looked up and nodded. He didn't look so much scared as dazed, as if he had no idea what was going on.

'Now Richard, we want you to talk to someone, to tell them what was happening in the house, to explain who really beat you so badly and, most importantly, to tell us what happened to Titus.' She paused again. 'We know you didn't kill him Richard, we know that, and we need you to tell us what did happen.'

Richard stayed silent but looked around the group. Lawrence had already disappeared outside but there were still too may of them for the boy to talk. Gloria was just about to suggest they leave him with Clementine when Richard pointed at Ambrose and said.

'I want to talk to him.'

They had waited outside for twenty minutes when Gloria's phone rang. It was the Chief and Gloria knew from the tone of voice that he was stressed again.

'Gloria we need to talk, where are you?'

'I am over interviewing Richard Varley sir. I should be back in an hour or two.'

'I need to see you now. The Varleys are kicking up hell. They claim we took a child from his house without any permission from his legal guardians, and without any warrants, and that we have effectively kidnapped him. They are also saying that even with a warrant or tacit permission, it would still be illegal as in Liberia no arrests can take place after six in the evening.'

Gloria took a deep breath. She knew she could easily lose this one. As Abu had pointed out yesterday, money and influence still talked in this town and the Varleys had lots of both.

'The after-six rule sir, we always used to talk about it before the war but I don't know if it's actually a law or just a custom.'

The legal system was a complex tangle of customary law, US imports and, since the end of the war, half-completed reforms to different kinds of legislation. The no-arrests-after-six rule was something they had all grown up with but she was pretty sure it wouldn't stand up in court, but the kidnapping charges might.

'Plus the fact is we did not arrest Richard Varley, we took him into protective custody, which is one of the new powers we have as the Family and Child Protection Unit.' The Chief didn't respond.

'Maybe I should go see them sir and convince them that any further publicity around this case is not going to look good for anyone. I think the fact they are so worried is a sign we are on the right track, and if we are correct, it would be dangerous to send the child back to them especially as it looks as if they –'

The Chief interrupted. He didn't want to hear too much that might make him responsible for the safety of a child, the tightrope between politics and justice was getting harder and harder to negotiate.

'Yes, go and speak to them, but do it immediately. And then get back to me.'

Gloria decided to leave Ambrose with Richard and just go with Lawrence, if he was still free. She called Alfred for the fourth time that morning and he told her they had finally found someone who had seen something the night the children were taken from the prison. He promised to let her know as soon as he had any more information.

'Lawrence, let's go.' Lawrence had been doing what he did best, namely chatting to people and getting information, but he left the group of teenagers he was with and came over. Gloria explained what had happened and he agreed they should go together.

'How is it you have so much time to follow me at the moment, the Head of Traffic and you can be spared to drive me around?' Lawrence said nothing and just accelerated up the road. 'Don't try avoiding the questions Lawrence you know it's useless, what is this arrangement?'

'I have my orders so don't worry about it.'

'Your orders? From whom? And why?'

Lawrence sighed. 'My orders are from the President. She is worried about you and is not sure if you always appreciate the kind of danger you might be in. So she has assigned me to you for the foreseeable future, but not to take orders from you,' he added quickly, 'to make sure you are safe, and report back to her if you are putting yourself in danger.'

Gloria was silent. She was battling her anger at this insult with her relief that her best friend was going to be with her for the rest of the case. Finally she simply said, 'Let's hope it's a quick case then or you might find yourself permanently replaced.' Lawrence grinned, confident that would never happen.

'Did the President give you her mobile number then? In case you have to report me.'

Lawrence looked puzzled. 'No, she told me to contact her private secretary but I suppose you could give me it if I needed it.'

Gloria relaxed a little and shook her head. 'There is no chance of that Lawrence.' She was the only one with the President's number. That must count for something.

They got through the traffic and back over the bridge to the marginally less congested roads before Gloria had to resort to any of her bullying tactics. They drove straight to the Varley mansion, Gloria explaining on the way that she would do the talking. The huge black gates swung open before they had slowed down and they drove straight into the hidden world of Liberia's rich and powerful. She had so wanted it to be ugly, or at least tasteless, but it wasn't. The drive wound its way through beautiful green lawns and dazzling displays of flowers and shrubs, all being continually sprinkled with a gentle spray of water that immediately made you feel cooler. Behind these walls there was no noise, no dust and no smells apart from the perfume of pampered plants. The front doors were of huge carved wood inlaid with antique iron hinges and brass handles and they swung open as they went up the steps. A small man in a white jacket and black trousers motioned them into a large hall and then into an airy library with spectacular views of the sea.

'Ok Lawrence, you can close your mouth now. They've got money and, although it hurts me to admit it, they also have good taste. We're not here to judge the décor remember so just keep your eyes open. I don't trust them an inch. I mean, how did they even know we were coming here?'

The library door opened before Lawrence could say anything and Africanus Varley strode in, but he wasn't alone. Behind him in a line were the election observers and Senator Gwedu.

It was an awkward meeting. The only person who looked relaxed was Africanus, looking every inch the senior chief and gracious host. When they had all sat down he looked pointedly at Gloria and asked how he could help. His voice matched the rest of him. It was deep, slow and authoritative.

Gloria began to explain the events of the past few days until Africanus put up his hand and stopped her.

'Now Inspector, let us get straight to the point. My grandson, a thirteen year old boy, is arrested for the killing of our houseboy and his trial is adjourned twice. The judge, by your own admission, has made a complete mess of it, and then last night he is taken away by one of your officers while both his father and I are out of the house. Given the current anxieties about the safety of children in police custody, you must understand how worried we are, and how irresponsible your actions are.'

Gloria knew that she had to keep the facts simple until they had heard from Richard himself what had been going on here.

'I do understand sir, but last night we received confirmation that your relative,' not your houseboy she thought, 'was killed before he was placed in the barrel. It is clear that Richard's story of how the death occurred is not true, and we concluded that he was afraid to tell us the real story. Given that someone in your household might be threatening him, we judged it best to remove him until we can be sure of his safety. I'm sure you'll agree that was the best course of action.'

She didn't mention the marks of the beatings on Richard's body or his obvious fear of this man in front of her, she could play him at his own game. She stopped and waited for him to challenge her further but the revelation about Titus's death seemed to have quietened him. Senator Gwedu was almost physically squirming at this exchange but the election monitors were alert and drinking it all in. Let them see the reality, Gloria thought.

'We have also asked the Attorney-General to quash the present case against Richard in the light of this new evidence and we are confident that is what will happen.'

'Of course Inspector, I appreciate your attention to detail but I hope you also understand our position. If you had just informed us about Richard and your fears, it would have been different but anyway I can see you did what you thought was the right thing. I hope you'll keep us informed further.'

He started to get up, clearly anxious to end this public discussion but Gloria chimed in.

'But you haven't even asked where your grandson is. Surely that was your major concern?'

'I think your explanation has served us well enough and, after all, if someone is threatening my grandson, the fewer people who know his whereabouts the better.'

But the smile had gone out of his eyes and there was a new edge to his voice. Gloria knew she had an enemy now. Just what she needed, another powerful man who took her seriously enough to see her as a threat. It was flattering in some ways, but her previous experience had shown her that when powerful men were threatened it didn't usually turn out well for her.

Lawrence shifted in his seat and moved in closer to her. For one horrible moment Gloria thought he was going to take her hand but instead he asked the election observers if they had had an interesting day, which broke the atmosphere and allowed the conversation to take a more neutral turn. Their over-eagerness to share the day's events showed they had felt the strain too, and they bubbled over each other explaining where they had gone and asking questions and checking with each other for clarifications on what this person had said or what part of town this other thing had happened. And through it all Gloria could feel Africanus Varley's eyes on her. She finally stood up and looking him squarely in the eye announced they would have to leave. He didn't make any veiled threats. In fact he said nothing as they were leaving except that it had been a pleasure to meet Inspector Gloria again. Gloria didn't think he was being totally sincere!

'Lawrence, please don't start.' She knew he had been going to make some suggestions about her safety. 'My only concern is to find out what was going on here and sort out Richard Varley. Oh, and to make sure Abu is kept out of it this time.'

Lawrence nodded. And Gloria went on. 'But why was Gwedu there with the election monitors? I'm pretty sure Africanus Varley's house is not on any itinerary.'

'I don't know but he looked so embarrassed, he knew he had been caught. I love to see a politician squirm. Secret meetings at the Mansion and private visits to the Varleys, I would say Gwedu is up to something. Anyway, Gloria, where to now?'

'I need to get back to the station and check with Alfred what new information they have managed to collect. Time really is running out for those kids, I know it. And get some feedback from Ambrose about what Richard told him. What are you doing?'

'Me? Oh I am doing all those same things with you.'

'Really Lawrence, I know you are assigned to me but don't you still have to check up on which parts of the city your men are harassing people for money, or if the tyres are still on the Presidential motorcade?'

There had been an incident the previous month when a German businessman had been conned into giving a lot of money to some police officers in the belief he was buying two of the Presidential escort vehicles for his classic car collection.

'Or if all the uniform buttons are still shiny enough?'

'Ok Glo, enough. Lord, you would drive a man crazy, can't you let anything go… the officers who sold those cars were not from the Traffic division as you well know, they were the President's own security contingent. And as for harassing… oh forget it.'

She had succeeded in riling him but Lawrence knew of old that this was one of the things she did when she didn't want to talk about what was worrying her. 'By the way what were you saying to those market women this morning to make them laugh like that?'

'I just made up some story, don't really remember what I was saying. Well, I think I did mention that you had eaten some meat, dog meat I think I said, which hadn't agreed with you and we were rushing to get you to a latrine before there was any embarrassment.'

Lawrence shook his head. That would have got them all laughing, big shot police inspector eating dog meat and then suffering because of it. He hoped he wouldn't have to go across the bridge again any time soon.

'I presume we have some time to eat before we get back to the station?'

Gloria looked at her watch. It would be an hour before any of the others got back and it was likely to be a very long afternoon so they might as well eat something. The nearest place they could find was the Daybreak Mouth Open food centre at the end of Randall Street, a place Gloria knew well.

Chapter Eleven

The shop was open but with only two other customers, a slim woman who seemed to be eating her own body weight in rice, and none other than Inspector Barnyou sitting alone nursing a bottle of Malt. When people said Monrovia was a fishbowl she knew what they meant. They joined him. Gloria figured a catch-up with him over some food was as good as tramping up all those stairs to his office.

'Gloria.' So they were on first name terms now, and Barnyou was even smiling, 'How are you? Inspector Boakai,' he nodded at Lawrence. 'This is lucky, have you got the time to talk?'

They ordered dry rice and fish, and listened as Barnyou poured out his story. He was not having much success. He had set up a panel to investigate what had happened at the school and was willing to include some of the students. He was confident that the man heading it, his deputy, would get to the bottom of it eventually but he was having more problems with investigating the 'rogue' unit of the riot squad. For a start there were no women in the riot squad, there never had been. It wasn't that they couldn't join it was just that apparently no woman to date had shown any interest in doing so. So there were still no clues as to who the mysterious female leader was. Added to that, all the members of the riot squad and all the equipment could be accounted for so, according to their records, there was nothing and no-one missing.

'And before you ask Gloria, I checked the equipment myself. That was a great job for a senior police officer, counting out sweaty body armour, dirty riot shields and as for the truncheons… I have told them to get it all cleaned up and there will be regular inspections from now on but that was the worst offence I could find.' Gloria just nodded as he talked. Somehow she hadn't expected there to be any obvious signs of a rogue unit.

'What about the murder investigation?'

'All we have established so far is the time. The body was left on the steps of the cathedral between two and four thirty in the morning. We have found his parents who are, understandably, in shock. It seems they are Catholics from Holy Redeemer parish so we are wondering if placing the body on the cathedral steps was deliberate. And the mutilations are nothing to do with any ritual killing, it was just torture, deliberate and skilful torture. If these are the same people who have the President's grandson it doesn't look good for him.'

'Or even less for the other child. And still no demands, no ransom, nothing? Do we have any idea if these people have some kind of political agenda or if they are just criminals?'

'I think we can safely say criminals. Psychopathic criminals.' Barnyou looked exhausted as well as depressed but Gloria didn't blame him at all. Child killings were always the hardest to deal with and their powerlessness at the moment to do anything to stop them, or to arrest those responsible, made it so much worse.

They had finished their food by now but it lay heavy in their stomachs.

'Ok Barnyou, let us know if there's anything we can do. Alfred may have a lead of some kind so I will let you know if it's anything solid.'

'Great, your man Paul is doing a good job, wouldn't mind having him on my team actually.'

Gloria could see where this was going but didn't say anything else. They were all adults and could make up their own minds but she wasn't going to make it too easy. She had spent a lot of time working with Paul, training him up, and felt a bit resentful that she was going to lose him, which she knew she was.

They all arrived back at the station at more or less the same time and met in the conference room. Gloria reminded them again about the need for confidentiality especially with the cases they were working on at the moment. 'Not a word to anyone, not your mother or brother or whosoever, children's lives are at stake.' She let Paul brief them on the developments in the murder case and then turned to Alfred but before she could ask him to speak Ambrose jumped in.

'The funeral of that little boy is tomorrow ma'am at the cathedral. I hear the archbishop will be taking the service himself. Do you want one of us to go and represent the department?'

Gloria thought for a second. 'No, I will go and one of you can come with me. Tell Inspector Barnyou, he may want to come as well. We need to show our respect too. Now Alfred, what's this lead you've got?'

Alfred, who looked as if he hadn't been sleeping either, started talking very rapidly.

'Slow down,' said Gloria, 'take us through it step by step.'

'We spent all day yesterday talking to everyone we could think of, in every shop and every house in the area but we got nothing, not even a rumour. It was as if they had all shut down. Then this morning Izena was following up on a domestic dispute in the same area. This woman had laid a complaint against her husband, said he beat her and she ended up in hospital. But the time she was going to the hospital was around the time we think the body of Anthony Kheimouth was put there. So Izena just asked if there had been anyone else around at that time of the morning and she said yes, she had seen a pick-up truck parked at the steps of the cathedral. Even though she was injured, she thought it was a strange thing to see there at that time. It was painted black as far as she could see and with no writing on the side as most of them have. Even the windows were dark she thinks but she saw someone getting into the car. She described him as tall and very thin, but that's all she saw. The other strange thing is that as soon as she started telling us this the husband became very agitated, telling her to keep quiet so she stopped then and wouldn't say any more. So whoever these people are, they have a hold over a whole area, and a place as rough as Ashmun Street is not easy to control.'

Despite its proximity to the cathedral, the area was described in the pre-war Monrovia guidebooks as being 'cosmopolitan', and since the war it had only become even more cosmopolitan, not an easy place to subdue. So this group must either have a lot of money or a fierce reputation.

'Good work Alfred but get straight back there. I presume you are looking for the taxi driver and –'

Alfred, rather daringly interrupted her. 'We are ma'am but we also want to send Lamine in there, it's where he's from and he could get us more valuable information.'

Gloria looked doubtful. The last time they had sent Lamine off to a gang to get more information they had very nearly lost him to the gang so enamoured had he become of their lifestyle. Maybe this would be different and anyway they didn't have a lot of choice.

'Ok do it, off you go then, there's no time. Go back and question everyone again as well, keep up the pressure. It's our only lead at the moment.'

They went off leaving Ambrose and Lawrence and herself.

'Your information is too sensitive Ambrose. We have to keep it to ourselves until we are sure who is involved in this one. Did Richard tell you anything?'

Ambrose looked at his notes and in a quiet voice began giving them the details of the story Richard had told him.

'Richard doesn't like his father and is absolutely terrified of his grandfather. He would only speak about him after I promised him he could stay at the hostel, and reassured him that no-one in his family had any idea where he was. By the sounds of it his father is an alcoholic who is also in awe of the grandfather. It was Africanus who made all the decisions about what should happen to Richard.'

'What about his mother?'

'He says he didn't see much of her and when he asked the last time about her – there are no photographs of her and she is never mentioned in the house – his grandfather slapped him and told him never to mention her. His father says the mother walked out on him when Richard was in the States to go and live with some servant who had been with her for years. But he has no idea where she went and why she doesn't at least contact him. She was the only person he was close to and when she left he says he knew there was no-one to protect him. His grandmother was a timid quiet woman who lived in fear of the grandfather too. The man sounds like a monster. He started beating Richard when he came back from the States... with an iron bar sometimes. He liked to boast to his friends that he rules his house with a rod of iron, literally, and on more than one occasion he beat the boy in front of his visitors to demonstrate. He has also been known to beat Richard's father when the mood takes him.' He stopped reading from his notes and looked up. 'These people should never be allowed near children. I think this is only the tip of what was going on in that house.'

Gloria was grim-faced as she listened. It was truly appalling and yet none of it surprised her in the least, the methods and the justifications maybe, but the facts themselves were depressingly familiar.

'Go on Ambrose, what about the day of Titus's death?'

'Well, he was right when he said Titus was his only friend. Apparently Titus tried to stop the grandfather beating Richard one day and was so severely beaten himself that he couldn't move from his bed for five days. Titus then tried to keep Richard out of the house as much as possible, taking him with him to football practice and trying to get him to go to some church with him on a Sunday and during the week.'

Gloria nodded. 'He played on Abu's team, he says Richard used to tag along with Titus for practice.'

'But nothing could stop the grandfather of course and the morning that Titus died Richard says his grandfather had sent for him, furious about some glass or dish which had been broken. He remembers Titus going with him and begging his grandfather not to beat him, to give him a different punishment. When the grandfather lashed out at Titus, Richard tried to defend him and got punched on the side of the head. The next thing he remembers is waking up in the kitchen and his grandfather sending him off to school. When he came home from school and Titus's body had been found, his grandfather persuaded, cajoled and threatened him into believing he had killed Titus for not preparing his breakfast. He says he doesn't know what really happened.'

'Well it wouldn't take Sherlock Holmes to work it out, now would it, but we have no proof. What we do need to do is get Richard seen by a doctor who can certify that the boy has been abused and then make sure he is somewhere safe. He can't stay at the shelter, I'm sure Africanus knows where he is by now and will go after him if he thinks the boy is telling these stories.'

'And you can't send him to the convent.' Gloria sometimes used the convent as a place of safety but a thirteen year old boy was not going to make it there.

'No, that's not going to work and my place is too public.'

'I would take him ma'am but I'm staying in a single room in a house on Old Road, there is just no space.'

Lawrence had been more or less silent during the entire proceedings but his shocked expression showed Gloria he had been affected by what he had heard. Most Liberians would be, she thought. There was a lot of casual cruelty in Liberia but deliberate torture, especially of children, was shocking.

'Look, if it's just for a few days, Richard can come home with me. My mother won't mind and our place is big enough and secluded enough. My mother's book club is enough to scare off any intruders believe me!'

Gloria was relieved. It wasn't ideal but she didn't have any better solutions.

'Thanks Lawrence, that will be great. Would you go and collect him Ambrose? Bring him here and tell everyone, including Clementine, that we are keeping him here for safety. The only people who will know where he is will be the three of us, and your mother and sister of course Lawrence.'

Ambrose left and Lawrence looked at Gloria. 'I don't know how you are able to do this work Gloria, day after day after day!'

'Come on Lawrence, you're doing it as well now. And besides, I often wonder how you manage all that traffic stuff you have to do, and all those shiny buttons…' Lawrence, who was secretly quite proud of the extravagant Traffic Division uniform, laughed again and reached over and hugged her. It wasn't awkward as she might have expected, instead it felt like the most natural thing in the world and she relaxed into it until the door opened and the Chief came in.

'Oh, it's you two.' Gloria didn't know who he had been expecting but straightened her uniform and gave him a brief rundown on the day's events. The Chief looked dismayed at the news about the Varleys but endorsed their plan to take Richard into protective custody.

'Will he be safe here though?'

'I believe so sir, we will be extra vigilant.'

'Well, please make sure he is, we don't want any more trouble from the Varleys.' He left them together and Lawrence suggested a cup of coffee which was exactly what Gloria needed.

The rest of the day passed very slowly, the build up of heat and humidity making any thought too much effort. By the end of the day most people were discussing if there would be a storm that evening and hoping there would be, the downpour of rain at least giving an illusion of cool and more importantly breaking the tension that always built up before a storm. Gloria thought that the increase of violence and aggression in the period before a storm broke warranted serious study. She was convinced there would be a direct connection.

At four thirty Lawrence appeared in her office to tell her that Richard Varley had arrived and he wanted to get him home as quickly as possible. Ambrose had agreed to stay in the office to keep up the pretence that Richard was being kept at the station.

'You may as well finish early for once as well,' said Lawrence. 'There's a huge storm heading in and you'll be struggling home in the dark and the rain. Let me drop you home, get some rest and we can start early tomorrow.' Gloria agreed reluctantly and got her papers together.

Richard, in a large coat and a hat pulled over his eyes, was already in the car when they got to it. He didn't say anything to her and she left him to his thoughts. What a few days that boy has had she thought, or what a few years more like. It was already very dark from the storm by the time Lawrence dropped her home, promising to call for her in the morning. She went upstairs and saw that almost all the apartment doors were open as people desperately tried to allow some cooler air in. The heavy storm clouds and rumbles of thunder promised a spectacular display. The first crash of thunder dropped like a bomb on the house as she got to her own front door. She went in and saw that Abu had already unplugged all the electrical appliances, standard practice in a storm, and she could now hear him in the shower.

'Abu,' she shouted, through the rumbling and growling of the storm. 'I'm going to light the gas cooker and heat something up. Better get the lanterns out too.' His reply was blotted out by another brilliant flash of lightning and an almighty clap of thunder and then the apartment was plunged into darkness.

Gloria stood for a moment to get her bearings and then walked gingerly towards her room hoping Abu had not moved anything around. She felt the handle of her door and went in, her torch was always in the drawer at the side of her bed and she managed to get to it without tripping over the clothes she never seemed to have the time to tidy away. She fetched the torch and was just about to switch it on when she heard a rustling behind her and she froze. The hairs on the back of her neck were standing up. She listened intently in the darkness, straining to identify the noise and then turned very slowly trying to see shapes or hear movements in the grey darkness all around her. The next flash of lightning flooded the room briefly with a sharp white light and then she saw it. On top of the cupboard in the corner of her room was a snake, a large angry looking snake.

Even while she felt her legs weaken and the sudden instant drenching of sweat, Gloria was calculating with another part of her mind what she could do. Her knowledge of snakes was sketchy but everyone was taught as a child how dangerous they were, and which ones in particular to be afraid of. And the one glimpse of the snake in her room had told her one very important thing: she should be very afraid. The Green Mamba was one of those creatures which even the snake handlers in the villages feared. She had been up in Tappita a few years earlier when a Green Mamba was spotted in a tree near the small clinic. Panic had ensued and in the end, rather than deal with it, the villagers had just watched from a safe distance and then breathed a collective sigh of relief when it slithered off back into the bush. Highly poisonous, very aggressive, very fast… and she had one in the confined space of her room. The next flash of lightning showed it was in the same place and when she heard Abu calling to her she called out to him softly.

'Abu, don't come in here.' She could hear his hand on the door.

'I was just bringing some candles aunt Glo, I can leave them here then.'

'Abu, listen, there is a snake in the room, it is a very dangerous one and it is now between me and the door. I don't know what I'm going to do but you must not come in.'

There was a pause and then he carried on speaking in a quiet voice.

'I'll go and get Mr Rohit, he was explaining to me about snakes the other day, I think he can help.' Abu sounded amazingly calm. 'Aunt Glo just don't move and don't try and shoot it, Mr Rohit told me that hardly ever works and the snake just gets mad.'

Gloria smiled briefly to herself at the thought of trying to shoot a snake in a dark room but just agreed with him quietly.

There was silence after she heard Abu leave and she didn't want to risk turning on her flashlight as she was convinced she could hear the snake moving towards her. She tried to remember everything she had been told about them. They moved very quickly or did they? Would light or noise startle them or stun them? She could feel her panic rising and the urge to make a dash for the door and take the consequences was very strong but she knew that way she had no chance. So she continued to stand as still as she could while the slithering noise got nearer and nearer. She was at breaking point when the next lightning flash revealed the snake in more or less the same position. It hadn't moved. It wasn't sneaking up on her yet apparently. And she had better get her nerves under control.

It seemed like hours before she heard quiet noises on the other side of her door and then Mr Rohit's quiet reassuring voice.

'Inspector ma'am, are you alright?'

'So far Rohit. It's just this snake that's bothering me a little bit.' This said with a bravado she didn't feel. Her legs were shaking and she really felt as if she was going to have to sit down.

'Inspector, do you know what kind of snake it is, and how far is it from you?'

'I'm pretty sure it's a Green Mamba and it's on top of the cupboard staring at me but it doesn't seem to have moved since I came in here.'

'Green Mamba...' she could hear the concern in Rohit's voice. 'But you say it hasn't moved at all.'

Gloria could feel the weakness spreading through her body. She really wanted to move, to sit down. 'No, each time I look it is in the same place.'

There was a silence then that felt to Gloria to go on forever.

'Ok Inspector, I think the only thing we can do is take a chance.

I will come into the room and if it stays still you should make for the door.'

Gloria's heart sank. She wasn't sure what she had been expecting except the hope that Rohit would have some secret device for dealing with snakes, like some spray to put them to sleep or music to hypnotise them... She gave herself a shake. That wasn't going to happen and if they waited any longer something worse might. She wasn't sure if she was going to be able to run or even move towards the door. She was afraid she might just topple over but she controlled her breathing and concentrated on the door opening.

'Ok Inspector, I am opening the door now.'

In the gloom of the room Gloria sensed rather than saw the door beginning to open. The flicker of light from the kerosene lantern in the living room made a huge shadow of Rohit as he put his head around the door. Still no movement from the snake. Rohit gestured to her to start moving slowly to the door which she did but the next flash of lightning showed the head of the snake beginning to rise, its eyes searching for something. Rohit was now standing in the doorway with a net in his hand. Gloria kept moving towards the door and Rohit very slowly came into the room.

'It's moving,' she hissed at him, 'it's rearing up.'

With a speed she would not have believed him capable of, Rohit pushed the door all the way open and more by instinct than sight threw the thin net in the direction of the snake as Gloria lurched past him and into the living room. Abu grabbed her, and then Lawrence – when had he arrived? she remembered thinking – took her and made her sit down on a chair at the other end of the room. She didn't have time to say anything about Rohit before he appeared around the door again with a thick sack in his hands, inside which something was wriggling and hissing.

'Don't worry Inspector I've got it. I'll get rid of it for you but it's very strange to find one of these in a house. And even stranger that it didn't attack you, these things are very dangerous.'

'Strange is the word Rohit, but thank goodness you know how to deal with them.'

'Oh no Inspector, it's my first time to even see a Mamba. I think I just got lucky.'

The old man shuffled off downstairs with Lawrence in pursuit while Abu hovered around her and then went off to see if he could heat up some coffee.

'Aunt Glo, I am going to search the rest of the apartment, just in case there's anything else in here.'

'I'd rather you waited for Lawrence, let him help you. When did he arrive here anyway?'

'Oh he came as soon as I called him. I couldn't think of who else to call since Moses isn't here.'

'It was a good idea but get me a coffee and wait for Lawrence before searching.'

Lawrence came back and a thorough search of the apartment by flashlight revealed nothing more. They both knew it was an attack or a warning. Lawrence explained that he had looked at the snake with Rohit and judging by its eyes and its behaviour it had been drugged before being put in her room.

'So they weren't trying to kill me then, just scare me or warn me?'

'Oh no, they were trying to kill you alright. Rohit reckons the drugs would have worn off in about an hour's time and then that snake would have gone for you as soon as you went into the room. And don't forget you arrived home early tonight, you never reach home before seven usually, and your enemies know that. If you had come home at the usual time, you would be dead by now.'

Gloria's overriding emotion now was anger. Once again, someone had got into her house with ease and put Abu's life in danger, never mind hers.

Lawrence stopped her as she tried to get up. 'There's nothing we can do tonight. The power is off across the city – well, the few places that had power – and the generator for your building has shorted. It's still pouring rain, the streets are awash and there's a gale blowing. We will do everything tomorrow.'

'What about young Varley?'

'Don't worry about him. He's safe with my mother and assorted relatives.'

They switched to beer when Abu had gone to bed and the combination of shock and tiredness was pushing Gloria to sleep. She tried one last time to outline a plan for getting Africanus Varley but it was no use and the image in her mind as she slipped into sleep was his face staring at her but with the black glistening eyes of the Green Mamba.

Chapter Twelve

Gloria woke with a start, her thoughts jumbled and going at high speed. As she sat up she felt a figure beside her in the bed and turned to see Lawrence lying next to her. Oh no, what had she done? What had they both done? Too much beer, too much danger, and now this very awkward situation. Not that Lawrence didn't look good lying there with his eyes closed, but this wasn't quite how she had imagined a romantic encounter. Try as she might she could not remember what had happened. But before she could untangle it Lawrence opened his eyes and grinned up at her.

'Don't worry, nothing happened.' He switched on the light and Gloria was relieved to see they were both fully dressed. 'It was the only way to get you to go to bed. At midnight you were all set to go and hunt Africanus Varley and other assorted rogues and criminals. Instead you got a few hours sleep and you are still alive, both of which I consider major triumphs.'

She relaxed back onto the pillow aware now that her head was hurting and that the light from the lamp was very bright on her eyes. She couldn't think straight at the moment and she had a feeling that Lawrence had a lot more ammunition from last night that he would use over the next few days. She groaned again. Lawrence was out of the room already, shouting that he was going to check on Richard Varley and he would be back for her in an hour. She heard him exchange a cheery greeting with Abu and groaned again. Minutes later Abu knocked and came in with a cup of coffee. He had never seen his aunt drunk before and had never known a man to spend the night. He was grinning from ear to ear. Gloria accepted the coffee gratefully and didn't even try to explain what had or had not happened.

'Oh aunt Glo, I have left that list of things we need for the memorial service, remember you said you would help with the refreshments. I'll leave it on the table. Oh and Mr Rohit is here with one of his men to change the locks… again!'

This would be the third set of locks they had put on their door. She had thought that living on the top floor of a respectable apartment block would be security enough but it seemed anyone could walk into her house when they felt like it.

Gloria finally got up, showered and changed into her best uniform remembering she would be at the funeral service this morning. When she came through, Rohit was supervising the lock changing and promised to keep the keys until she got home that night.

'I have some work to do on the building today so I will be around.'

She knew there was no work to be done on the building but he had done this the last time too, making sure the place was safe, and that she felt safe. She was very grateful to him.

'Thanks again Rohit, you always seem to be saving me from something.'

'Not at all Inspector. I feel very bad that someone managed to get past us all and put this thing in your apartment. It should not have happened, it won't happen again.'

Gloria nodded wearily. 'Anyway, when is your nephew arriving?'

'My nephew gets in the day after tomorrow, I hope you will meet him in the next few days.'

'Not "the next few days", please you must come for supper the day he arrives. You won't have time to cook. Well, neither will I of course, but I think I can persuade Abu to prepare something. And please don't blame yourself for the snake, I am a police officer and I don't seem to be able to even keep myself or Abu very safe. That's not your fault.'

'Thank you Inspector, but I have been living in this building for more than twenty years. In fact I built it, did you know that?' Gloria hadn't known it. 'And I kept this place safe for most of the war. So I take my responsibility very seriously. No-one will get up to your apartment again, I promise you.'

Gloria knew he meant it and she believed him.

'Thanks Rohit. And remember, the day after tomorrow you and Rahul will come for supper.'

Lawrence was waiting for her outside. 'The snake story is already doing the rounds, just so you know. And no, it was not me who told anyone. Actually the story is that you were bitten and killed last night,' he was grinning, 'so it might be your friends in high places who spread it around, in anticipation of their plan succeeding. And the Chief wants to see you.'

Gloria listened in silence. She was still outraged at what had been done to her last night and more so that Abu had been dragged into things again.

'Look Lawrence, I have nothing to say to the Chief at the moment. So let's skip that one. How was Richard last night?'

'My mother said he ate some food and quietly went off to sleep. He was still sleeping when I got there so she said to leave him. She will stay with him today and no-one will get near him. She didn't believe the snake story either. She says as an excuse for staying out all night, it's one of the worst she's ever heard!'

Gloria then called Alfred and Ambrose and told them to meet her in the conference room and not in her office. 'And find out what Paul is doing, I can't reach him on his phone.'

'And if I hear any rumours around the office about you and I sleeping together...'

Lawrence smiled. 'Well it's not a rumour, we did actually sleep together but don't worry my main concern at the moment is to keep you safe, that's all.'

Everyone knew about the snake by the time Gloria got to the office, and she was touched that there was real concern for her safety and genuine relief that she was still alive, although she knew the jokes would start pretty soon as well. But she didn't have time to waste on that. Alfred and Paul were waiting for her in the conference room. She made it clear she wanted the snake incident investigated but she did not want it to become the focus of the investigation.

'It is obviously connected to one of the cases we are working on so when we solve those we'll find the people who did this.'

She told them she was trying to get the case against Richard Varley dropped but Judge Weah was making it difficult. Despite the evidence, she was still intent on making an example of Richard and pushing the 'children are out of control and need to be disciplined' agenda. Alfred and Paul listened but were clearly not that interested. Maybe they agreed with the judge, thought Gloria.

Alfred continued talking. 'Lamine has gone back into Ashmun Street to see if he can learn anything else about who is threatening them all there and if there are any better descriptions about the people who were seen in the area that night. Paul,' Alfred nodded at him, 'is going to be in the crowd at the funeral this morning along with Christian and Ambrose. I believe the criminals sometimes come back to see the victims, or the family's grief, so we might spot something.'

Gloria thought that seemed more the behaviour of arsonists but she didn't say anything. Alfred had thought about all of this very carefully and she didn't want to dampen his enthusiasm. He looked exhausted and she felt guilty. She hadn't meant for him to take full responsibility for the case but he, well, all of the team, had immersed themselves in these cases, and it was taking a toll. But even with all of them working at full throttle, it seemed like a pitiful response to a terrible murder and kidnapping.

'Thanks guys, I need a report on my desk of progress so far... before we all head off for the funeral.' They groaned but went off to get it done.

Holy Redeemer cathedral was packed to the doors and even with all the fans whirring noisily on full power, the heat lay like a wet blanket on the congregation. Gloria and Barnyou had been shown to seats quite near the front and from her place Gloria could see the family on the front row. The small white coffin looked lonely and insignificant even with huge piles of flowers around it. She had just sat down when a thunderous wave of organ, drums and tambourines announced the start of the service. The roar from the choir was the signal for the family to start wailing and the noise filled the cathedral.

The archbishop, despite trying to give the family some hope, looked grim. He banged the pulpit and demanded that they all take responsibility for a society where these kinds of things happened. People clapped and whooped and the choir hurried to join in as the archbishop launched into 'Blessed Assurance'. It went on like that for what felt to Gloria like a very long time and then abruptly it was over and everyone sat down.

The tributes followed including one read by Matilda Wesley on behalf of the President. Matilda was followed by scores of tributes from family and school friends, teachers, team members and representatives from the Ministry of Education until Gloria began to feel that people had forgotten they were talking about a ten year old boy and not some old man who had lived his life to the full.

As they were singing the final verse of 'What a Friend We Have in Jesus', Gloria felt a discreet tug on her elbow and turned to find the President's head of security. In his dark suit and tie and the shades he was never seen without – day or night, inside or outside – Amos Toweh, or The Colonel as he was known by everyone, had been head of security for the last three Presidents and, amazingly, had survived their various departures from office. One had been executed in a gruesome fashion, one had 'retired' suddenly after being found taking bribes from rebel commanders and the last one had gone into exile. He's either very good at his job, she thought, which, judging by the fate of the last three Presidents wasn't the case, or he knows too much to be allowed too far from the seat of power. At the very least, with that outfit he was always ready for a funeral.

'Inspector Sirleaf,' he spoke in a quiet whisper, 'the President needs to see you urgently so you have to come with me right away.' She caught Barnyou's eye and gestured that she was leaving and would call him later. 'No, the Inspector needs to come too.' She gestured back at Barnyou and they left together.

'Can you tell us what's going on then?'

'We received a message at the Mansion this morning. The President wants you to see it.'

'A message, you mean a letter or a phone call? Surely you could trace a call.' For all its faded grandeur the Mansion did have a very sophisticated electronic surveillance system.

'You better see it for yourselves.' The Colonel was famous for his reserve. It was said he lived only for his work, was never seen at social gatherings and wasn't known to have any close friends. According to Lawrence anyway, and he was the police force's very own living breathing information collection service.

The road took them along the side of the army barracks, with the ocean on their right and then swung into a very ordinary looking entrance at the back of the Mansion. So it was to be a low key visit then, she thought, except it wasn't. As they got out they found themselves in a large courtyard with store rooms and workshops with an opening onto what were the kitchens. The courtyard was completely empty with the look of those villages Gloria had sometimes come across during the war where everyone had panicked and run off at the noise of advancing fighters, leaving food on the fire, storerooms open, doors unlocked. This had the same air of a hurried departure except for a figure standing in the corner. In amongst the rice bins, bags of charcoal and tins of oil stood the President of the Republic of Liberia. But with her slight stoop and worried expression she looked like any Liberian grandmother, not out of place at all amongst the debris of everyday life. She was already walking towards them and was speaking before she had reached them.

'Welcome Inspectors.' She kept walking obviously expecting them to follow which they did to a small brick building in the far corner. It looked as if it hadn't been used for anything for many years.

'This was a detention cell in the good old days of my predecessor Inspectors, and after a tip off this morning my security searched it and found...' she pushed the door open and then seemed to shrink into herself, 'this poor, poor child.'

The boy's body lay at an awkward angle as if he had been struggling to free himself from the ropes around his ankles, but the expression on his face was of pure terror. Even at first glance it was obvious he had bitten through his own tongue as he was being tortured. Gloria had pictures of other children tortured in the same way seared on her memory. This had to be the other kidnapped child, Tony Cole. She remembered the details. His family had arrived from neighbouring Sierra Leone during their terrible civil war but had decided to stay on in Liberia judging it to be safer than returning to their own country. His mother and father were both teachers in Central High out at Twelfth street. They were people who had already lost a daughter and an older son in the fighting in their own country, most likely under the most savage of circumstances, and now their last remaining son lay here on a pile of rubbish, in a place which had probably seen more torture and bloodshed than she cared to think about.

Unexpectedly, the words of the last hymn they had been singing as they left the cathedral minutes before came into her head. 'What a friend we have in Jesus', and Gloria shuddered. She hoped these children had a friend now.

Barnyou remained impassive but his stiff movements as he went towards the body told her he was near to breaking point.

'Who found the body ma'am?'

'Sorry Inspector, that is not all. I will leave you to do your work. These people,' she indicated the security guards one of whom, a short young-looking man, was openly crying, 'can give you all the details. I need to show Inspector Gloria something.' They left without any further word and without any security, Gloria walking beside the President.

'I don't know what to do Gloria, I have never had to make a decision like this.' They were in the President's office now and, as if she couldn't bear to bring herself to talk about it, she placed a brown envelope in front of Gloria and nodded to her. Gloria found six glossy photographs inside all taken as Tony Cole was being tortured. The look of terror, the silent screaming, begging and crying of this small child as he was killed, was matched only by the look of horror and frozen trauma of the small skinny figure beside him. The President's grandson, hands tied around an old school chair and a hand pulling his hair back, forcing him to watch his friend die, was seated next to Tony Cole for the whole grisly event.

When Gloria looked up President Helen Sirleaf had tears running down her face but her voice was steely.

'These are monsters Gloria, I don't need to know or understand any more about them. They have to be caught. You have to get my grandson back, whatever condition he is in.'

Gloria nodded, her head hanging, for once out of words and feeling like such a failure. They had failed, whatever happened from here on, they had still failed.

'Right Gloria let's put aside the tears and recriminations and see what can be done right now.' The President was brisk now.

'Did these pictures come with any message ma'am? Any demands that might help us to identify them?'

'No, nothing at all, no demands. The pictures seem to be the only message.'

What kind of message, Gloria wondered? We are ruthless. We don't care. We don't want or need anything from you? Kidnapping and torture she knew from her friends in the Nigerian police force had long been a weapon of criminal gangs, especially in the Niger Delta where violent action to try and get justice for the people in the region had quickly deteriorated into plain old kidnapping and extortion. But it had never been a feature of life in Liberia, even during the war. This was the stuff of nightmares.

'The pictures might give us some clues ma'am. We will follow it up with everybody we have.'

'I am going to see the parents of that child myself. I feel responsible for what has happened to their son. Keep me informed Inspector, and please do not allow this story to reach the press.'

Her words were almost drowned out by a loud rumble of thunder, and the lights in the President's office flickered for a moment. Another downpour was on its way. Gloria nodded that she understood and left the office. Matilda Wesley was outside with her clipboard and a pile of papers she seemed to be poring over. She ignored Gloria completely and made a beeline for the President's door.

The rain had started and was coming down in sheets, bouncing off roofs and roads and filling the gutters. She knew the main roads would soon have small lakes on them and then the breakdowns and accidents would start. The traffic would be backed up within the hour. She found Barnyou standing in the rain. The boy's body had been covered up. There was water pouring in through the roof, washing away any clues they might have found, and with the help of the security men they lifted Tony Cole's body onto dry ground on some slabs higher up.

'You're going to learn nothing here Barnyou. If there was anything it's gone now but you should get someone to examine the body immediately.'

'I know Gloria, but who? You know we have almost no resources and no-one trained in forensics.'

'I would take him to Dr Brown. He is excellent, and he is discreet. If you explain the circumstances to him, he will do the examination and the information will not be leaked to anyone else.'

'Oh right, yes, that's a good idea,' he seemed dazed. 'Where are you going?'

'We have to get everyone onto this now. There is still a chance we can find Pri... the President's grandson alive. I will see you back at headquarters.'

The back road from the Mansion was already awash with water and Gloria could see nothing at all through the pounding rain. She hoped the Colonel had a better view of the road, especially as the steep ocean side cliff seemed to be much nearer than she would have liked. The Colonel, on the other hand, was clearly of the opinion that speed was always the answer and they raced down the road. When the high grey wall of the army barracks came into view, he promptly slammed on the brakes. They slid along the last ten feet of the road before coming off completely, twirled gracefully in the mud and came to a stop just inches from the wall. The Colonel, who still hadn't uttered one word or stopped chewing his gum, calmly put the car in reverse and forced the vehicle back onto the road and then, as if this was just standard driving, he revved up and sped off again in the general direction of police headquarters.

Although the roads were clogged with rain and debris from the drainage system, and littered with broken down vehicles, everyone scrambled to get out of his way. He made no gestures, never used the car horn, and didn't even look left or right, but still managed to cut a way through the chaos, and at top speed. In spite of herself, Gloria was impressed.

'I could have done with you yesterday when I was trying to get through Duala market.' She contrasted his speedy direct passage with her clown tactics of yesterday. 'Do you slow down for anyone or anything?'

There was a silence and Gloria thought he was going to keep up his strong silent image for the whole journey. Then he turned and grinned at her.

'Force of habit Inspector, if you slow down there's a good chance your enemies will catch up with you. This way they are always behind me trying to keep up.'

'But the way everyone moves out of the way for you, isn't that a bit strange?'

'Strange, what's strange in this town Inspector? It's still all about survival. You should think about that yourself a bit more often.'

They had arrived at the entrance to headquarters and the Colonel had snapped back into security mode. Looking straight ahead he said, 'Take care of yourself Inspector, and please find that child, we must get him back at all costs.'

She got out and he was gone before she could even wave. Another man of mystery, Gloria thought, this town was full of them. She had hardly gone a few steps when a familiar voice was calling her and when she turned there was Rufus Sarpoh, Liberia's foremost investigative reporter – by his own estimation. He was waving a small voice recorder under her mouth.

'Inspector, can you confirm that the body of the other missing child has been found in the grounds of the Executive Mansion, and that demands have been made for the safe return of the President's grandson?'

Gloria was stunned. Even for Monrovia this was fast. Too fast.

'Put that thing off Rufus.' She looked around to see if anyone had been listening but luckily for her a fight between a taxi driver who had been arrested and his passengers who wanted their money back had distracted everyone.

'Come with me.' If she just fobbed him off he might go ahead and print a story that would complicate things so she took him to her office instead.

'Where did you hear this Rufus? This is serious, I need to know.'

Rufus had helped her in some of her other cases in return for a good story but she knew he was no 'tame' reporter. He did have a nose for the truth and was not afraid to confront corruption wherever he came across it.

'I can't say Inspector. I have my sources, you know that.'

But the only thing Gloria knew was that she was heartsick from the killing of these children and from her powerlessness to do anything about it.

'Look Rufus, open your ears and listen good. We have helped each other in the past but that will not stop me throwing you in jail if you are obstructing my investigation. I thought you were concerned about justice man. Do not play with me-oh, this one is too big, too big for either of us.' Her voice had risen as she had fallen into Liberian English, it was so much more expressive.

Rufus wisely could see where this was going.

'Ok, the truth Inspector is that I received a call to my private mobile number. The number was blocked and a muffled voice told me the child's body had been dumped at the Mansion. That's all I know.' He took out his phone and showed her the last call received from 'Unknown number.'

'Was it a man or a woman?'

'It's hard to tell, it was muffled, as if they were speaking through something. But is it true?'

Gloria thought for a moment. 'Here's how this is going to work Rufus.' Usually they had a debate about terms that suited both of them but not today.

'The body of the other boy was dumped there but no demands have been made. You don't print any of this until I tell you. That way you won't obstruct the investigation but you also will get all the inside information on the story when it's released.' Rufus had started to object. 'Oh I'm not finished Rufus, keep listening. You will find out if anyone else has been given the story and, if so, you will let them know that if it goes to print we will come after them for obstruction, non-payment of taxes, traffic violations, dropping litter or urinating in public.' She knew she sounded like some hackneyed fictional cop but decided it wasn't a bad sound.

Rufus had never heard her like this. Gloria was known to be fair and straightforward in dealing with the press.

'It must be bad Inspector.'

'Not just bad Rufus, it's the worst.'

'You can count on me. And if I hear anything else, I will let you know too.'

'Good.'

'But I still get access to the story first when it breaks?'

Her answer was cut short as Lawrence burst in. He stopped when he saw Rufus. Rufus and Lawrence enjoyed a mutual contempt which meant they were not able to discuss anything in a calm way. Rufus wrote a weekly satirical column for The Eye newspaper on local political and civic issues in the fictional town of Bigmanville, in which he referred to everyone by a nickname or title. Lawrence was always known as Glamour Cop and the Traffic division as Wacky Races. Lawrence hated it but Gloria thought it was quite funny. She hadn't escaped herself, Rufus always referring to the Family and Child Protection Unit as the No.1 Lady's Detective Agency and to Gloria herself as Mother of the Station, in mockery of the President's Mother of the Nation tag. Gloria just laughed at that, it could have been so much worse.

'I'll come back later,' said Lawrence.

'Don't worry Inspector I was just going. Later Gloria.' They shook hands and he was out. Lawrence sat down.

'I saw you and Barnyou leaving the cathedral with Toweh. Any news?'

Gloria threw the packet of photographs across her desk. 'There's news alright.'

Lawrence opened them and jerked back in his chair.

'The news is that we are failing completely. Two children tortured and killed. Bodies left inside a church and inside the Mansion, no demands and no clues as to what's going to happen next. We have really failed.'

Lawrence was speechless. 'No demands whatsoever?'

'Nothing. I'm meeting the team now to try and redouble our efforts but we have to be cautious. The President doesn't want any publicity yet, she's very sure of that and that doesn't give us much room to manoeuvre. We are no further forward.'

'Well, we are a little Gloria. It's clear these are not ritual killings so this is either political or criminal or both. These people want money or power.'

'Or both.'

'Yes, or both, and we can stop saying that now! That's a step forward. But what's the next step?'

'I need to speak to the team, see if they found out anything more from that eyewitness. And I need someone to examine the photographs for clues but –'

'I'll do that.' He lifted the packet.

'Ok, thanks Lawrence, don't really know who I was going to ask on the team. Are they around?'

In ten minutes they had gathered most of the team together. Gloria explained what had happened. There were two pieces of information though that had been gathered from the crowd at the funeral and from the people in the area. The first was from Lamine who was clearly bursting to tell everyone what he had discovered. The night the body had been left at the cathedral one old ma who had been selling food there in the day had fallen asleep right on the street, worn out with malaria and fatigue. She had only woken when the pick-up had drawn up outside, but her instincts and her experience of the war told her that people driving around in the night could only be bad news so she stayed hidden. She had seen two men and heard them arguing. One, the tall one, had called the other one stupid for not filling the tank. She heard him say that if they ran out of fuel before they reached Clay Ashland, he would be in big trouble.

Clay Ashland, a definite clue at last but not a place Gloria would have associated with kidnapping. She had visited Clay Ashland the last Christmas before the war had hit them. Though there had been rumours of war even then it had seemed very far away. It was, or had been, a picturesque, almost pretty place surrounded by hills, with a river running through it.

'There was a famous Baptist minister there, I remember, Walter Pritchard. He knew everything about the area. I remember we went out there to buy one of his famous pigs for our Christmas.'

Lawrence coughed. 'Gloria, the Rev Pritchard died. He was shot right at the beginning of the war in front of his church.'

She remembered that now but she was distracted by another memory. She had passed through Clay Ashland a second time when the war was on. She and Abu and some of her family had been running from the fighting and had ended up there. It was a different place then. Most of the houses had been burnt, the few shops looted and there were young rebels lounging under trees at makeshift checkpoints. She remembered they were standing in line at a checkpoint outside what remained of the lovely old Baptist church when a young woman had driven up in a 'technical', a pick-up that had been adapted to carry a rocket propelled grenade launcher. This woman was like some kind of Amazon, standing at the back of the truck issuing orders, firing in the air and then choosing people at random from the line and questioning and humiliating them before killing them. An elderly professor from the university, two young boys travelling with their sick mother, their neighbour from Westpoint who had worked at the Ministry of Finance – all killed because they couldn't speak Gio or Kpelle, or were too fat which meant they had been 'enjoying' before the war, or because they were too smart like the old professor. Actually it didn't matter what answer you gave or how quickly you crawled on the ground, or licked her shoes or the even more humiliating things you were ordered to do, you would still be killed. She remembered desperately trying to shield Abu from view and hoping she wouldn't be spotted as a police officer. Momentarily she felt again those feelings of fear and anger.

'Alison Matthews,' the name came back to her.

The others looked puzzled.

'That female rebel leader, she was really famous, what was her war name?'

'Queen of the Night ma'am.' It was Alfred. 'She was terrible.' They all agreed. 'And after the elections she was given some kind of security job.'

'At the airport ma'am.' Alfred again. 'She was head of security at the airport, total madness after what she had done, and the fact that she was completely crazy. She only lasted for two months before she was fired for assaulting the German ambassador.'

'You remember a lot about her Alfred.'

His handsome face clouded over. 'She's somehow related to us, she is my uncle's daughter.'

There was no shame in that, given that most people in the country had relatives on both sides of the madness, killers and victims. Even in this room she thought. Lamine, Ambrose and Christian had all been fighters but Alison Matthews was a special case. Her brutality was legendary.

'She was based in Clay Ashland for a while, she had family there but I don't know what happened to her after the airport job. Apparently she was very angry when she got fired and there were stories of her still operating her unit illegally. We don't talk much about her.'

'Well, it's only a lead but if we are looking for a psychotic woman trained to kill and ruthless enough to torture children, and in the Clay Ashland area, she sounds like a good fit. So we go now, we can't wait for Barnyou's team but I'll call him and inform him. We will go in quietly and try and trace her first, we don't need a full-on battle until we know she is there and how many men she has with her. Alfred, you and

Christian will come with me.'

'And me.' It was Lawrence. Gloria nodded.

'Ambrose you need to stay on the Varley case, but don't put yourself in danger. Remember, they are dangerous people the Varleys. And Paul, you go back and talk to Lamine's contact, see if you can get more out of her.'

On the way out Gloria could see Pascal waiting for her by her car. He looked worried.

'Aunt Glo, I need to talk.'

'Pascal I am too busy mehn, no time for chi chi poly now. I'll see you when I get back.'

'No old ma, this one tha not gossip, it's Alex. You said you would look for him and he keeps asking about you. He is very sick but the doctor won't tell me anything.'

Gloria remembered how sick the little boy had been and her promise to look for him. She never broke a promise, especially to these children. She looked at Lawrence.

'We can call in. Is he still at the clinic?'

Pascal nodded. 'The Chinese clinic on Center Street.'

'We won't stay long Lawrence.'

'Hope not, you have a psychopath to apprehend.'

Chapter Thirteen

The Chinese clinic was up six flights of stairs and squeezed into four large rooms. The reception desk was empty and Pascal led them down a dark corridor into a room with four beds but only one patient. Alex looked even smaller now, his body shrunken and his eyes huge. Gloria was shocked at the change in him in such a short time.

'Hello Alex, how are you?'

Alex opened his eyes and smiled at her. 'Eh old ma, you lost from me. I thought you finish forgetting about me-o.' Gloria took his hand and knew how sick he was when he didn't pull it back.

'After all the trouble you gave me, how would I forget you.'

'Auntie, I sick-o.'

'I know, I know. Let me go speak to the doctor and then I will come back.'

Lawrence, true to form, had already found the doctor, a young Chinese man, who took Gloria into a small side room. Gloria explained who she was and assured him he could tell her what was going on. The young doctor looked at the table and then at the ground.

'Actually Inspector, the child has AIDS and there is nothing I can do for him, he is approaching the last stages.'

'AIDS! But a few days ago he was out running around.'

'Well, the boy who brought him in said he has been sick on and off for months now, gradually losing weight, no energy and hardly eating anything. My tests confirm that it is AIDS. We can keep him comfortable but there is no medicine that will make any difference at this stage. Maybe if he had come in a few months ago he could have started taking ARVs but with his lifestyle the chance of controlling it would still have been very small. I'm sorry, he is so young but your government hardly seems to take the HIV problem very seriously.'

Gloria was stunned. She thought she would have noticed, or someone would have noticed but that was the life these children had been forced into. Scavenging and hustling for a living any way they could and only appearing on people's radar, even caring people like her, for a few moments outside the supermarket or at the car wash.

The doctor was still speaking. 'We have no facilities here for him Inspector. This is a clinic not a hospice. As soon as he is stabilised a little he will have to go somewhere else.'

'But how long has he got left?'

'I can't say, but I don't think very long. An attack of any other illness will finish him off very quickly. That's what usually happens in these cases.'

She thought quickly, juggling all the things she had to do. 'Doctor, I have to go, I am on a big case right now but I will come back tomorrow and I will make arrangements for him to go somewhere.'

'Don't worry Inspector, he needs to stay here for a few days. I won't put him on the street.'

Gloria took her leave of Alex promising to come back the next day and bring food. She could see now that his shining eyes and glowing skin were not a sign of health but rather the sickness eating him from the inside and soon to devour him completely.

Pascal followed them out. 'So what did the doctor say auntie?' Gloria hesitated.

'He's very sick Pascal.'

'I knew it. He's got slim sickness hasn't he?' The local name for AIDS had never sounded so appropriate. Gloria said he did and there was nothing they could do to cure it.

'So he's going to die.'

Gloria nodded. She knew better than to offer these children false comfort. She sat him down in the small reception area.

'Pascal, the best thing we can all do now is make sure he is comfortable, we don't know how long this sickness can take. You did the best thing for him, you are a real big brother and you need to keep on being one. I have to go somewhere now but I promise I will be back tomorrow morning.'

'Ok, I will stay here with him. The Andersons said it would be fine like that.' He held out his hand as if they had made a formal agreement and she shook it. Pascal nodded to Lawrence and went back to Alex without any further discussion.

Lawrence knew there would be no talk of this in the car so he didn't even try. Clay Ashland was only ten miles from the city but it felt like a very long ride. It was now late afternoon and the intense muggy heat after the rain weighed heavily on all of them. Their arrival in Clay Ashland did nothing to dispel that heaviness. The once pretty little town, home to several past Presidents and the place where the now infamous True Whig Party was founded, was a shell. Many of the houses were roofless, some were broken down completely and there were still burnt-out shells of cars and a tank in the main road. The town hall had been patched up and seemed to be the place where government business was being conducted from so they avoided that. Instead Gloria sent Alfred off to see if he could find any of his family members while she and Christian set off to talk to any long term residents, if there were any. She knew word would spread quickly so there was no point in trying to be discreet or go in undercover. Better just to get the information they were looking for and if they needed back-up they could send for Barnyou. She hoped they could avoid that but Lawrence would stay in the vehicle just in case.

The tattered remains of the once famous Clay Ashland Gardens with its statue of President Coleman still standing, was where they came across Annie Richards sunning herself in the late afternoon glow. She looked to be in her nineties but Gloria knew that war could do terrible things to people and remembered to be tactful. Annie however needed no tact, she was ready and willing to talk. She had lived all her life in Clay Ashland and was indeed in her early eighties.

'If I sit here with my eyes half closed I can imagine I am back in the old Clay Ashland. So that's what I do each day and for a few minutes I can forget all the war and destruction. How do you cope with it?'

'I work,' said Gloria.

'Yes, that's good too,' the old lady said, nodding her head.

Gloria knew the old lady wanted to talk but time was running out and she pressed her for information on what had happened during the war.

'Do you remember Alison Matthews at all?'

The old lady looked puzzled. 'Was she from here? I don't remember that name.'

'The Queen of the Night,' Christian chipped in helpfully.

Annie Richards' eyes opened wide. 'The Queen of the Night, who could forget her? Wicked, wicked woman. She killed many people here, including my son and my grandson.' She paused again, as if searching back into her memories. 'Do you know why she killed my grandson, my youngest grandson?' Her words were tumbling out now. 'He was fifteen years old and she recognised him because he had played for the under-16s national football team. He had a great career ahead of him but he was just a boy. She said he and his friends had laughed at her during a football match when the ball hit her. She said she hadn't forgotten. Saul said sorry, he begged her, said they were just being foolish and finally she said she would forgive him… all he had to do was kill his father.' The old lady paused but her voice was still strong. 'She gave him a machete and told him to kill his father in front of everyone and then he could join her unit. Saul begged and begged, we all begged, he said he would do anything else but he didn't know how to kill. So she took the machete back and she killed his father in front of all of us.' She stopped again. 'But that wasn't enough, oh no, her wickedness couldn't finish. She made Saul lie down next to his father's body and with the same machete, with his father's blood still on it, she hacked off his right foot, the foot that had kicked the ball which had hit her. I will never forget his screams as long as I live.' The old lady was crying now, quietly, as if she didn't even have enough energy left for that.

Gloria shuddered. 'Where is Saul now?'

'Oh, he died a few days later. They said it was an infected wound but I was with him, he just stopped living. He never spoke another word, but I knew if he couldn't play football his life wasn't worth anything.' The old lady came to herself then. 'But why are you asking about her, what has she done now?'

'We just need to find her Annie, some other children's lives are in danger. Is she around here?'

'Here? No, that witch is not here, it wouldn't be safe for her. She destroyed this community. No, she's certainly not here.'

They got up to go and Gloria, uncomfortable at having stirred up such painful memories for the old lady, patted her awkwardly on the shoulder. Christian on the other hand, who had said almost nothing while the old lady was telling her story, leaned down and put his arms around the old lady holding her in a tight hug. She held on to him for a few seconds and then, as if sensing his turmoil, she patted him on the back and then gently pushed him away.

'God bless your search my son.'

Gloria was taken aback at the normally reserved, even uninterested Christian, but she didn't mention the hug. She had no idea what was going through his head but clearly something private had passed between him and the old lady. She sent him over to the small bar at the end of the main street to ask around while she headed for the church to see if there was a pastor there who knew anything about Matthews. Her phone rang as she was walking. It was Rohit. Surely she hadn't invited Rohit and his nephew for supper that evening.

'Inspector ma'am how are you.'

'I'm fine Rohit. Look I am very sorry about supper…'

'What supper Inspector? My nephew arrives tomorrow and that's when we are eating with you. No, I have been thinking about that snake incident and I am still puzzled how someone could get that snake up to your apartment. I spoke to everyone in the building and the only person who saw anyone go up to your floor is Dr Jupiter.' Dr Jupiter, now retired, was famously nosy and spent his days sitting by the open door of his apartment asking everyone their business. 'He swears the only person who went up to your apartment that afternoon, apart from Abu, was a young girl called Fatu. He questioned her of course and she said she was your colleague's young sister, and she and Abu were studying together.'

'Fatu?'

'Yes, isn't that Lawrence's sister? Abu told me she was at the dinner the other night and that she was "good fun for a girl".'

Gloria was puzzled. Unless Abu was sneaking girls up to the apartment which was unlikely, this was a ploy. 'I will ask Abu Rohit, thanks, but I don't think that was Fatu.'

'Dr Jupiter did say she was wearing so few clothes and had no bag' – he had an eye for detail, thought Gloria – 'that there was nowhere she could have hidden a snake and especially not such a dangerous one.'

'Thanks Rohit, it just gets more puzzling.' By this time Gloria had reached the church but she could see Alfred running up the hill to her and she stopped. He was out of breath and embarrassed to be so.

'Ma'am, I think I have found her.'

He stopped and took a few more breaths. 'My auntie says no-one has seen her in town but the story is that she is living in a disused farm a few miles away. She never comes to town and no-one wants to see her, but she is in the area.'

A lonely isolated spot and her fearsome reputation enough to keep people away. It sounded like the ideal place to keep prisoners.

'Good work.' She started down the hill to the car.

'Eh, where are we going ma'am?'

'We're going to find her of course, where do you think we are going?'

Alfred grimaced. 'It's just that we don't know how many people she has there, and we are only four and with only three revolvers,' Christian wasn't allowed a weapon although he was probably the best shot of all of them, 'so do we need to call Inspector Barnyou?'

'Yes we do, of course. I've just spoken to him and he is on his way but we're not going to sit here until he arrives. We will go and investigate and he can meet us there. If that's ok with you?'

'Of course it is ma'am. Let's do this.' Despite the heat, the tiredness and the terrible stories they had heard today Gloria grinned at him. 'Good for you Alfred. Let's go meet this cousin of yours then.'

The road quickly shrank to a track and although there were some signs that a vehicle had passed that way recently, the grass was still very long. The four of them had fallen silent until Gloria outlined what they were going to do.

'We are only going to go and look, we need to see how many of them there are and how well armed they are. I wouldn't be surprised if they had people in town so they might well be waiting for us. Keep alert.'

It was Christian who suggested they park the car a good way back. Lawrence wasn't sure how much further they would have got it anyway so after twenty minutes they pulled off into a clump of bushes and set off walking. By Gloria's calculations they should be able to get close without being seen as long as Matthews hadn't been warned in advance. They were under a wide green canopy of trees and the late afternoon sun slanted through, lighting up the path in front of them. Lawrence had taken the lead but they were following so closely behind that every time he stopped to check the path, which was often, they bumped into each other like some slapstick comedy routine. Gloria's exasperation finally got the better of her fear of stepping on a snake or of alerting the gang ahead and she straightened up.

'Lawrence, let's just go for it. At this rate it will be dark before we even get near the place and we are going to wander into the witch's den like Hansel and Gretel.' Their blank looks indicated they had no idea of that particular story and as she fished around in her head for the Liberian equivalent. Lawrence just nodded and started moving at a faster pace.

Three minutes later they were on the edge of the farm staring at a dilapidated house with a large barn attached. It was silent. They couldn't see any guards, and there were no vehicles.

'Looks like they have gone out. This is our chance to get closer.

Christian you stay back and cover us, you too Lawrence. Alfred you come with me. She might not shoot her cousin.'

'Well, we really weren't that close ma'am…'

'Come on, before the rest of them come back.'

They made their way around the back of the farmhouse. There were no signs of life at all. The rough kitchen at the back was quiet and there was no fire burning. I hope they are not out doing more mischief while we tiptoe around their house, Gloria thought. The closer they got to the house the more uneasy Gloria began to feel. Just as they reached the kitchen lean-to they saw some movement at the window. A tiny old lady, who would have done well as a witch in any of those children's stories, opened the back door and stared at them.

'Auntie Selma,' she heard Alfred say.

The old lady squinted up at them but even at this short distance she was clearly having trouble seeing them. 'Who is there? What do you want?'

'It's me auntie, your nephew Alfred.'

The old lady gave no sign that she recognised either his voice or his name. 'Who are you people, why can't you leave us alone?'

'We are looking for your daughter Alison.'

'I know who you are looking for, who everyone is looking for. Why can't you leave us alone I say?'

'I'm sorry but we think your daughter is mixed up in a very serious crime. We need to see her. Do you know where she is?'

The old lady made a strange noise that could have been a laugh. 'Oh you want to see her, well come with me then.'

Guns at the ready they slowly followed her, but there were no more people and certainly no security. They passed through a sitting room with no furniture in it and then into a dark stuffy room at the back of the house. A figure lay in the bed wrapped in a blanket like a shroud.

'There's Alison,' the old lady said, 'there's your dangerous criminal.' A weak voice asked from the bed who they were and Gloria told her. She started to laugh.

Gloria opened the shutters and she and Alfred stared at the figure on the bed. She was recognisable as the terrible Alison Matthews but only just. She was little more than a skeleton, her teeth had fallen out and her face had sunk in on itself. Alfred took a deep breath and stepped back a little. Gloria sent him to tell the others and then sat on the bed. Alison Matthews stared at her.

'Yes it's AIDS, maybe you've never seen anyone with AIDS before.' Gloria thought back to a few hours ago and young Alex at the clinic.

'We are just here to investigate a crime Alison, maybe you can help us.' She outlined the story and Alison laughed again.

'You thought I was the genius behind it? Maybe a few years ago but not now.' She claimed to have heard nothing about it and then drifted off into sleep or unconsciousness again. The smell in the room was almost a taste, a terrible taste of decay. When she opened her eyes again she was crying.

'I have done some wicked things Inspector but I am sorry for them now. The war was madness, we were fooled by the big people, by the devil. But look at me now. I don't want to die with all that on my soul, I am sorry.'

Gloria thought back to Annie telling the story of her grandson's mutilation and to Alex dying of a disease caught through no fault of his own and then looked back at the woman lying on the bed.

'Sometimes the madness was of our own choosing Alison. I can't forgive you, I am not a priest and neither am I an old lady whose grandson you killed. You better just keep praying.' She stood up and signalled to Alfred if he wanted to say something but he shook his head. She felt nothing for Alison Matthews. She couldn't hate this shell of a human being but neither could she offer her any words of comfort. She just wanted to get out of this place now and shake off the smell of death and despair.

Matthews struggled to sit up a little and stared at Gloria with mad eyes. She was clearly in the last stages of the illness where the dementia had set in too.

'Oh and Inspector, if you are investigating these killings you would do better to look closer to the President instead of coming all the way out here, closer to the President is where your answer is. Pray for me, please.' Gloria made no promises and Matthews fell back on the bed her lips moving but no sound coming. It was impossible to say if she was praying or remembering her glory days during the war, but it didn't seem likely they would get any more useful information from her so they left.

There was silence in the car again on the way back to town, each of them occupied with their own thoughts stirred up by their investigations. Alfred may have been wondering if he should do something for this woman who was a member of his family, Christian maybe remembering some of the things he had done during the war, and Lawrence very probably wishing he was back in the Traffic division where it was all a lot more straightforward.

Gloria broke the silence by telling them about the mysterious Fatu going up to her apartment. Lawrence was furious until they checked the times and realised it couldn't possibly have been his sister. It was an impostor trying, and succeeding, to get to the apartment. An impostor who knew enough about their families to use Fatu's name.

'I wonder where she hid the snake though.' Alfred finally said what they had all been thinking about, although clearly from different points of view.

Gloria then called Abu and told him what had been said. He confirmed that a girl had been at the apartment that afternoon but she was very young and she had been collecting money for the Girl Guides.

'Was she carrying a bag or anything?' There was a pause.

'I don't think so auntie.'

Gloria knew there was little chance of Abu noticing what she had been wearing and she was right. She asked but the exasperated silence told her Abu was really thinking how on earth she expected him to notice that.

'Where are you auntie?'

'On the way back to town, I'll be home soon. And remember Rohit and his nephew are coming for supper tomorrow.'

'Ok, do you want me to fix some food then?'

Gloria could hear the others sniggering behind her as they listened in to the conversation.

'We can talk about it tonight.'

'Ok, later auntie.'

Gloria glared at Alfred and Christian but she could see even Lawrence was desperately trying not to laugh and she gave in.

'Alright, I won't be cooking for them so you needn't worry.'

Gloria had invited the team to her house a few weeks previously, just before Moses had left for the States, and had been determined to prepare all the food herself. It was a disaster, and she still shuddered at the memory. It was still a discussion point at the office how she managed to reduce even simple dishes like fried plantain to a soggy unrecognisable mess.

They were all laughing now and that helped to cheer them a little after the day's misery. They passed through the last checkpoint and were once more crawling though Duala market which was still teeming with people and noise, the small market stalls lit by candles or lanterns and the music from the booths selling CDs and DVDs booming out in competition with each other.

'Alfred, if you don't object I will contact Fr. Garman.' Father Garman was known to be eccentric but he was kind and he was the only person in the Clay Ashland area Gloria could think of who might be able to give Alison some help now. 'I'm sure he would go and see Alison, it might help her.'

Alfred nodded gratefully. 'Thanks ma'am, maybe he can do something for her.' Alfred attended the Burning Bush Tabernacle church himself but he knew none of the pastors from there would go within ten miles of someone like his cousin. 'I'll talk to my mother too. We need to do something for auntie Selma. She has suffered too you know.'

They all silently agreed. Civil war in a small country like theirs had broken so many ties of family and community that repairing them had to be done at that level too. National reconciliation was a nice idea but the real work of reconciling had to be done between families and communities torn apart by violence, anger and revenge. That was going to be a long process.

They dropped Alfred and Christian off and Gloria asked Lawrence to take her to the clinic again before she went home. Alex was sleeping when they went in but Pascal was sitting upright on an old wooden chair staring at him. Gloria did not even suggest that Pascal go home, she knew how fierce his loyalty was and what a developed sense of responsibility he had. He had never given up on his friend Boyes who had been missing for months now, and he still felt he had let him down. She knew that he would sit here all night with Alex, keeping watch over him.

'Pascal, you have my number yes?'

'No auntie, how would I have your number?'

She wrote it down for him and told him to call her at any time if there was any change and then, promising to call back in the morning, she and Lawrence left.

Lawrence dropped her at the front entrance but said he had to go and check on Richard Varley. He had been calling his mother during the day. Richard seemed to have settled down there and was very quiet and respectful.

'Are you sure it's the same person? That doesn't sound like him at all.'

'My mother can be very persuasive Gloria, you know that.'

'Well look, don't come for me tomorrow. I am going to forget how to drive if we go on like this. I'll come to your place in the morning and see him and then we can take it from there. I can't think straight at the moment. So much misery Lawrence, so much misery.'

'Get some rest. I'll look at the photos tonight, see if I can see anything – and I just want to check with Fatu. If you need anything during the night though, call me. Don't be going to that clinic on your own. There are people who know a lot about your movements, they could easily trap you.'

Gloria was climbing the apartment stairs when Rohit opened his door. Gloria looked up at him wearily and then jumped. He was holding a snake.

'Rohit, where did you get that? Not from my place again I hope?' She had her back to the wall as far from the snake as possible.

'Sorry Inspector ma'am for giving you a scare, I just wanted to show you this.' He held the snake out to Gloria and in the dim hall light she could see it squirming. The thought flashed through her head that Rohit had gone mad or that he was part of the plot to kill her and she stumbled back further until her back was pressed against the wall.

'No, Inspector please, look carefully.' Rohit was embarrassed at having scared her and held out the snake again, close enough for Gloria to see this was no snake. 'Lord,' she breathed out noisily, 'it's a belt!' It was a belt, an imitation snake skin belt.

Rohit was talking quickly explaining his theory to cover her fright and his blunder. 'I found these in the market Inspector. In daylight they look cheap but in a dim light as you saw they are quite lifelike.

'So that wasn't a real snake in my room, it was a belt.' She realised the foolishness of what she was saying before she finished the sentence. Rohit had carried a real snake out of her apartment and it had been examined.

'No Inspector, I am saying that in a dim light the belt and the snake look very similar. We have been wondering how the girl, as it looks as if it must have been her, managed to get the snake into your apartment. She had no bag, she was wearing only very few clothes but she did have a belt on. I checked with Dr Jupiter, he remembers the snakeskin belt she was wearing. And that snake in your room had been heavily drugged a few hours prior to your arrival, in other words at the time the girl was knocking on your apartment door the snake would have been comatose.'

'And the girl was wearing it as a belt?'

'I think so. As your Sherlock Holmes would say, "when you have eliminated the impossible, whatever remains, however improbable, must be the truth". I don't see there's any other way anyone could have got a snake into your room.'

Gloria looked at the belt again. 'But even if it was comatose she would still have to be very brave to wear it like that and then talk her way into the house. I don't know anyone who would want to try that.'

'Ask Abu if he let the girl into the apartment, I bet he did. But you should rest Inspector, you look exhausted.'

'Thank you Rohit, thank you for this, at least it makes some sense of it, in a crazy kind of way.'

When she got in, Abu was in his room but on questioning him he admitted shamefacedly that he had let the girl into the apartment.

'She started talking about how she was so embarrassed and needed to use the restroom. I didn't want to ask her anything and because I was washing clothes in the other bathroom I let her use yours. She was only in for a few minutes so I thought it was ok.' He tailed off.

'No, it's fine Abu, I would have done the same thing. Who's going to suspect a young girl of setting a trap? These people are very clever. But it means we have to be even cleverer.'

'I don't think they will try again here auntie, and it looks like it's really you they're after this time so there would be no point in them hurting me,' he paused, 'so I think I'm ok, if you know what I mean.'

'Yes I agree, I don't think there's any danger in you going to football practice.' Abu looked relieved. 'And I don't think there's any need to have Morris or Leo stay here either.' Abu looked up and grinned, that was going to have been his next request but aunt Glo had seen him coming this time.

'Eh aunt Glo, you got me. Agreed. But let's eat.'

Gloria thought guiltily as she tucked into boiled cassava and a delicious gravy which Abu had prepared, that she had quietly allowed this situation to develop whereby Abu did the cooking and so also did a lot of the shopping for the ingredients he needed on his way home from school. And, when she thought about it, he did most of the cleaning in the apartment as well. While she had no problems about Abu doing his share of the work around the house and had no intention of taking on a houseboy or any other kind of domestic help, she didn't want to feel she was taking advantage of him. She looked up at him but he was clearly thinking of something else. Before she could broach the subject he looked up at her.

'We are having that service tomorrow Aunt Glo, you remember that?'

Gloria hadn't remembered and couldn't help thinking of the very serious issues she was dealing with. 'Well, tomorrow...'

'No Aunt Glo please, you have to be there. Even if you just come for ten minutes at the end and say something. Really it means a whole lot for you to be there. You know there are some terrible rumours going around about Titus, that he was into witchcraft, that he used to torture his cousin, that he was lazy and used to steal from them. All nonsense. If you come then people will believe he wasn't a bad person.'

Gloria looked at her nephew and wondered again where this burning sense of justice came from. He took his duties as manager and captain of the team very seriously.

'Ok Abu, of course I will pop in and say something. I think it might even help us to get the message out that not only is Titus innocent but that Richard is innocent too. As far as I can see he's not guilty of anything either, he's just scared.'

'Of his grandfather, yes, he is a scary man. Is that why Richard is staying with Lawrence?'

Gloria looked up at him. 'How do you know that Abu? He's there for his safety, no-one's supposed to know. Is nothing secret around here? How did you find out?'

'Well, I was talking to Fatu –'

'You were talking to Fatu?'

Abu looked a bit awkward. 'We were just talking about football, you know, I was giving her some advice about her team and what they should be doing.'

'So you were giving Fatu football advice and she told you about Richard Varley? She wasn't even supposed to know who he was or why he was there, this is a mess and it puts all of you in danger.'

'But I haven't told anybody else and I'm sure Fatu won't. In fact she even told me she hasn't.'

'So just you and Fatu?' she raised one eyebrow.

Abu seldom looked embarrassed but he did now and Gloria relented a little. 'Are you sure you have not told anyone, this is really important?'

'I know it's important aunt Glo, we haven't told anyone.'

Gloria noted the 'we' but let it go. She called Lawrence who had already discovered that Abu and Fatu had been talking. He was sure Fatu would not have told anyone else. 'She's famous in the family for being tight-lipped Gloria. I would stake my name that she's told no-one.'

'Well I wouldn't stake my name on Abu not talking but if you're sure. Just be doubly careful, maybe we need to move him. Ok, I'll see you tomorrow Lawrence.'

Chapter Fourteen

At seven-thirty sharp the next morning Gloria was outside Lawrence's house. It was a modest place, tucked away on the side of the hill with a view over the ocean and with only a few small houses around it had the feel of a small village in the middle of the city. The gate was open and she drove in and found Lawrence standing outside in his t-shirt and shorts drinking a cup of coffee.

'Morning Lawrence, you having a day off today?'

'No, just waiting for my uniform,' Lawrence looked a bit sheepish as he gestured towards his mother who was pressing his uniform shirt with the coal iron. Everything between him and Gloria seemed to be about scoring points these days.

'Gloria, is that you?' Lawrence's mother still had her teacher's voice.

'It's me ma, how are you? I see he's still got you working.'

Edith Boakai was a lady in her early sixties who had survived deaths, coups and civil wars and still insisted on all the formalities of a previous era. She was tall with grey hair but a fresh complexion and sharp eyes that told you everything you needed to know about her: intelligent, kind, strong.

Edith glanced at Gloria's not-so-neat uniform and said with a twinkle. 'Well, if you ever need anything done dear, just let me know.' She finished the shirt and handed it to Lawrence while inviting Gloria in, ignoring completely her protests that they were in a hurry.

'How is Richard getting on? I hope he's not giving you any problems ma.'

Edith gave her a look. 'He's outside feeding the chickens, he's a big help actually – especially since these two are always too busy to help.' Lawrence looked indignant at being put in the same category as his younger sister but said nothing. 'Richard helps me with chores round the yard and then we do some school work, the boy is very smart you know, and then he helps me to cook.'

Gloria was impressed but thought that maybe Richard was also a good actor. She looked up then as Richard came in the back door and had to blink twice at the figure in front of her. He looked quite different, younger and happier. He definitely wasn't acting.

'Come and greet the Inspector child, then go and wash and have your breakfast.' Richard came over and shook her hand, not meeting her eyes. He was quiet but seemed to have lost his agitated restless manner.

'How are you Richard?'

'I am good ma, thank you.' He said nothing more.

'And you are behaving yourself here, you're not giving the old ma a hard time?'

She saw Richard glance at the stick in the corner and then smile a little. 'I tried to at first but the old ma is a very good teacher. I only needed one lesson.'

Behind him Fatu was grinning and even Edith smiled. 'Now, don't be giving the Inspector the wrong idea child or she will take you somewhere else.'

Richard's head jerked up and Gloria saw panic in his eyes.

'No you can't take me from here ma, please, I will try harder, I can do more work, please.'

Edith pulled the boy to her and gently rubbed his hand and arm. 'Ah, my child relax, no-one's taking you from here, we are only joking. And you don't have to do any more, you are doing just fine.'

'He is Inspector,' Fatu had decided to join in, 'he is helping me with my lessons too.'

'You girl, go and get ready for school, you are going to be late again. Go on, no-one asked for your opinion.'

'So you have Richard *and* Abu helping you Fatu ?' Gloria laughed. 'You are lucky.'

Fatu scowled and quickly disappeared leaving Richard with them. Edith got up to fix some coffee for them and for the first time since they first met Gloria was alone with this confused boy.

'Richard, you like it here and it seems like the old ma likes you too. We just need to talk about what happened and why you are so scared. Let's be honest now, we know you didn't kill Titus, he was already dead by the time he was put in the barrel.' Richard winced. 'So we know it can't have been you who did it. What we don't know is why you said it was you, why did you make up that story?' There was silence and then Richard started talking in a low voice.

'I was confused. The last thing I remember is my grandfather beating

Titus when he was trying to protect me. When I woke up my father told me I had to go to school, that I had done something very bad but they would sort it out, all I had to do was do what they told me. I could see my father was scared, he is always scared of my grandfather. He just kept saying to me I should do what they told me, he was shaking me really hard and shouting at me, so I agreed. I had to. Then when I came from school the police came for me and I had to go to the police station and I just told you all the story they told me to tell.'

'So you don't remember any of it?'

He shook his head. 'Not really.' He put his head in his hands. 'I just want to forget about it.'

Gloria let him sit for a moment and then stood up. 'Well, all you have to do is stay here and be good to the old ma, do what she tells you and keep inside the yard.'

He nodded, clearly relieved that he was going to be left with Edith and the family.

Gloria took a cup of coffee from Edith and joined Lawrence outside. It was a long time since she had used a cup and saucer and she was having trouble balancing it. Lawrence took the saucer off her.

'Mum always uses these, I don't know why since no-one knows what to do with them.' It was already hot and the thought of the long day ahead filled her with some dread. She felt again that she wasn't on top of things, that, in fact, the situation was slipping away from her.

'I know you probably should be discussing this with one of your deputies but maybe it would help if we just sort out where we are up to with all of these things. If I can help with any of it you know I will.'

'That's half the trouble Lawrence, I don't have a deputy. They're a good team but too young and too inexperienced. And you're supposed to be just on protection duty.'

'Let me set up a meeting with Barnyou to start with and see how much progress they've made on the case of those children. That's a priority I think. Then set up a team to follow up on young Richard and his grandfather and the whole crazy household.'

'And find out what's happened to the election observers, I don't know if I am supposed to be showing them around. And Alex?'

'Well that's enough for any person to do in a day.'

'Yes, but I also have to turn up for the memorial service Abu has organised for Titus, and,' she groaned, 'Rohit and his nephew are coming for supper tonight. I can't miss that.'

There followed a series of calls and in ten minutes Gloria had meetings set up and the rest of her team put to work. By eight-thirty she was in Barnyou's office.

Barnyou looked angry and tense as he always did but his habitual air of despair seemed to have vanished.

'I heard about your raid on Alison Matthew's house. It would have been good if you had waited for us Gloria. It could have been dangerous, plus the fact is that it is our investigation.'

'There wasn't time Inspector,' Gloria couldn't remember his first name to reciprocate his new informality, 'and I thought it was more important that she didn't get away. I wouldn't have proceeded if I had thought it was dangerous. And you know the story now anyway, it's definitely not her.'

Barnyou let it drop. 'We took the body to Dr Brown. He confirmed that the child was tortured while he was still alive but that the mutilation had nothing to do with ritual killing. They are designed more to inflict the maximum suffering on the person. The amount of blood at the scene is evidence that the child was not killed there but somewhere else and then his body was dumped there. That's about it. We still have almost no leads.'

'How can a body be dumped inside the Executive Mansion and no-one see anything. That's very worrying for those security people surely. Unless they're involved.' She told him what Alison had said about looking closer to the Mansion for the solution.

'Toweh,' they said the name together.'

'He certainly has the access but what about motive and everything else? And it doesn't fit in with this mysterious woman the first children told us about.'

'Well, when you have eliminated the impossible –'

'Please do not quote Sherlock Holmes at me Inspector. I had enough of that last night.' She told them Rohit's theory about the snake and the belt thinking they might make a joke of it but Barnyou seemed interested.

'It sounds like one of those tricks they do out at the Cultural Village, at Kendeja. Before the war they were famous not just for dancing and drumming but also for playing with snakes. It might be worth investigating.'

Gloria looked sceptical, 'If we have time maybe. The Cultural Village has gone now anyway hasn't it? Didn't Prince Julu's boys attack it thinking it was the Executive Mansion compound during their "Operation Free Monrovia"?'

They laughed at the thought. There had been a lot of stories of young rebel fighters who had never been to the capital before, attacking places they took to be the Mansion. It was Monrovians' way of emphasising how ignorant these children had been, and a way of laughing at them and thus reducing the terror.

'I don't know about that but it was certainly destroyed. My cousin used to work there and is selling used clothes now down at Waterside. I could ask her.'

Gloria agreed. 'But we need movement on these child murders Barnyou, the child's life is at stake. They must want something, whoever they are, even if it is only attention but I know there's something else they want. And now they have the President at breaking point and all of us running around getting nowhere.'

'There is one thing,' Lawrence spoke for the first time. 'When I examined the photographs last night the first thing I noticed, well, apart from the horror, was the light. There is a small patch of light slanting in from somewhere onto the wall and the light shifts by the end of the photos so it is at the opposite end by the last photograph.' Neither Barnyou nor Gloria had noticed the light in the background of the photos and even now couldn't see its significance.

'Well, as it is light in the first of them and then gets dark we know they started in the morning and finished at night,' he paused at the thought of the child being tortured for so long, 'and it means the room they were in was facing east as the morning light is coming from the left of the picture and the light is at the opposite end in the last of them.' Barnyou and Gloria looked at each other. It was smart of Lawrence to notice this but not much help. He could read their thoughts.

'The other thing is, this is not a barn or a hut somewhere in the bush, the light is too clear and the angle of that beam of light, given the small window it's coming from, means it is quite high up. So these children are in a tall building with windows all round.'

'You can get all that from those close ups?' Gloria was incredulous.

Lawrence preened himself a little as he explained that part of his job in planning the routes for the President's motorcade was not just about stopping traffic but looking for potential dangers, and blind spots from the sun were some of the main dangers.

'Did you know that the height and angle of the sun is one of –'

Gloria stopped him quickly. He could go on at length when he got the chance.

'No, that's great Lawrence, I'm impressed.' She said and she meant it. 'I don't suppose you know how tall the building is?'

'No, there's not enough of the room in the picture. I would say taller than three storeys though.'

Barnyou was writing it all down. 'Well it's not exactly fingerprints or face recognition but it will narrow the search Inspector.' They were not on first name terms yet. 'Really useful… and impressive. We should collaborate more. I hadn't really thought about that before.'

Gloria interrupted before the two of them got involved in mutual admiration. 'What about the schools now Barnyou, are they back to normal?'

'Not quite normal. It's quiet in most places but that is because a lot of them are half empty. You know a lot of parents are keeping their children out of school with this panic about ritual killing. Swift FM are reporting every hint or sign of anything to do with ritual killing, most of it is nonsense but people are scared. And we have daily scares about attempted abductions of children from schools. All of which so far have been mistakes or confusions but tensions are high and there will be a fatality soon if it keeps on like this. A taxi driver was beaten very badly yesterday when he parked outside a school in Sinkor to collect his own children and people saw a rolled up carpet in the boot and thought it was a child.'

'He's lucky he wasn't over in Duala, he would definitely have been killed.' Lawrence was still nervous of the crowded market areas.

Gloria agreed. 'There was a similar incident outside Wilton High yesterday as well. It's always the same at elections but this is making it worse and these elections are still two months away.'

'Now we have the taxi drivers protesting about being targeted and claiming we are not protecting them. They plan to drive around in convoy today with the boots of the cars open and blow their horns every time they pass a school which will add to the mayhem. I've got patrol cars going around as many schools as possible but we all know that's just a gesture. There could be big trouble at any time.'

'What about the committee investigating the initial trouble at GW Horton, have they started yet? It might help if they got going and we could divert attention to them.'

'No, they are still selecting the committee members. The President appointed Sr Laurita to head it up and she is working on putting the committee together. She is going to announce today that all the children who went to hospital have been released and that no charges will be brought against any child. That might defuse things a little.'

They split up then. Barnyou was keen to follow up on Amos Toweh. 'He's been head of security at the Mansion for years. He probably knows more about government than any of us.'

Gloria agreed he was an obvious suspect but there was something about the way Toweh had urged her to find the President's grandson that had struck her as sincere. And there was still the question of the woman but I suppose, she thought, the woman could just be an accomplice. He is too clever to get his hands dirty, that's for sure.

Back in her office the election observers were sitting patiently around her desk. Except for Loretta Howsing. Gloria couldn't remember if she was supposed to be doing something with them, and if so what it was.

'Good morning Inspector.' Lex had become the group spokesperson. 'We thought we would just make our way here this morning so you wouldn't have to pick us up.' Yes, Gloria muttered to herself as she sat down, because picking you up was my priority today. 'We will be here all day with the local election staff to observe their training and maybe even give some advice if we're asked.'

Gloria remembered with relief about the training and that they would not be trailing behind her today. That relief made her a bit more amenable.

'Where's Loretta?'

'I'm afraid she has to go home. Her stomach...'

'Oh sorry to hear that. Well, Liberia's not the place for you if you have a weak stomach.'

Only Lex laughed, obviously feeling they were Africans together and could share a joke his colleagues couldn't. 'You are right Inspector. It's quite a country you've got here.'

Gloria stopped and looked at him. She had found this before with visitors from other African countries who thought their common heritage gave them the freedom to poke fun at Liberia. While most Westerners were either polite or focused on Liberia's food, friendliness or music, her fellow Africans seemed to think they had the right to make unfavourable comparisons. She was tired and she just couldn't stop herself.

'So in South Africa Lex, you've sorted out all the violence have you, and the corruption and your HIV epidemic?'

He looked very uncomfortable while the others were clearly pleased to see him taken down a peg.

'It's quite a country *you've* got there. But maybe we need to focus more on the matters at hand.' She then spent twenty minutes getting them to summarise their experiences so far, noting any questions they had and their observations.

Magda started straight away. 'I very much enjoyed watching you deal with Mr Varley the other day Inspector. You were very direct. I think it is still,' she paused obviously wondering if she was going to insult Gloria as well, 'very difficult to challenge some of these people in many countries today. I thought you handled it very well. But is it not a bit dangerous for you? The Senator told us that Africanus Varley is a very powerful man in this town.'

'I don't know about dangerous but, yes, power is still a big issue for us but I thought, and still think, that his grandson is in danger and that is our priority. Even big people have to live inside the law.' They nodded and the discussion moved on to other things.

Overall they were worried about the fragility of the election process, the causes of the riots and the treatment of the children involved although Gloria was able to reassure them all the children had been released and an official enquiry had been set up to look into the causes. They were also very concerned about the uncertainty around the kidnapping of the President's grandson and the implications for Liberia's new democracy. In summary, they were struggling with how they were going to fit Liberia into the DRAS – which Gloria learnt was the Democracy Rating Assessment System. It would be funny if only the international community didn't take it so seriously. Based on their score on the DRAS, Liberia would receive more or less money in international aid. It was madness, she thought, that these three inexperienced individuals had that kind of power. She had better be a bit kinder to Lex though, or just keep her mouth under control.

When they had gone off to their training she went into the main office where Alfred and Izena were huddled over something on her desk. They stood up looking guilty when they saw her.

'We were just on our way out ma'am.'

'Your way out where?' She noticed that Alfred didn't look quite so exhausted as he had the day before. 'Come on, what's going on?'

They looked at each other and then Alfred stammered something about it not being the right time, and it wouldn't interfere with their work but they could forget about it for a while if she preferred. Izena glared at him.

'We're getting engaged ma'am. We hope to get married at the end of the year.'

Gloria was a little taken aback. She thought Izena and Ambrose had something going on. But she recovered quickly and gave them both a hug, even though Izena wasn't really comfortable with hugging, and wished them all the best.

'No-one else knows yet ma'am, well my mother and Izena's family do but no-one here. It won't interfere with our work and if you think we should postpone –'

Gloria put up her hand.

'Whoa, stop. I know it won't interfere with your work because I won't let it. As for postponing, don't even think about it. You need to get on with your lives or this job will take over.'

'Like you…' Izena stopped herself but not in time. She looked very embarrassed but Gloria shrugged.

'We all make our choices Izena. Make sure they are your choices that's all. Now are you two working today at all or are you just going to stare at each other?'

Alfred grinned and went out. They would make a handsome couple, Gloria thought, but she hoped Alfred was strong enough for the young princess – and the Cooper family!

'Ma'am, we got some good news yesterday though, about the children from the mine in Sierra Leone. The ones who were in hospital have gone home and two of the other families turned up. There are only the three children remaining but I don't think anyone is coming for them. Should I take them to St Luke's?'

'Well done Izena, that is really good news.' Gloria felt a momentary glow of satisfaction. 'If they are small children though,' Izena nodded, 'better take them to the place we used the last time, was it the Princess Diana something?'

Izena nodded again. 'Yes, ma'am, the Princess Diana Home for Girls, it's the one on Snapper Hill. Yes, they were kind to those children.'

'Great work. Can you and Ambrose get me a full report by the end of the week? And we need the names, or the identities, of as many of the children who died there as possible. They are to have a special section in this new Memorial Garden. Ambrose is busy at the moment though so maybe you can start on that.'

She called Ambrose as she was leaving with Lawrence. She had decided to visit Tony Cole's parents before going to the service for Titus.

'I can't believe it's almost lunchtime already?' She said to Lawrence as they got into the car again.

'Lunchtime? When was the last time you had a lunch break?'

When she got through to Ambrose it was clear he was a bit stuck.

'I don't really know what to do now ma'am.'

She told him what Richard had told her. 'I will be with you this afternoon. Meet me outside the Varley house at three. We will have a chat with dad and granddad. And I'm sending Paul down to you as well. We need to start putting more pressure on these people.'

Lawrence looked at her. 'Is there any point in me asking you what your strategy is for the Varley meeting?'

'Strategy? Yes, get them to tell me the truth. Why they forced that child to take the blame for Titus's murder, and anything else they're up to. I don't like it Lawrence.'

As a strategy it, well, it wasn't really a strategy at all, but Lawrence let it go. He hadn't really expected much more.

'You still have to call in at the clinic don't forget.'

'That's right, let's go there first.' Then she was on the phone directing Paul down to join Ambrose.

The Chinese Clinic was full of people when they arrived. A long line snaked down the stairs and out onto the street. The receptionist explained it was half-price day.

'Half price for what? Consultation, treatment, drugs?' The receptionist didn't know the answer to that. 'It's just half-price day,' she kept repeating as if that should be enough information, which it seemed to be for the bulk of the people queuing.

A mixture of pushing, begging and excusing got them onto the floor where Alex's room was. Here it was very quiet. Only one other bed was occupied in Alex's room, an old man who lay perfectly still his thin frame hardly making a bump in the sheet covering him. Pascal was still in the chair. He looked exhausted.

'Hello auntie.'

'Pascal, how is he?'

'He hardly moves now auntie. He was crying in the night and the nurse gave him something, now he's just sleeping.'

Lawrence rubbed the back of Pascal's head. 'Come on old man, we'll go get some food and anything else you need.' Pascal looked at Gloria who nodded.

'I will be here.'

She sat in Pascal's chair and looked at the little boy who was sleeping peacefully. All his years on the street seemed to have dropped off him leaving his face smooth and unlined. She took his hand and his eyelids fluttered a little and she felt him squeeze her hand.

'I'm here Alex. Do you need anything?' She wondered how aware he was and what his thoughts would be as his life slipped away. Was he thinking of his family in some rural town or village, she wondered. He said something and she leaned in closer to hear him. 'I wan soft drink.' That she could do, she thought, guiltily relieved he hadn't asked for his mother or grandmother or someone. 'Pascal is bringing it Alex. He will be here soon.'

When they came back they looked as if they had enough food for a month's siege and Pascal looked a bit brighter.

'Did you speak to the Andersons?' Gloria didn't want him annoying his foster family.

'Mmmm,' he nodded, his mouth full and then swallowed noisily. 'They came last night and brought me food and then the old ma came this morning again with breakfast. She bathed Alex and gave him new clothes. They will come back later.' His eyes were filling up. 'They are too nice, auntie.'

'Hey, hey Pascal, that's a good thing eh.' She wished she had been able to do something practical instead of just dropping in for a few minutes.

'And the old ma talked to the Chinese man. She says Alex will come home with me when the doctor says he is ready.'

Gloria glanced at Lawrence who gave a small 'I-wouldn't-be-sure-of-that' shrug.

'That is a big thing Pascal. Are you sure that's what she meant?'

Pascal was suddenly back to his sharp self. 'Of course I am, I can't make a mistake on something big like that.' Gloria was not totally surprised but she was very happy. She knew her countrymen and women and most of them were big-hearted and generous. Even the war hadn't crushed that out of them.

She got up to go and with one last squeeze she let Alex's hand go. 'He was asking for a soft drink.'

'Bro. Lawrence bought juice. I will give him some when he wakes up. He can't drink soft drinks now.'

'I told Pascal I will come back later Gloria. You have Rohit round tonight. Pascal and I can play cards.'

'And you can lose your money bro. Lawrence.'

'Great, thanks Pascal, I look forward to that.' They left Pascal organising his supplies.

'How much food did you buy anyway?'

'Oh, about four bags full, I've never seen so many biscuits!'

'And it's all for Alex?'

'Well, it's mostly for Pascal obviously, but I couldn't really argue with him every time he picked something and said, "Alex might like this". He knew he was on to a winner with that one.'

'But he will take care of him so who's caring that he gets some supplies out of it.'

'Exactly.'

Chapter Fifteen

Tony Cole's parents lived in an apartment behind the Better Buy supermarket on Newport Street. As they climbed the stairs Gloria began to hope they wouldn't be in. Now she was here she wasn't sure what she wanted to ask them. The door to the apartment opened on the second knock and a man who had obviously been crying answered. He invited them in calmly enough though. The sitting room was dark, the curtains closed against the sun and also, she supposed, the wretchedness of the world.

John Cole asked them if they wanted a drink but they refused. He then sat down and looked at them expectantly. Gloria was uncomfortable. The intense heat of the room and the heavy atmosphere of resigned despair was almost like a physical weight. The only light came from a small candle burning in front of a framed photo of a smiling Tony Cole. She hoped they would never have to look at the other photographs of the last hours of their son's life. She had the feeling that John Cole was waiting for some good news although quite what would constitute good news for him at this stage Gloria could not imagine.

'Mr Cole, I am truly sorry for what happened to Tony and to your family. It is beyond words and we will find the people responsible.'

'Not the people, the animals Inspector. These are not human beings, they can't be. He was only a child, happy to be out of the war in Sierra Leone and to go to school. We thought we had saved him,' his voice was bitter now, 'that by staying here we could keep him safe, give him a normal childhood. He ended up worse than his brother or sister. His condition is so bad they will not let us look at him. The President came here, the President herself, and said sorry, but it is not her fault.' He seemed to run out of words. 'Anyway, what did you want Inspector?'

Gloria asked him if he or his wife had noticed any changes in Tony's behaviour or his moods in the previous few weeks. John Cole shook his head. If anything he was even happier than he had been.

'Not happy, he was excited.' The voice from the room was that of

Martha Cole and, despite what she must have been feeling, it was calm and measured. If she was 'sitting on the mat', part of the traditional mourning customs, she wouldn't come out but she had been listening. 'He was always a happy child Inspector but in the last few weeks there was something making him more than that, as I said he was excited about something.'

'Did he say what he was excited about?'

'Well not really, you know children get excited about lots of things. He was coming from school at the same time, he didn't have lots of money or expensive new toys we hadn't paid for.' As teachers and parents the Coles were obviously aware of some of the signs to look for that your child was being dragged into some dangerous or unsuitable activity. 'He was just more, well, more buoyant.'

'Was he friends with Prince Sirleaf at school?'

'Oh yes, very good friends. Prince came here a few times. Tony and Anthony Keimouth and the other two children called themselves the Praetorian Guard. They had been learning about the Ancient Romans at school, they were like a harmless gang with Prince as their leader. They made badges and shields and all that stuff that children do.'

Gloria didn't comment on the appropriateness of the Ancient Romans being on the curriculum of schools in post-war Liberia – she had found Abu struggling with an English assignment about the Loch Ness Monster two weeks previously.

'Were there any other children in this gang?'

'No, it seemed to be just them and the main ones were Prince, Anthony and Tony. Those other two children were more on the margins if you know what I mean.' There was silence then and Gloria sensed rather than heard Martha Cole crying quietly in the next room.

'She is a very private person Inspector. She is trying to be strong but this is killing her.' Her husband was clearly very worried about her.

'Give her time Mr Cole. Do you have friends or other family here?'

'Not family but we have so many friends, too many. We have received so much food and so much advice. In Sierra Leone it is not our way to be so…' he paused.

'Pushy and blunt.' Gloria suggested.

John Cole smiled for the first time. 'People mean well Inspector but if one more person tells me that this is God's will and He knows best I may commit murder myself.'

They took leave of the Coles and once outside in the glaring heat of the afternoon Lawrence talked excitedly about the connection between the children. 'Did no-one pick up on that before Gloria? It seems like such an obvious thing to ask about?'

Gloria was thinking that too but she remembered that the two children who had been released had been very afraid and had not said anything about being friends with the others.

'Well, we thought originally that they were taken just because of their ages. Then we focussed on the fact that Prince Sirleaf had been taken and remember we never got the chance to talk to the three of them who were, according to Mrs Cole, the closest.'

'But the people who took them knew who these children were. They took a very specific group of friends, one of whom was the President's grandson.'

'Well, more than that, the people who arrested them knew what they were doing. Remember how surprised we were when we found those young children in the cells. So out of all the children rioting that day someone managed to arrest this group of friends, the Praetorian Guards!'

'Right Gloria, so there is nothing random about this. Someone who knew these children well, from school or from home, set it all up. But who?'

Gloria was scribbling notes as they drove off. 'I need to try and think this through. It seems like a very elaborate plan, all those school riots, to kidnap just one boy, and the violence against the children seems so gratuitous and excessive. They could just have kidnapped Prince Sirleaf from school. No, his kidnap is a part of the picture but it's only a part and we still can't see the whole picture. That's what we need to work on.'

'Isn't that Barnyou's remit though?'

'I suppose so, but based on our last meeting with him do you think he's going to be able to do that? He is completely stretched just trying to keep a lid on things and carry out a basic investigation.'

'While you have lots of time?'

Gloria didn't answer, her mind whirling away somewhere else. He knew the signs. This was the time when Gloria detached herself from the emotions and politics of the case and started to fit the pieces together, to complete the jigsaw and see the whole picture. It was what made her a formidable police officer. But he also knew there was no way she would let it go now. She had her teeth into it like one of those killer dogs he had read about. The only way to get them to let go apparently was to shoot them. It was the same with Gloria, and Lawrence knew there were a lot of people out there who would happily do just that.

'Gloria, we are at the beach. Have you thought about what you are going to say to these people, I'm sure they are expecting great things? Well, Abu is anyway.'

'What, oh I'll come up with something. I'll tell them to stay out of trouble and work hard at school.' She was still distracted. Lawrence didn't think that sounded too appropriate for a memorial service but said nothing.

'I'll wait in the car for you. Just shoot your gun in the air if you need me to rescue you.' That got him a grin.

Abu had organised the memorial service for the hottest time of the day and as Gloria approached over the hot sand she could hear the loud and slightly off-key singing more associated with the football field than a funeral service. There was a large group gathered under one of the thatched beach huts and from her place at the back she could see Abu to one side and a short boy who seemed to be leading the service. After another two hymns and then the longest prayer Gloria had ever heard, she managed to catch Abu's attention and point at her watch. He whispered something to the boy in charge who stopped talking and then announced that Madame Inspector Sirleaf was going to say a few words.

In spite of her reluctance to attend, and her distraction on the way there, Gloria was moved by the sincerity of the team and its supporters. She had planned to say a few words about Titus and then a few stock phrases about keeping out of trouble. Instead she found herself telling them about Alex and Pascal and how Pascal was able take care of Alex so much better than she would have been. She used Titus's death to remind them how dangerous their society could be and how easy it was for powerful people to take advantage of others.

She ended with words she hadn't planned and which sounded sentimental afterwards but which in the moment struck the right note. 'Be a team on the field and be a team off the field. Stand together, take care of each other and look out for your brothers and sisters who can't take care of themselves.' They applauded and cheered.

Gloria left them to their refreshments and made her way back to the car. Lawrence was grinning from ear to ear. 'Wow Gloria, stirring the mob are we. I could hear the clapping from here.' Gloria glared at him. 'You can do it next time then.'

'You have to admire them though. That nephew of yours is a great leader and he really believes all those things you say.' Gloria ignored this.

Lawrence's belief that Abu hung on her every word and was so proud of her was not something that rang true for her. He was a teenager. You could be his hero today and his tormentor tomorrow. Wait till Fatu gets just a bit older, she thought to herself.'

They were pulling away when the boy who had been leading the service ran up to the car.

'Inspector, I need to tell you something.' Lawrence stopped the car so that he could speak. 'It's about Titus.'

Gloria got out of the car and walked to the back so they could talk in private.

'Ok, er…' She wasn't sure if she was supposed to know his name.

'I'm Anthony.' He looked at her expectantly but when she didn't react he carried on.

'Titus and me, we were good good friends. It was me who brought him to the team. My old ma used to work in that house in the kitchen and I went there one or two times. My ma left the place soon after Richard's old ma disappeared, she said there were funny funny things going on there but she wouldn't talk about it, she said she were too scary. I met Titus in the market one day and I told him to come to practice with us. After that he came most of the time except when the old man stopped him.'

'And Titus was afraid too?'

'Titus? No, Titus was not afraid of anything. He didn't talk much but he said the place was not good, and he was always worried about Richard. He really had patience for him but when I told him to come and stay with us he wouldn't. He said if he left the house he was scared what would happen to Richard.'

'But you don't know what he was talking about?'

'Well, all the people in that area say they can hear things at night, sometimes lots of cars arrive very late and stay until daybreak. People say its witchcraft.'

It sounded more like one of the 'private' parties she had heard about, not uncommon among Monrovia's elite. Drugs, girls, drink and gambling. It wasn't very wholesome but behind closed doors there was little Gloria or anyone else could do.

'Thanks Anthony, it's good you told me and if you hear anything else you will let me know? You can tell Abu.'

'Ok ma, but seriously that house is not correct.'

She told Lawrence what he had said as they drove to the Varley residence. Both Ambrose and Paul were waiting for her at the gates. She told them to get in and they drove up the long drive once again. They were met by the same man at the door who took them straight to the same room.

Africanus Varley kept them waiting for twenty minutes. Gloria was ready to burst by the time he came in but she showed none of that on her face. Africanus was accompanied by a tall thin man, obviously Richard's father, and another man Gloria recognised as one of Monrovia's most famous lawyers.

'We were just on our way back from Titus's memorial service, thought we might as well drop in and tell you about it.'

Africanus didn't even blink. 'Very commendable but hardly necessary Inspector. I actually sent someone to the service with a very large donation but it was refused. Your nephew apparently is as impulsive as you are. He sent the money back with a message that it was a private service.' Africanus seemed to find this very funny and roared with laughter for a few seconds. Gloria didn't think he found it all that funny really and made a mental note to have a word with Abu.

'Well, now we are here, I thought it would be a good time to interview the staff.'

'Look Inspector, whoever you are,' Richard's father had joined in now, 'I want my son back. You have no right to keep him. I am worried about him. We have been discussing this with our lawyer.'

Africanus was obviously displeased at the interruption and a withering glance at Richard's father was enough to make him physically shrink back into his chair.

'If you want to interview the staff Inspector you are welcome to do so. Martin will bring them.'

'Thank you but there's no need, we will go to them.' She stood up and indicated to Paul to come with her. 'Maybe my sergeant can ask you both a few questions in the meantime?' She looked at Ambrose whose expression hardly changed and indicated to Lawrence to stay with him.

The inscrutable Martin had appeared as if by magic and Gloria and Paul followed him through the house. A long corridor took them past a series of closed doors towards the back of the house. Nothing unusual in that until they turned a corner and came up against a heavy wooden door. To their surprise Martin produced a key and unlocked the door. The door led them down into a large modern kitchen and Martin sent the young girl who was sitting there to go and bring the staff. In a few minutes there were three women sitting around the table.

'Is this all the staff?' Gloria was surprised.

'We are a small team but very hard working.' Martin hovered around, seeming to have adopted a referee position between them and the staff.

'Well thanks Martin, we'll bang the door when we need to be released.'

Martin was uncertain but when it was clear that Gloria was not going to begin until he left, he did precisely that – and locked the door behind him. Gloria faced the three women, who looked terrified, and tried to lighten the atmosphere a little by asking if the locked door was to keep them in or the rest of the house out.

'Oh to keep us in here,' was the very earnest reply from the oldest of the three.

'So it's locked all the time?'

'Oh yes.'

'What about cleaning?'

'I do the cleaning,' one of the younger girls replied this time, 'and I am supervised all the time by Mr Martin. When I am finished I am locked back in here.'

'Is there a way into the house from the garden?'

'Yes there is but we can't get into the garden.'

Paul who had gone to look around confirmed that the outside door from the kitchen led into a small courtyard where the clothes were washed and dried and a row of small rooms where, presumably, these women lived.

'It must be like being in prison.'

The two older women said nothing but the youngest nodded her head.

'And you all live here?' Again the nods. 'But don't you ever go home to your families?'

'Well, this is our family. We don't need to go anywhere.'

It turned out that the older two were mother and daughter. The older lady, Miatta, was a cousin of Africanus, from the same village as Titus, and the youngest girl was from the same village and some kind of distant relative too.

So, more poor people with family ties that the Varley family could exploit and control. Gloria was furious but she was sure if she asked them they would say everything was fine for them and they were happy to work there.

'So what can you tell me about Titus?'

'Titus put us all in trouble.' It was the oldest lady, Miatta, again. 'He was always questioning the master, he could be very rude. And he was too close to the young master.'

'So what happened the day he was killed?'

'We don't know. We came in later that day, it was a different cook at that time and she's gone now.'

'So you didn't see anything?'

'No, we noticed Titus wasn't around but we thought he was off playing football again or something. Only when the cook opened the barrel and we heard her screaming did we know something was wrong. Then when Richard came from school and the police came we knew it must have been him.'

The youngest girl had her head down during all this talk but she suddenly looked at Miatta and burst out. 'Old ma, that thing you talking, it not true. You know it not true. It not good to lie about the dead.' She had a thick country accent but kept going at full speed as if scared to pause for breath in case she lost her nerve. 'Titus was a good boy. He was strong and he was brave. He was the only one to defend Master Richard against that nasty old man. That's why they wouldn't send him to school but still he found a way to get out the house and go play football. Master Richard didn't kill him, he cried like a baby when they told him that Titus was dead. This house is full of evil, myself I am too scary all the time. I don't like it.'

She started sobbing but neither of the two women made any attempt to comfort her. In fact they seemed to move away from her as if to put some distance between her accusations and themselves.

Gloria stretched out her arm. 'Paul, why don't you talk to Miatta and her daughter in the courtyard and I'll have a word with…'

'My name is Fanta.'

'I'll have a word with Fanta.'

Miatta and her daughter were clearly very unwilling to leave her alone with Fanta but they were conditioned to obey authority and reluctantly went outside with Paul.

'Now Fanta, you liked Titus yes?'

'Yes ma.'

'How old are you?'

'I don't know ma, maybe fourteen or seventeen. I have been here since I were small.'

'Do you like working here?' Stupid question she thought to herself, the girl was clearly terrified.

'I used to, when the Mistress were here, she were nice.'

'Richard's mother?'

Fanta nodded.

'And when she ran away with her houseboy things got difficult.'

If Gloria had uttered some terrible blasphemy she couldn't have got a stronger response. Fanta stood up her eyes blazing. 'The Mistress not run away-o. To leave her son here, his one. It not possible. She cried bitterly when they sent him to America. No, no, she loved the boy too much.'

'So what do you think happened Fanta?' Gloria felt she was disappearing down a bewildering maze.

'Witchcraft.'

'You mean here in the house? How did that involve Richard's mother?'

Fanta would say no more. To even talk about witchcraft could cause you big problems.

'Ok, where is Richard's mother now do you think?'

Fanta looked at her again. 'She's dead of course. I tell you these people are wicked.'

'Fanta, do you want to leave here? If you do, I can take you with me. I'll find somewhere for you to live.'

'Leave? They will never let me leave.' It was said as a statement, with utter certainty.

'Think about it. I am a police officer. If you want to go we can leave together right now. I don't think it's safe for you here.'

Fanta didn't seem to understand. 'You are a police officer but big big police people come here all the time, and people from the government. This family are too powerful. If I try to leave they will kill me too, like they did to the Mistress.'

Gloria could not persuade her. In some twisted logic Fanta believed that it was impossible for her to leave but also that it was safer for her to stay here.

They banged the door and Martin opened it instantly and without a word took them back to the library. There was what only could be described as an atmosphere in the room. The lawyer had left and Africanus Varley was sitting stiffly in his chair. As soon as they entered he stood up. His forced politeness was gone.

'You will regret this Inspector, I promise you. You clearly have no idea what you are dealing with here.'

'Well, I had a very interesting chat with your staff.'

He looked blank. She wondered if he even knew who they were.

'The relatives you keep locked up in the kitchen?'

'I know who they are Inspector. Don't play games with me. If you have any real evidence of anything then you need to do something about it. As I said you have no idea –'

'Yes, I get it,' she interrupted, 'I have no idea how important you are and how powerful you are. Power is very important to you obviously. I may as well warn you, I will have more questions.'

'Of course you will. Contact my lawyer and don't send a youth and your boyfriend the next time you want to ask some questions. Have some respect.'

Chapter Sixteen

They were in the car before Gloria apologised to Lawrence and Ambrose about the insults. Ambrose was completely unperturbed, he was used to the insults. Lawrence said nothing although Gloria thought she could see a smile on his face.

'How does he know so much? Not that Inspector Boakai is my boyfriend,' she added in for Paul and Ambrose in the back, 'but he knows we are friends. It sometimes feels as if everyone is one step ahead of us.'

'Anyway ma'am it was actually quite interesting. Richard's father said nothing at all. Even when we asked him a direct question he looked at his father who answered for him. Africanus, you are right, he loves power. That is the most important thing to him.'

'Sorry I didn't give you much time to prepare. What did you ask him?'

'We asked him to tell us again what happened that day which he was very willing to do. He says Richard has been very troublesome since he got back from America and they had brought Titus down to try and be a good influence but that Titus was instead influenced by Richard. He had become rude and disobedient, sneaking out the house and not doing his work. He says he was first alerted to something being wrong when he heard shouts from the kitchen and the police at the door. He was annoyed that the cook had called the police but she said, apparently, that she had panicked, thought she might be blamed and that there was no way for her to get into the main house anyway.'

'That's true enough. They are kept locked in the kitchen and only allowed into the house under supervision.'

'When Richard came from school his grandfather asked him what had happened and he told him the story he later told the police. The grandfather says he could have used his influence to keep the case out of court but that he knew Richard had to learn a lesson about the consequences of his actions.'

Gloria snorted. 'Rubbish. By all accounts Titus was a good lad and they handed Richard over to the police because they persuaded him to take the blame. Ambrose, I want you to try and find out everything you can about Richard's mother and her disappearance. I heard a very strange story today about that. Ask around, see what you can find out. And we need to get that girl Fanta down to the station for her own safety as much as for her statement. She wouldn't come with me today but we need to go back for her with authority to take her into custody. You should work on that Paul as soon as possible.' Paul pointedly looked out the window where it was already dark. 'Ok, I know it's late so do it first thing in the morning then. Ask Inspector Barnyou to send some of his men for her since it is in connection with a potential murder case.' She could feel Paul's eyes on her. 'Alright, I will ask him officially but you follow it up first thing.' Paul was getting more officious by the day, she thought.

It was after eight when she got home. By the time she got upstairs she could hear talking and laughter from the apartment. She found Rohit and Abu sitting with a tall skinny teenager, the famous nephew, she thought. As Gloria was being introduced Abu disappeared into the kitchen. She knew he was annoyed at her lateness but it couldn't be helped. Rahul, Rohit's nephew, was obviously tired after his journey but being very polite. Rohit was explaining to him who she was and telling him the story of the snake. Gloria excused herself and went into the kitchen where Abu was putting rice into a serving dish.

'Sorry I'm late Abu. It was a very busy day.' Abu just grunted and carried on putting food onto dishes. 'Can I help with anything? It looks great.' It did. Abu had prepared rice, fried plantain and palm butter.

'No, it's fine aunt Glo, just go and talk to them. They have been here for an hour already. I was running out of things to talk about and that boy is so quiet.'

'Well he's just arrived, he must be in shock I think.' Abu didn't respond so Gloria retreated from the kitchen. She wasn't Abu's hero at the moment anyway and had a lot of making up to do to. But that wasn't going to be in the next few days either the way these cases were going.

They had just sat down at the table when her phone rang. It was the President. She ignored Abu's glares and got up to answer it.

'Inspector, I have just received a demand. Finally we know what they are asking for. It's not good. Can you come to the Mansion now?'

Gloria made her excuses as best she could but, even to her ears, saying the President had phoned her at home and asked her to come to the Mansion did not sound real. Abu's reproachful look – he did reproachful very well now – stayed with her as she headed to the car. She knew Lawrence would be angry if she went out alone so she called him in the hope that he was still at the clinic with Pascal. He was, and agreed to meet her at the Mansion.

The Executive Mansion at night was like any other office building. Lawrence and Gloria had got through the security at the main gates very easily, as if criminals knocked off work at five o'clock. Amos Toweh met them in reception looking grim. He greeted them with a nod of the head and they went up in the lift to the fifth floor. At the end of the corridor the door to the President's office was open and the noise of a loud discussion could be heard very clearly. When they went in they saw Chief Inspector Kamara, Barnyou and, much to their surprise, Paul sitting opposite the Minister of Justice, who looked as if she had fallen out of bed. The head of the Cabinet, Dr Fofana was there and Matilda Wesley was hovering in the background. The discussions stopped as they entered. Apart from the President, Gloria had the feeling that no-one else was very glad to see her. The President made some brief introductions and then placed a disc on her desk.

'I received this disc this evening. It explains what these people are looking for.' She handed it to Toweh who put it into the machine. There was a brief flicker and then the small figure of Prince Sirleaf appeared. He looked very tired and thin but when he spoke his voice was strong.

'Grandma, this is Prince,' around the table there were a few smiles at the familiar introduction, 'the people are treating me fine but I want to come home.' Treating him fine apart from killing his friends in front of him, thought Gloria. 'The people say they will allow me to go if you do one thing. They say you must cancel the elections. If you do this I will come home,' he gulped and they could see him holding back his tears, 'but if you haven't cancelled them by twelve noon on the third day…' his head went down and a hand suddenly shot out from the side and slapped the boy hard across his face. They all gasped and there were mutterings around the table. Prince raised his head again, a small trickle of blood visible on his cheek. 'If you don't cancel them then the people will kill me the same way they killed my friends.' Prince had tears rolling down his cheeks now but he carried on speaking in a steady voice. 'I know you will do the right thing.' The screen went blank.

There was no awkward silence. As soon as the picture had disappeared everyone started speaking. But the chatter of sympathy, questions and suggestions couldn't disguise the smell of self-interest around the table, a lot of those present asking themselves what this could mean to their political careers and reputations. The President looked, for a moment, as if she was lost. It was Gloria who brought some order to the discussion by loudly asking the President what Prince had meant by saying 'I know you will do the right thing'.

'That sounds like a very grown-up thing for a boy to say under those circumstances.'

Her question got through to the President who nodded at Gloria.

'Well spotted Inspector. It is a very grown up thing for any boy to say but I believe he was sending me a message. It is no secret that Prince and I are very close and he and I spent a lot of time talking about many things. He used to ask me why I even wanted to be President of a country where there was so much trouble and where so many people seemed to hate me. Why didn't I stay in America and enjoy my old age?

'I won't bore you with my political philosophy but I told him that nothing changes if everyone leaves it to someone else to make those changes. We talked about duty being more important than personal comfort or ambition and that sometimes *doing the right thing* meant putting your country first before your family or yourself. It's a phrase I used a lot and he used to tease me with it. I believe my grandson was telling me,' she looked round the table at the people who had been arguing about their own futures moments before, 'to remember my own words and not to do anything that could jeopardise the country, anything that might derail our fragile peace. I'm glad you picked that up Inspector.'

'Brave as well as smart your Excellency. You must be very proud of him.'

'No, I am very scared because I don't know what to do, I don't know if I am strong enough to put my own philosophy into action, or even if I want to. I want my grandson back.'

Dr Fofana was next to speak. Fofana was an old man, too old for personal ambition, and trusted by the President.

'Why do they want the elections cancelled?' No-one said anything, they knew he was going to answer his own question.

'The international community is watching us closely. They have backed us only because we promised to restore democracy, and we claimed to be strong enough to take on all the warlords and all the mess left by the war and in three years make Liberia a democratic country again. It is based on those promises that they have given us all the money and the support which we rely on. The local elections are a strong signal to them that we are on track and if we have to cancel them under pressure from some random criminal group we will lose credibility. It won't be immediate, you know how international relations work, but very soon some of these same people who are our supporters now, will start having talks with the opposition. It will be the beginning of the end for us and, I believe, for Liberia's future.'

'Surely the international community will understand the pressure the President is under,' Barnyou jumped in. 'Surely they will agree that cancelling the elections to save her grandsons life is a price worth paying. They won't abandon us immediately.'

The President answered for Fofana. 'I'm afraid Dr Fofana is correct. Oh they will sympathise on a personal level, they couldn't do otherwise, but what they will see in foreign policy terms is a weak government at the mercy of criminals. They will switch sides very quickly if they believe another candidate can deliver what they want more efficiently.'

'And we all know that will be the end of the peace. We will be at war again by the end of the year. No-one else is strong enough to take the peace forward and all the players who prefer the chaos of war will have won. There are a lot of people whose business is much easier conducted in war than in peace.' Coming from Albertine Bull, the Minister of Justice and a member of the opposition, this was convincing.

It was back to Gloria who asked, 'What are you going to do?'

'I don't know. I know there is no guarantee at all that cancelling the elections will ensure Prince's safe return and will almost certainly result in war but I am not sure I can take the risk. My question to the police is 'What are you going to do? Can you give me any hope at all?'

Gloria explained their efforts so far and the Chief and Barnyou outlined what they knew to date. She realised they couldn't say too much with Amos Toweh in the room but their efforts sounded pitiful compared to what they were up against. Three hours later the meeting broke up with a solemn promise from the President that they had two days left otherwise she would make her decision public.

Although it was now after midnight the Chief pulled them into a small meeting room on the bottom floor.

'I know you are all working flat out but we need to do more.

Follow up the leads you talked about but I want a meeting in my office tomorrow at three sharp, and I want to hear some progress.'

As they left he said to Gloria, 'Have you given your sergeant to Barnyou's crowd then?'

Gloria made a face. 'He is supposed to be liaising but I think he feels the CID is more for him than our unit.'

The Chief agreed. 'Maybe it is. And by the way, I will take on the election observers from now on so don't worry about them.' Gloria hadn't been, but was relieved to have it officially taken off her shoulders. The Chief looked at Lawrence. 'Unless you feel you could take them on Inspector.'

Lawrence's face didn't change but he pointed out that he was acting as security for Gloria on the President's orders. 'We could always check with her sir.'

'Very funny Boakai. I hope you are doing something useful that's all.'

'Well, Inspector Gloria is still alive sir. That's quite useful.' But the Chief was already heading out the door into the warm dark night where the distant flashes and rumbles promised another storm was coming.

'Let's go home Gloria.'

'No, since we are already in town Lawrence I'm going to the clinic first. Was Pascal there when you went?'

'No, Mrs Anderson had sent him home to sleep. She was going to sit with him instead.'

They drove down in Gloria's car for a change. 'I had no idea it was so serious Lawrence. I mean a demand for money would have been more manageable, all this political stuff is beyond me.'

'Looks like it's beyond most of the people in that room. What a decision she has to make, her grandson or her country.'

Gloria snorted and then tried to turn it into a cough when she caught Lawrence's look.

'Her grandson or her country! Honestly Lawrence, as if those people will return the boy even if she cancels the elections. If we don't find him she can cancel the elections, resign from the presidency and go into exile and they will still kill Prince. Even the child knows that, could you not see his eyes? We have to find him.'

'Did you speak to Barnyou about getting that girl from the Varley house?'

'He wasn't very enthusiastic but I think I persuaded him. Paul wasn't going to mention it to him obviously. That young man needs a change, he wants to go and play with the big boys.'

'Will you let him go?'

'Let him go? I'll give him a free pass – when this case is over. See if he likes it.'

The Clinic was quiet but the night watchmen let them in. The stairs were full of sleeping bodies, patients waiting for the clinic to open or family there to take care of a sick relative. The room at the end was lit by a single bulb, the only fresh air coming from the breeze which was getting up, a sign of the storm.

'Mrs Anderson, how are you?'

Ma Anderson was sitting in Pascal's chair. She didn't look surprised at seeing Gloria and gave her a warm hug. 'He's sleeping, he sleeps most of the time but he's not in any pain Gloria. I will try to take him home tomorrow or the day after. The doctor says he probably won't live very long and there's nothing more he can do.'

'You know it won't be easy ma, and you've already got your own children and Pascal.'

'Don't worry about us Gloria, we'll be fine.'

Gloria stroked Alex's hand. He looked very peaceful. 'If you take him then ma, I will sort out all the paperwork with Social Welfare, just to make sure you don't get into any trouble. I'll get the Minister to sort it out himself.'

'Thanks Gloria, please do that.'

Chapter Seventeen

Breakfast was a very quiet affair in Gloria's apartment at the best of times but the next morning was not just quiet but tense. Abu muttered that Rohit and Rahul had stayed for a few hours and that, yes, they had enjoyed the food. He ate some bread quickly and left saying he would be late home and, as he closed the door, added that he would eat with his friends that night.

Gloria had too much to think about at work to worry about Abu for long. The events of the previous night had driven everything else out of her mind. How was she going to move on the case urgently? She was just packing her bag to go when the phone went. It was Barnyou.

'Gloria, I am at the Varley house now. That girl has gone.'

'What do you mean?' But her heart was sinking even as she asked.

'I was here at seven with all the paperwork. Some person named Martin told me that Fanta was very upset after your talk yesterday and has left to go back to her village. I suspect that isn't true of course but there's not a lot we can do here.'

'I'll see to it Barnyou, thank you.' She called Lawrence and they agreed to meet at the Varley house.

She called Paul to instruct him to stay at the house until they arrived but he told her he hadn't been part of the unit who had gone there, and that in fact he was working hard on the other case. The one concerning national security, he added. Just before she hung up.

Gloria was furious. She had no real objections to people finding and then moving to their real place of interest in the police, but Paul's tone and his attitude was unacceptable. She related all this to Lawrence as they made their way once again up the drive to the Varley's front door. Part of her anger she knew was displaced from her sense of responsibility for what had happened to Fanta. She was sure that talking with Fanta yesterday had put her in danger. She should have insisted the girl come with them.

When the door to the house was opened, Gloria pushed past the 'steward' and went straight to the library. Africanus Varley was sitting in his usual chair as if waiting for her. He remained impassive when she all but accused him of murder, demanding to know where Fanta had gone.

'I knew your temper would get the better of you eventually Inspector.' He paused. 'Women...' He said this with such contempt that Gloria finally got the sense that his mask had dropped and she was seeing the real man. 'They should never have let you in the police or anywhere else. But when you fail spectacularly, as you are going to do, people will see that. I should congratulate you really. By the time you have finished this mess, no-one will want to see any woman in any position of authority, well except for those decorative ones of course, you know the ones Inspector; a nicely dressed woman,' he eyed her crumpled uniform, 'who can talk about children or family or something.' He stopped, sensing he had given too much of himself away.

Lawrence had stepped between them. 'It's very interesting to get your ideas Mr Varley, but at the moment we are more interested in the whereabouts of this girl Fanta who has lived in your house for a number of years, and who disappeared immediately after she spoke to Inspector Sirleaf – after she told the Inspector a number of things about Titus, and your son's wife in fact. People disappearing from your house has become a bit of habit.'

Africanus had resumed his impassive stare but the mention of his son's wife made him frown. 'I have no need to tell you people anything, you have no authority to come in here and make your insulting remarks. However, let me be clear. This girl Fanta worked at my house and yesterday she decided she wanted to go back to her village, she wants to get married or something. That's all I know.'

'And the name of her village?'

'The name of her village? You must be joking Inspector, I hardly knew her. I do not encourage the staff to mix in the house.'

'But this girl was a relative of yours, surely you knew where she came from?'

He paused. 'Well, my relatives come from a number of places. I'm not sure where she is from exactly.'

'So maybe the staff can help us then.' Africanus indicated brusquely they could make their way to the kitchen and they left.

'Thanks Lawrence. I was losing that one.'

'No you weren't, you got him to show his real self. What a man, loves power and hates women.'

'And has lots of money, now that's dangerous. If he thought Fanta was telling the real story about what happened to Richard's mother, I'm sure he would have no problem getting rid of her. I think we have more than one murder on our hands here.'

Lawrence nodded. 'Me too.'

The door to the kitchen was open but as they went in they only saw Martin sitting at the table.

'Where are the others?'

'They are very upset after your visit yesterday, they don't want to talk you.'

Without exchanging another word Lawrence and Gloria turned and left.

'We would get nothing from them anyway.'

'I agree. Let's get back and see the Chief. He needs to know there's a potential triple murder here, and he won't like it.'

The meeting with the Chief did not go well. The pressure on them all from the kidnapping case and the implications for national security was taking its toll.

'So, you have the hearsay of a disaffected relative and a mish mash of stories, no bodies and no evidence, and on that basis you want to harass one of the most influential people in Monrovia, and one of the President's biggest supporters, and take resources away from this kidnapping? Honestly Gloria, we do not have resources for this, we need to find this child and, for goodness sake, get some perspective.'

Lawrence poked her in the back, a reminder that this was the response she expected and to control her temper.

'I do understand sir but I am sure that Richard Varley's mother, this maid and Titus were all killed by someone in the house and we can't ignore it. At least let me leave one officer to continue investigating. He is very discreet and very thorough.'

The Chief reluctantly gave his permission, with the proviso that Ambrose steer clear of the Varley senior.

'Now what about our main case? Barnyou told me you think Amos Toweh is the most likely suspect so what are you waiting for?'

'I'm not sure sir, there are a –'

'INSPECTOR!' It was a roar. 'Enough speculation, get out there and find this child and give Barnyou any support he needs to investigate Toweh.'

Gloria and Lawrence left quickly feeling like schoolchildren.

'So how are you going to do this then?'

'I'm not sure. Let's find Barnyou and see what he is up to, and if he's got any further with the Toweh investigation. Time is running so short though and I feel this is the wrong way to go.'

'Well, the sooner we investigate the sooner you can be proved right.'

'There is no sooner Lawrence, we're out of time already.'

She called Ambrose and gave him very precise instructions about investigating the Varleys.

'I'm afraid you are going to have to be discreet.' Being discreet was not a great virtue in Gloria's eyes. 'There is a lot more background information but you will need to dig around for it, find out everything you can about that family.'

'I think so, ma'am. I am on my way to the Catholic hospital. That lady who used to work at the house said Richard's mother was at the hospital before she left. They were told she was pregnant and went there to 'move the belly' because the houseboy was the father of the child but –'

She finished his sentence for him. 'I know, there's no way she could have had a termination at the Catholic hospital, they don't do them. What does it mean do you think?'

'I don't know but I will see if I can talk to someone who remembers.'

'Good start. And remember to keep your head down, the Varleys are on the warpath.' She rang off and looked at Lawrence.

'Don't worry Gloria, Ambrose is about the smartest person on your team and loves a cause. He will ferret out any information and he has the advantage that he doesn't care what anyone else thinks of him. He would have been a bit of a ferocious priest though. I would never have gone to him for confession.'

'Well that's because you're not a Catholic isn't it? But you're right, he's a good investigator and he...'

'...cares. I know, not like us traffic police.'

'Will you stop finishing my sentences? It is too annoying. And don't feel bad Lawrence, we know the traffic police care about things too.' She said nothing more and Lawrence, sensing he was on shaky ground again, decided not to pursue the discussion.

Barnyou was very happy to meet with them. He was energised and explained enthusiastically that he had officers, including Paul, watching Toweh's every move.

'Paul is supposed to be liaising not playing a key role in your operations.'

'Come on Gloria, he's very good and we need to use his skills.' Then

Barnyou hesitated. 'He is actually heading the surveillance. I was going to talk to you about him after the investigation. He really wants to transfer to us and I think he would be useful.'

Gloria, even though she had been expecting this, was taken aback. Paul had effectively transferred behind her back and there was little she could do. If she made a fuss or refused to agree to the transfer she would have a very unhappy team member or potentially more opposition. But she wasn't happy.

'I think we need to move on, we can discuss the details of this later.' Barnyou nodded quickly, grateful not to have to deal with an angry Gloria.

'Let's go to my office then.'

As expected Paul was sitting at the small conference table with a whiteboard behind him on which were names, lines and arrows – a strategy of all things!

With a terse nod Barnyou asked Paul to explain what they were planning to do which he did with the aid of the whiteboard and lots of references to 'saturation surveillance' and '360 degree observation'. Gloria restrained herself for ten minutes after which she interrupted his flow.

'I get the picture, you are going to follow Toweh everywhere. What about the other suspects?'

Paul was not pleased at being stopped in mid-flow. 'Well, there are no other suspects Inspector. That's why we are putting all our resources onto Toweh. I thought that was ob...' He tailed off in the full blast of Gloria's glare.

'Inspector Barnyou, I appreciate that Toweh is a suspect and we have to follow him but he can't be the only one. We are putting a child's life in danger here.'

Barnyou got in before Paul could interrupt again. 'He's our best lead and we don't have the time or the resources to spread ourselves too thin.'

Whatever Paul had done to impress Barnyou it had worked. This was clearly his plan and Barnyou was backing him all the way.

'Inspector Barnyou, you seem to have forgotten that my sergeant here is,' she paused, looking for the right word, 'still undergoing training, hardly suitable to lead a big operation like this.'

Barnyou nodded again. 'I know it's unusual Gloria, but the fact is he is smart and, more importantly, I can trust him. At the moment I don't know who else in my section I can trust.'

Gloria shrugged and decided to leave it there, especially since Lawrence was digging her in the ribs again with his fingers. 'Well, we will back you up on this of course. I'll get an officer along to join you. Just make sure this one comes back to me.'

The laughs couldn't hide the tensions in the room and Gloria and Lawrence left soon after. To Lawrence's surprise Gloria didn't mention Paul's actions. She was focussed on the case now and nothing else.

'We need a mobile team Lawrence. With Ambrose following up on the Varleys, we need to assign Alfred and Izena to work with Barnyou's people and we'll have Lamine and Christian with us to go wherever they are needed. Old Alfred can coordinate and we will move between these cases while we pursue any other lines of enquiry.' Lawrence raised an eyebrow.

'So you really think Toweh is not involved in this? He just seems to be the most obvious and –'

'I know Lawrence, sometimes the most obvious suspect is in fact the criminal but despite all that I feel Toweh is not. It's the motive. I don't see what he gets out of bringing the government down. It's not as if he has any friends among the opposition. Everybody is suspicious of him because he has been so close to every President, the good, the bad and the ugly, so he has no political affiliations. And if it was for money he could have made a fortune over the years just from stealing or blackmailing. This is so extreme and would require him to work with other people – that's the other part that's out of character.'

'But people change, Gloria. The facts are that someone from inside the Mansion, or with very good connections, has been orchestrating all this and he is the only one who has been here long enough or who has the training and the ruthlessness to do it. We'll find out his motives when he is arrested.'

Gloria shrugged again. This wasn't just a feeling she had. She thought back to Toweh urging her to find the President's grandson and was still convinced he had been sincere when he said that. And the case lacked logic. The whole thing had been put together in a very detailed and planned way. This wasn't some random act of revenge or kidnapping, and Toweh just did not fit.

Her phone rang as they were leaving. It was Sr Laurita.

'Inspector, can I have a few moments of your time?' It was very hard to refuse a request from Sr Laurita. Apart from the fact that she appeared to have taught everyone's mother at Holy Redeemer High School before her promotion to President of the new Catholic university, she was also a Kru woman and not afraid to use her kinship connections. 'I know you are very busy but I just need ten minutes.'

Gloria agreed to call in, all the time aware of Lawrence smirking at her.

'What are you making those faces for? Sr Laurita is heading up this commission and needs a bit of help obviously, I think we can spare her ten minutes.'

'And she'll tell your mother if you don't turn up…'

'Oh let's just go.'

Sr Laurita's office was large and full of books and papers. She sat behind the desk in her brown dress and short veil looking for all the world like everyone's ideal nun. But when she spoke it was different. Gloria introduced Lawrence who was greeted politely enough but she made it clear that he wasn't party to the discussion.

'How is your mother, Gloria?' Gloria muttered something non committal. It had been a while since she had been down to Westpoint, as she suspected Laurita knew only too well.

'Perhaps a visit sometime soon might be a good idea. Anyway,' her tone changed, 'I know you are under a huge amount of pressure with this terrible case, those poor children. I want to ask you to join the commission of investigation.' Gloria looked up at her, polite deference gone. 'No, hear me out Gloria. I want you on the commission but I know you will not be able to do anything until after this case is closed.'

Then why drag me in now, Gloria thought.

'Gloria, there is something strange about these riots and I wanted to let you know, it might be of some help to you. I have already started interviewing some of the children from the schools, especially the ones who were in hospital. You know I have done this kind of investigation before.'

Gloria knew. Sr Laurita had headed a similar commission of enquiry in 1985 when a strike by teachers in government schools had led to students invading the campuses of the private and mission schools, and a lot of destruction of property. She had also headed an internal enquiry into corruption in the Catholic school system, and a further incident in 1986 when students at Central High on Twelfth Street had held a number of teachers hostage for a few hours. Yes, she had a lot of commissions of enquiry under her belt, or her rosary.

'I can tell you one thing straight away. These riots were not initiated by students. I know that even though I can't tell you any more than that at the moment. In every enquiry I have headed up it was clear that trouble started because of some real or imagined grievances by the students. Corruption, injustice, poor food, or in the case of Central High, dissatisfaction with the uniforms provided for the band for the Unity Day parade! There was always something and that complaint was central to all the stories I heard. In this case I have already talked with over fifty students and not one of them can tell me why the riots started or even what the reason might be. All their stories start with the actions of the police provoking them to further disturbance. No-one seems to have any idea what happened beforehand to cause the initial protest.'

Gloria nodded. 'Thanks Sr, that is very useful. And of course I will be happy to join the commission as soon as this case is finished.'

They got up to go and Sr Laurita shook Lawrence's hand. 'Tell Edith I will see her soon Inspector.' Lawrence looked surprised at the message.

'I didn't know you knew my mother.'

'And you know all your mothers friends? Your mother was a few years ahead of me at Kakata Teachers Training Institute but she was very good to me. And besides, I don't just talk to Catholics and Kru people you know.'

'When I said she knew everybody, I meant everybody.' They were heading back out on to the main road.

'I see what you mean. Does that information mean anything though?'

'Well Sr Laurita obviously thought so, and she's one of the smartest people I know. Let's just keep it in mind.'

They had reached the boulevard when they ran, almost literally, into a crowd outside the City Hall. Gloria slowed down and wound down the window. The crowd was fairly quiet and it didn't take long for Gloria to recognise the voice booming over the loudspeaker. 'It's Senator Gwedu, I'd know that voice everywhere. Now why's he out rabble rousing at this time?'

They pulled over and got out the car.

'...so what is the real story eh, what really happening in the country today? Every day we hearing different different ting, but we not force to believe what the big people tell us. They tell us this is the new Liberia eh, it not too new-o, it more like the old Liberia with new clothes. Instead of the coat suit they wearing African dress... but the news is the same. Ritual killing, police arresting children, corrupt politicians. Is any of this new?'

The crowd laughed and shouted back, 'No.'

'I say is any of this new?'

They shouted back a louder, 'No!'

'You need other suspects, there's one right there.' Gloria nodded towards the small figure on the steps of the City Hall. 'So why did he choose today to come down here and talk about this. He is making the most of the uncertainty and the fear and,' she indicated some reporters, 'to get some news coverage. Nonsense.' She made to push through the crowd until Lawrence pulled her back. 'What are you going to do, arrest him? Leave it.'

They got back in the car and as they were driving off they could hear Gwedu moving on to talk about the kidnapping and the dangers to national security. Gloria was furious. 'Put his name on the list. Senator Gwedu, a man hungry for power I would say.'

The rest of the boulevard was empty and they reached the Catholic Hospital in a short time. Ambrose was waiting for them just outside the Emergency area with a short grey-haired man at his side. He introduced him as Dr Kiwanuka.

'Dr Kiwanuka remembers treating Richard Varley's mother that night.' Gloria was sceptical that this old man could remember one patient from so many years ago.

'Nice to meet you sir. Would you mind telling us the story?'

Kiwanuka looked at Gloria as if he could read her mind and then recited in a monotone.

'The woman was brought in about nine in the evening. I was the doctor on call in Emergency and as soon as the staff saw her they sent for me. I have never seen a woman so badly beaten. I could list her injuries but it would take a long time. I tried to patch her up and then to admit her. I tried to get her to tell me what had happened but she was only semi-conscious and in great pain. She was also very afraid. She would not let go of my hand.'

'Who was with her?'

'Her husband. He said she had been coming home when she was attacked in the street outside her house.'

'But you don't think that's what happened.'

'Not unless she was wearing her night clothes for a night out. She still had on one slipper and a badly torn nightdress. The woman was beaten in her own home and if it had been by intruders why would her husband not say? He was untouched.'

'So her husband thought you wouldn't notice the nightclothes?'

'The husband didn't care what I noticed. He was simply telling me what to put in the report. He made it clear to all of us when he was leaving with his wife, that it would be very bad for us if we tried to tell anyone else what we had seen.'

'Right, so that's why you kept quiet.'

'The next morning, Inspector, the hospital authorities told me that a young woman had made a serious complaint about me and my 'inappropriate' behaviour. I was suspended pending an investigation.'

'But you were cleared right? Otherwise you wouldn't be here, so they didn't succeed.'

'Ay ay ay,' he laughed at her, 'they weren't trying to destroy me Inspector, it was just a lesson. They were letting me know they could destroy me anytime they wanted.'

'So why now doctor?'

'Because they are not concerned with me now. Who is going to listen to the ramblings of an old doctor? But the memory of that terrified woman has stayed with me. If you can make those Varleys pay for her death then I will get some peace as well.'

'So you think she died?'

'Inspector, her injuries were terrible and in all probability inflicted by the same people who brought her here and took her away. If she didn't die from the beating I'm sure they finished her off to stop her talking. In my professional judgement,' he paused as if waiting for someone to challenge him, 'there was no way she could have run away, or whatever the story they spread. She died and they disposed of the body and, because they are Varleys, no-one investigated.'

He looked her in the eyes for the first time.

'I need forgiveness Inspector. I handed her back to die and never said a thing, but I have never forgotten her.'

'Thank you doctor.' Gloria stood up, torn between feeling sorry for him and angry that he could have done something all those years ago but had chosen not to. She made a vague gesture with her hands.

'Ambrose here will take a detailed statement from you.' She indicated to Ambrose that she would call him later and told Lawrence they needed to go back and talk with Sawyer, the principal of GW Horton School.

'Based on what Sr Laurita said he might have something more he can tell us about how the riots started. And I am tired of old stories and regrets.'

Chapter Eighteen

On the way to the school Gloria's phone rang again. It was Alfred this time, and he sounded excited.

'Ma'am, Inspector Barnyou is ready to go for Colonel Toweh, I thought you should know. They are planning to hit him at the Mansion and at his home at the same time. They are just waiting for permission from the President to arrest Toweh on the grounds of the Mansion. Barnyou wants to see you back at the office.'

'Already? But what happened to saturation surveillance?' There was a silence at the other end of the phone. 'What I mean Alfred is on what grounds are they going to arrest this very high profile figure who is so close to the President? There isn't a scrap of evidence.'

'I don't know about that ma'am. They seem all geared up for it anyway.'

Gloria and Lawrence drove straight back to police headquarters in silence. As they entered the building Lawrence made one last attempt to calm Gloria down.

'Look Gloria, if this isn't successful then it's Barnyou and his men who have made the mistake not us, so just go with it.'

'It's not about getting away with something Lawrence. All the focus on this one man means the real criminals get away with it and the life of a child is even more endangered. If I thought he was the one responsible I would have arrested him hours ago, never mind permission from the Mansion. I just don't think he is.'

The meeting in Barnyou's office was short and bad tempered. Gloria asked for the evidence base for the arrest. It was Paul again who spoke.

'We have watched Toweh go in and out of a disused security tower on the grounds of the Mansion. Only he has the key. He makes frequent trips home during the day as well, and never has any visitors at home – in fact, the family doesn't seem to socialise at all. And only he has the access to be able to dump the body of a child in the grounds of the Mansion. It seems clear to me that he is a man with a secret.'

'It's not exactly rock solid, more like a few observations strung together to paint a picture. I think we are making a huge mistake here.' She went on to explain what Sr Laurita had observed but was met with blank looks. 'Whoever has organised this has to have a team and a wide sphere of influence to be able to carry it out. By your own words, Toweh does not. Everyone knows he is a loner and he has only kept his job by deliberately not trying to influence people or set up some patronage system. That is unusual here I know but it's not illegal. Are you sure you are not going after him for completely the wrong reasons?' Silence again. 'What about Senator Gwedu, if you're looking for someone with influence and motive?' She told them about Gwedu's impromptu rally on the steps of City Hall. 'There is a man desperate for power. He was the first person on the radio questioning the government after Anthony Keimouth's body was found. He's stirring up people against the President and we met him at Africanus Varley's house with the election monitors on an unscheduled visit. And he disappeared off to the Mansion last week when he should have been taking them to dinner. He is up to something.'

'Gloria, Senator Gwedu is one of our most respected politicians, the international community love him and he's got no scandals attached to him. He is allowed to disagree with the government and to question its policies and its effectiveness. In fact, that's his role as opposition leader. We may as well arrest the city mayor, the captain of the national football team and Archbishop Gray, they have all criticised the government this past week as well.'

'You know what I mean Barnyou, this is different. He is angling for power.'

Barnyou seemed to take offence suddenly and turned very formal.

'You promised you would support us Inspector. We are going to observe and arrest Colonel Toweh. So are you going to keep your word?'

Gloria looked at Barnyou and then at Paul who had a small smirk on his face.

'Of course we will support you.' It would be better to be close to this operation, she thought. 'I will go to his house then. He does have children and a wife I presume?'

Barnyou shrugged. 'I'm not sure but you lead on that one and I will lead the arrest team at the Mansion with Paul here.' Gloria knew that by letting her lead the arrest team Barnyou now had her fully implicated in the operation. They were not bystanders.

At six that evening Inspector Barnyou and his team entered the Mansion grounds and arrested Colonel Amos Toweh as he was coming out of the old watch tower in the far corner of the compound. He was charged with murder, kidnap and treason. As Gloria heard from Barnyou later, Toweh's expression never changed while the charges were being read out. He looked neither surprised nor shocked and remained impassive until Barnyou informed him that his house was being searched at the same time. At this information he became furious and had to be restrained and bundled into the back of a pick-up while the tower was searched.

The old watch tower was dank and humid with fungus growing on the walls of the stone stairs. There was only one room in the tower, the watch room itself which had one wide window looking out to sea. There were no children in the room, no evidence there had ever been children in the room and no furniture except for a desk, a chair and a cupboard stacked with boxes and boxes of papers, documents and photos. It looked like the room of a professor in some run down educational establishment and not much like the headquarters of a criminal gang. This much Gloria found out afterwards.

At the same time as Toweh was being arrested at the Mansion Gloria drove into the grounds of Toweh's modest house on Coleman Ave. in Sinkor. It had a high wall around it but no security on the gate and in front of the house two small children were playing with an old football. They hardly looked up as Gloria, Lawrence, Alfred and Izena got out the car and covered the various entrances. Gloria knocked the front door which was opened by a young girl in a simple lappa and t-shirt.

'We need to talk to Mrs Toweh. Can you tell her it's the police?' As the girl went in Gloria and Alfred followed, not waiting for an invitation. The sitting room was long with doors opening onto a veranda and a beautiful garden. Mrs Toweh was already standing to greet them. She looked very worried.

'Mrs Toweh, I am Inspector Gloria Sirleaf and I have a warrant to search your house right now. Can you please stay here in this room while my officers go through the house? Nothing will be disturbed.'

Mrs Toweh looked both terrified and angry. 'Do you know who my husband is? How dare you come here with this nonsense. What are you searching for?'

'The search is in connection with the kidnap of the President's grandson.' Gloria didn't elaborate on the other charges. There would be time for that if they found anything incriminating.

Lawrence and Izena had already gone through most of the rooms on the ground floor and Alfred was upstairs in the bedrooms when the scuffle broke out. At the end of a short corridor off the sitting room a man was standing in front of a door refusing to move.

'You mun kill me-o, you mun kill me. I not moving from here.' Lawrence and Izena were explaining that he would have to move but the man had been joined by the cook and two other staff who had all assembled in front of the door. The others said nothing but their message was the same. No-one was getting past them into that room.

For the first time since they started Gloria began to doubt her assessment of Toweh. What were they hiding here? 'Mrs Toweh, whatever is going on here you must not make matters worse. We will get into that room, the easy way or the hard way.'

'Inspector, you have to understand –'

'Understand what?' Gloria felt time was running out but Mrs Toweh had nothing more to say. Gloria took out her gun and walked down the corridor.

'Now, everyone out the way or I will arrest all of you. NOW!' The shout, combined with the waving gun, seemed to do it and there was a shuffling as they moved away leaving the door free. 'Now unlock the door.'

The staff looked bewildered.

'The door not lock ma.'

Gloria turned the handle and found it wasn't locked. She pushed the door wide and went in. In the corner sitting hunched on the floor was a terrified child. But instead of the President's grandson Gloria found herself looking at a face so deformed that, in spite of herself, she shivered and turned away. There was silence. So this was the big secret, not a kidnapping but a child whose deformity could not be shown in public. She put away her gun as Mrs Toweh brushed past her and knelt down to cradle the sobbing child in her arms.

'It's alright DG, it's ok. Don't worry, you are safe. Nothing is going to hurt you.' She looked up at Gloria. 'Now you see? Eh? You happy now?'

It was half an hour later that Mrs Toweh was able to tell Gloria the story of her first born son Deogratias or DG as he was more commonly known. He had been born nine years previously with a genetic deformity and, despite all the medical consultations, the trips to other countries and even a visit by the doctors from Operation Sunshine, no-one had been able to do anything. During the war when the rebels had smashed their way into the house they had found the child and called him a witch, poking and kicking him until Amos had got back from the Mansion and shot two of them. The child had been badly traumatised and never left the compound, rarely going outside at all.

'That is why we live so quietly here, Inspector. We don't have time for social visits and we rarely invite people to come here. We are trying to make a safe place for DG, he is our whole life. I know that seems suspicious to some people but that is our choice.'

Gloria had rarely felt so wretched. Not only had they got it so badly wrong with Toweh but they, the Family and Child Protection Unit, had succeeded in increasing a child's trauma. This was turning out to be a great day's work!

Mrs Toweh, or Mercy as she had told Gloria to call her, was still explaining.

'Our staff have been with us for a long time and they are devoted to DG. They thought you were coming to do him harm.'

Gloria apologised for the tenth time in the space of half an hour while cursing Barnyou under her breath. What a mess, and they were still no nearer to finding Prince. When she thought she had apologised as much as she could and restored some calm to the household, Gloria gathered the team and left. She managed to get a wave from DG as they were leaving and promised she would come back and see him.

The news from Barnyou was not good either. There was no evidence of any criminal activity. Toweh claimed to be writing a book on Liberia and its recent history and was using the tower as quiet place to work. His only crime was collecting and keeping papers and photos which had been looted from the National Archives, the National Museum and the various Ministries during the war. A quick glance at the papers showed they were all connected with Liberia's social history.

'The only photographs are black and white pictures of President Tubman in a top hat and tails and meetings of tribal chiefs and elders in Pleebo in 1929.' Barnyou sounded bitter down the phone.

'Well, there's nothing treasonous about that although you might want to question his sanity, spending his time writing about the old days. I take it you've let him go then?

'These are government papers. I could charge him with theft except –'

'Except he says he saved them from being destroyed during the war like everything else in the Museum and the Archives, and he intends to return them to government ownership when there is a safe place to store them.'

'Exactly what he said.'

'Barnyou, you need to let him go. We already look ridiculous arresting the President's head of security and terrifying his wife and family. If we try and hold him for preserving the nation's heritage we will look even worse. Let him go, and pray he doesn't come after us.'

'I know, you are right.'

'Can I suggest you start looking around for other leads? I still think Senator Gwedu needs investigating and we are running out of options and time. Two days left.'

Barnyou conceded wearily that it was worth pursuing in the absence of any other leads, but the mistake with Toweh had taken the edge off his appetite for pursuing prominent people, and no-one was more prominent than Gwedu at the moment. Any mistakes there and Barnyou knew his career would be over.

'I am going to see Principal Sawyer at GW Horton again tomorrow to try and get more information on the riots. They started with his students at his school maybe there's more he can tell us. And we are running out of options here.'

They did not agree to meet later. There was no time for that.

It was almost nine by the time Gloria reached home. She had thought of inviting Lawrence in but he was anxious to get home and check on his mother. Gloria sensed he was more worried about her safety now that he had seen how powerful and how ruthless the Varleys could be. How hard would it be for them to track Richard down? And he was being protected by an old lady and a teenager. The more she thought of it the more Gloria became convinced that the tension they were all under was affecting their judgement.

'We need to find somewhere else for Richard to hide, and if we don't get a breakthrough on that case soon we will be charged with kidnapping as well.' Lawrence nodded wearily. 'And remember to pass on Sr Laurita's greetings.'

Despite his anxiety, Lawrence waited until she was in her apartment and had waved from the upstairs window before he drove off.

The apartment was quiet and Gloria realised it was late and Abu was still not home. She called his phone but it was switched off or 'out of coverage area' apparently. She hoped it wasn't out of coverage area. After half an hour of telling herself he would be home soon Gloria gave in to her anxiety and called Leo and then Morris. Abu had eaten with Morris but then left to go home. Feeling slightly desperate she then called Lawrence on the off chance that Abu was up visiting Fatu.

'At nine o'clock at night? You have met my mother haven't you?'

'I know, it was just a try.' She sat in silence for a while wondering if Abu was punishing her for how she had treated him, but that's wasn't really his style. Thoughts of her enemies and what they might do to someone she loved kept pushing their way in until finally Gloria could take no more of it. Grabbing the keys to the Polo she went downstairs. On the first landing Rohit's door was open and she could hear voices laughing and talking including, if she was not mistaken, Abu's. She knocked the door and went in. Abu and Rahul were hunched around the TV playing some game while Rohit sat by the window reading his newspaper. Abu looked up and waved at her while Rahul nodded politely. Rohit was already bringing her over a coffee.

'Ah Inspector ma'am, you are here.' He led her over to the window. 'Inspector, please to sit down. You were looking for Abu?'

Gloria nodded. 'I was beginning to get worried Rohit.'

'You had a visitor earlier on this evening, a lady. I just happened to be here when she was going upstairs and I knew Abu was there alone. I thought it best to ask her business.' Gloria smiled at him.

'She wasn't one of my family?'

Rohit shook his head. 'I think I know most of your family Inspector, this was a stranger. She was heavily veiled, very mysterious. She asked for you and said it was a private matter. She says she will look for you tomorrow.'

'You told her to come to the office?'

'She said she can't do that, she has to meet you here. Inspector, you will please be very careful. All these strange visitors and this one was wearing enough clothes to smuggle a python up to your apartment! That's why I told Abu to come down here and wait for you.'

Gloria thought for a moment. She couldn't recall any connection with any ladies and thought that Rohit was probably right, being careful was the best tactic.

'I'll have a think about this Rohit. I am not too happy about people coming here to see me, they always seem to bring trouble.'

'Well, I'll be around tomorrow anyway.' Gloria sometimes wondered when Rohit did any work at his store, but was grateful for his vigilance. She stayed and enjoyed the food Rohit offered while the two boys finished their game. It was after ten when she and Abu walked up the stairs to the apartment. Abu was describing in great detail the plans he had for Rahul and Gloria had lapsed into her usual state of semi-awareness when Abu was in full flow, when a figure stepped out of the shadows beside their door. Abu instinctively moved in front of her to block her coming any closer to Gloria but Gloria pulled his shoulder sharply. If this was an intruder she didn't want Abu shielding her.

'Inspector Sirleaf,' the voice was low and educated, 'I need to have a word with you, urgently.' She paused, looking at Abu and then back to Gloria. 'I am Richard Varley's mother. I think you have been looking for me.'

Chapter Nineteen

In her brightly coloured dress and veil, her gold chains and rings and dramatic make-up the woman would easily be taken for a member of the Fulani people but once in the apartment with her veil off it was easy to see this was no northern lady. Gloria, on instinct, had invited her into the apartment and took a good look at her. They had only a blurred photo of Nessee Varley standing with a very young Richard. The lady in front of her could be her or just as easily might not be.

'We thought you were dead Mrs Varley, it's a surprise to see you.'

'Who told you I was dead? My husband I suppose.' She spoke through gritted teeth. 'That half-man.'

'Well no, they told us you had run away... with your houseboy. We thought they were lying.' Nessee Varley looked at Gloria and then at Abu again who was sitting on the floor staring at her.

'Maybe I should start from the beginning, I'm not sure...' she looked at Abu again but Gloria's mind was made up.

'As long as you are not going to confess to murder then he can stay, he knows half the story anyway. I trust him.' Abu's smile was reward enough for this statement. Nessee Varley half rolled her eyes in an expression Gloria couldn't read but started talking.

'I was, I still am I suppose, married to Daniel Varley and we have one son Richard. I will spare you the details of the hell I went through in that household but suffice it to say that I consider Africanus Varley one of the most wicked people in this country.' Her eyes clouded over as she remembered details of life lived under the total control of the Varleys. 'I stayed in that house only to try and protect my son. I had only one friend in the house, my houseboy, Kwame.' She looked at Gloria. 'Forget the lies they have told you. Kwame had lived with my family since he was a small boy. He was like my younger brother and when I married I asked if he could come with me to the house. They hated him. They hated him because he was honest and cheerful, and he was loyal to me. They called him the Ghana boy because his late father was from Cape

Coast, and did everything they could to make his life a misery.'

Gloria couldn't help thinking the story had all the elements of the traditional stories her uncles used to tell her when she was little: wicked family, loyal servants, beautiful victimised wife. She looked at Nessee closely but could see no emotion on her face. Her eyes were closed and her voice had sunk even lower.

'The Varleys, although they go to church every Sunday, are into ritual and magic, more for the sadistic pleasure it gives them than from any belief, but they have also used it to snare some big people in society here, so the magic does work for them. They get the contracts, the protection, the power and influence they want.'

Despite what she had said, Gloria was not sure now about Abu listening to all this. She signalled him to please bring some drinks for them and he reluctantly pulled himself away from the small circle of light they were sitting in and what he knew was going to be a grisly story.

'Are you sure you want to tell me all this Mrs Varley?'

'I'm sure – do you want to listen to it though?'

'No' was the honest answer, thought Gloria but she signalled Nessee to continue.

'I don't know what the rituals were, I was never allowed anywhere near the library when they were having one of their sessions but the noises and the atmosphere in the house were terrible. Anyway, to cut the story short I came home one evening very late from meeting a friend. Richard was already in the States by this time so I was a little less worried. I couldn't find Kwame anywhere which was very unusual. I remember his books were open at the table but he was nowhere around. In fact the whole house was quiet.' She gulped and her voice shook a little. 'After I had searched all the usual places I went down to the kitchen. The door was usually locked but that night it was open and I went into the yard thinking he might be outside. The only light was from the small room at the side of the kitchen. I pushed open the door and the first thing I saw was Africanus Varley with a wild look in his eye and blood all over his gown.' She gulped, her eyes screwed up as if in pain. 'He had his head flung back and he looked as if he was frothing at the mouth. There was only one lamp in the room so it took me a few seconds to really see what was going on. There was a body hanging by its feet from the ceiling from one of those big meat hooks. It was Kwame.'

Gloria swallowed. She had heard so much already today but this sounded like a horror story. She could feel the sweat on her neck and her palms were moist.

'His throat had been cut and the blood was draining into a basin on the floor. And then I screamed. And kept on screaming. I ran to him and tried to lift up his head even though he was surely dead. That was when I saw Daniel in the corner. He and his father jumped on me and started beating me. The beating went on until I passed out. When I came to I was in a hospital.' She stopped. Abu was frozen on the edge of the circle of light. Gloria suggested they stop for the time being and have a drink of something. Her mind was racing too. It was terrible and yet not at all surprising.

'Nessee, that is a terrible story, really terrible. But for now it is getting late. I don't know where you are staying but I think it is too late for you to go home tonight.'

Nessee looked at her. 'Go home! I have no home Inspector but also I have so much more to tell you and I need to see my son, I need to make sure he is safe.'

It was going to be a long night.

Gloria pulled Abu into the kitchen on the pretext of preparing food for their new visitor. 'Abu I think you should go to bed. This story is a lot worse than I had expected. It would be wrong of me to let you listen to this.'

Abu had clearly been expecting this and looked a bit relieved. Despite his bravado he did not relish violence and gore. He just nodded again and said. 'Those Varleys, I told you they were bad.'

'You did, and I hear you refused his money the other day as well. You will be happy to know that made him very annoyed. It might be the first time anyone has refused to take it.'

'You heard about that.' Abu sucked his teeth. 'Does he think we are so cheap that we can be bought off with dollars the same day we are burying our friend that he killed? And I wasn't the first to refuse his money. When he wasn't beating Titus he was always trying to give him things. Titus would take nothing from him.'

'Well, you made me proud again but I don't want you to listen to any more of this story. I know you are involved so I promise to tell you about it in the morning.'

Nessee had moved out on to the balcony and was staring out at the dark where the white flecks of the incoming tide were illuminated by the lights of Mickey's Bar.

'I need to see Richard Inspector, that's why I risked coming back. That's the only reason I came back.'

'Look Nessee you need to tell me the whole story before we do anything else. Where have you been these past few years and why come back now?'

'You mean when I heard Richard was being accused of murder or manslaughter, I should just have stayed in hiding? That's the one thing I had counted on, that Africanus would protect Richard. He's the only male heir to their whole sick empire. I reckoned he would be safe as he was in the States and then when they brought him back I got more worried, but still I thought they would keep him safe. I knew they would not initiate him until he was fourteen so I thought I had until then.'

'You seem to know a lot.'

'I have a few good contacts Inspector who keep me informed, the same people who helped me escape from that house.' She looked at Gloria. 'And no, I won't be telling you who they are. But when I heard that Richard had been accused of killing his cousin I knew I had to come back.'

'That's what I don't understand. Why did Africanus not just cover it up, he obviously has the power to do that?'

Nessee laughed bitterly. 'You really don't know him at all do you. He wants to break the child the same way he broke Daniel. He's happy enough to let him go through that ordeal so that he will have another pliable broken human being at the end of it.' She was crying now. 'You have no idea how evil this man is.'

'I think I have some idea. When you say you "came back", does that mean you have been living outside the country?'

Nessee smiled then. 'At first I went into Guinea but it is still full of refugees and I had to make a living. I became a business woman. I started buying goods in Guinea and then selling them in Voinjama and I found I am very good at business so I extended all the way to Kakata and right to Waterside. Money is not a problem for me Inspector and the business means I am able to move around and I get to hear a lot of things. I've got used to the costume as well,' she indicated the rings and veil, 'and no-one ever looks at me twice. They just see a trader.'

'It's quite a story Nessee. Apart from the problems with the Varleys there is also the problem of the court case. The Attorney General has halted the proceedings but the case is still pending and the judge is pressing for it to continue. She is on a mission I think to "punish" criminal children. If you meet Richard you will want to take him away presumably, and if you do that he will be breaking the law.'

'It's Judge Weah isn't it?' Gloria nodded. 'She's not exactly blameless is she?'

'Her personal history doesn't come into it Nessee.'

'Well, not her personal history but her specific involvement in criminal acts surely would have some bearing on things.'

Gloria didn't say anything at first. 'Look Nessee I don't like Judge Weah and she doesn't like me, come to think of it, but she is still a judge. If you have real evidence of her illegal activities you need to let me know, but we can't use that as pressure on her to change what she is saying in this case. It doesn't work like that.'

'What she is saying and doing is wrong. It's obvious Richard is not guilty but she wants to press ahead just for her reputation. And you don't even know what her crimes are yet.'

Gloria could feel herself getting annoyed. This woman was dictating terms to her.

'Maybe you should just tell me what you know before we go any further.' What she heard took her by complete surprise.

'You never did find out who signed the papers authorising all those children to be taken out of the country, all the children who ended up in the mine, abused, exploited or even dead.' She was staring at Gloria questioningly.

It was true. All those papers had been removed because of a threat to national security before they could be examined closely. Gloria had supposed the signatures were those of someone at the Ministry and had thought she knew who it was when the Minister herself had resigned for 'personal reasons.'

'What are you saying? That Judge Weah was involved in this?'

'Not just involved. She personally signed every one of those papers basically sentencing a child to slavery and death. And she was paid for it too, very well paid for it. But she is too well connected. She pleaded ignorance, claimed she had acted in good faith. She also knows too much to be allowed to go on trial or even removed from the political scene.'

'How do you know all this? I never even heard her name mentioned. If this is true then she needs to be brought to book.'

'I told you I have contacts Inspector. You don't have to get the papers just confront the judge and she will cave in.'

'It's not that simple. If I confront her I will want her to answer for all the children whose lives she destroyed, not just to get Richard off.'

There was a silence then. The lights had gone off in Mickey's Bar and the last drinkers had gone home.

'Inspector, I am sorry. I have pushed my way in here and foisted all this information on you. But I am desperate. You can have no idea how guilty I have felt these past years leaving my son in the care of those people, and when I heard what was actually going on I felt even guiltier. I can't think of anyone else, I just want my son.'

More guilt.

'Then you more than anyone else should know we have to get the Varleys for these crimes and finally get justice for Kwame and the others.' She told her about Fanta's disappearance from the Varley house.

'She was brave enough to speak up for Titus and for you. Titus defended your son even though he suffered for it. You say Kwame was loyal to you and that's probably why they decided to get rid of him. And besides, if you don't do it for them then do it for yourself. If you just spirit Richard away where will you go? To Lofa? Richard will not be happy and the Varleys will search for you everywhere. This is hard, but we all have to make sacrifices.'

She told her about the threats against Abu and the incident with the snake.

'Nothing comes cheaply in Liberia, you must know that Nessee, and challenging the power these big people have costs more than anything else.'

'Do you really know who you are dealing with Inspector? I know you removed the Minister of Defence and all his cronies but Africanus Varley is more dangerous than all of them.'

Gloria sat back exhausted. This was not even her main case. There was still Prince Julu and the future of the country at stake!

'I will get some blankets for you to sleep. I can't think any more.' And that was the end of their discussion.

The few hours left till daybreak were not very restful for Gloria and she woke from a dream-filled sleep as the first rays of the sun started to heat up her room. It was only five but she knew there would be no more sleeping. As she went through to the kitchen she noticed the blanket neatly folded on the couch. Nessee was gone and Gloria wasn't surprised. As the whole encounter had taken place at night she wondered briefly if it had been a dream but knew the details were too sharp and the information too precise for that. What was she going to do with it though and, more to the point, what was Nessee going to do? A resourceful woman driven to her limits by her fears for her son's safety and her hatred of the Varleys, she could do anything.

Although it was still very early she called Lawrence and gave him the details of the conversation.

'I know it's a lot to take in at this time of the morning but I think we need to move Richard. His mother is desperate and if she tracks him down which, believe me, I think is very possible, it will be dangerous for him and for your mother. I will come up there as soon as I am ready.'

Abu, emerging blearily from his room, looked at Gloria with a puzzled expression. Instead of asking what had happened the previous night he just said, 'I'll make coffee auntie, you go get ready.'

She hadn't realised how hungry she was until she smelt something being cooked in the kitchen. When she was drinking the coffee and eating the pepper omelette and fried potatoes Abu had prepared, Gloria, after first marvelling again at her nephew's cooking skills, gave him a summary of what Nessee had said.

'Rituals and magic! How can people believe that killing someone and drinking their blood will help you, and they are supposed to be the smart ones!' Abu had a healthy scepticism for most belief systems, traditional, religious or political. 'Do you believe in any of that stuff auntie?'

Gloria was taken aback at the question and hesitated. She didn't spend a lot of time thinking about life's deeper questions but before she could give her measured answer Abu was up clearing the table.

'You are born, you live, you die, that's all there is.' Gloria wondered when Abu had become such a philosopher.

'Anyway, you keep your eyes open Abu. We don't know what these people are going to do.'

'Eh, don't worry about me Auntie. But what about Richard? If you leave him with Auntie Edith, his mother or the Varleys might find him and it would be dangerous for Fatu,' he stumbled, 'and for the family I mean.'

Gloria ignored his slip. 'I have thought of that but there is nowhere to hide someone in this town unless we tie him up and put him in the back of my car.'

Abu grinned.

'And being with Edith, *and Fatu* is good for him. I'll talk to Lawrence and maybe put someone in the yard with them.'

Chapter Twenty

In the end, with Lawrence's agreement, Gloria sent Christian up to stay with Edith and keep an eye on Richard. She explained to him the dangers from the Varleys and enough about Nessee for him to grasp the seriousness of the situation. Christian, who had been one of the most unwilling new recruits last year, listened seriously and promised he would make sure they were safe. She had obtained a pistol for him, although it was against the rules, but Gloria figured Christian, who had often boasted of his glorious exploits as a rebel during the war, could be trusted with it. Edith had been trickier to deal with. She had been outraged to start with at the thought of having someone guarding them but Christian, who was often surly and aggressive with his colleagues, had won her over in a matter of minutes and they had left them drinking coffee in the yard.

'How does he do that?' Lawrence had been surprised at the change in his mother.

'I don't know, but I've seen him do it before.' She told him about the way Christian had hugged the old lady in Clay Ashland when she had just felt awkward and out of place, and how good he had been with the terrified children in the slave camp.

'It's just us he doesn't like then?'

'Mmmm yes, all other adults.'

'Well it's not bad, Ambrose smiles a few times now and Christian actually likes some people. You're making progress.'

'They're making progress, it's nothing to do with me.'

Lawrence laughed out loud.

'So modest Inspector. What about Lamine?'

'Lamine is just… impressionable.'

'I heard old Alfred telling that story of one of our late Presidents and how stupid his wife was, you know the one. They are at an official function. He's drinking orange Fanta and she's drinking coke. The reporter asks him how he's feeling and he says *'fantastic'* and then asks her the same question and thinking he had used his soft drink to give his answer she says, "I am cokeastic". They both laughed again. 'But Lamine didn't get it and by the time Alfred had explained it, it wasn't really funny any more.'

They were pulling into GW Horton by this time.

'Yes, Lamine is not the sharpest but he really really tries.'

The school looked deserted although the main entrance was wide open. The doors were still lying inside where they had been pulled off their hinges during the fighting but the rubble of broken desks had all been cleared away. They walked down to the principal's office where Mr Sawyer was having a meeting with three other men – and Matilda Wesley. Matilda greeted her coolly while Sawyer bustled around for more chairs. Gloria explained that she just wanted to go over things with him again but Matilda had already stood up.

'I am just here to pass on the president's sympathy to the Principal and teachers and to assure them that Her Excellency is following the case very closely.'

'Of course she is, her grandson's been kidnapped.' Lawrence was whispering in Gloria's ear.

But Matilda hadn't waited for a response and was already out the room followed by the other men, teachers Gloria presumed, and Sawyer was staring at her expectantly.

'I just wanted to ask you if you remembered any more about the riots last week.'

Sawyer was silent for a while.

'Sounds like you are getting desperate Inspector. With all that tension up at the Mansion and you are here asking if I can think of anything else. Is that all you have to go on?'

Gloria ignored his tone.

'Well, is there anything else you can think of? How did the trouble start?'

'As I explained, I was in here talking with some of the students because there had been a complaint about some of the teachers cheating in the exams, you know the kind of thing Inspector, girls exchanging favours for good grades or students just bringing in money.'

'Yes, and we never got to talk to those particular students at the time. Maybe we could meet them now, you could give us their names. And the teachers' too.'

Sawyer hesitated.

'I don't think that's such a good idea Inspector. I am sure they can't tell you any more than I have said, unless you have time to investigate their complaints that is. But I don't think they will be able to shed much light on this case. And I have to tell you, they were quite badly wounded by your colleagues when they broke in here, and are still in shock. I am in contact with their parents and guardians and I really don't think it would be advisable for you to look for them at the moment. There are a lot of very angry people out there.'

He was standing now and Gloria thought he was going to bang the wall or stamp his foot. He looked furious.

'They will not be able to tell the difference between the kind reasonable people of your unit and the rogues who broke in here. And most of the teachers are out looking for new jobs anyway. I don't think talking to the police is going to help their chances of getting work.'

He stopped and took a deep breath.

Gloria thought she could have forced the issue but decided it wasn't worth it yet.

'Thanks for your advice Mr Sawyer, and your time. I will let you get back to your teachers' meeting then. Are you re-opening the school soon?'

'Haven't you heard Inspector? GW Horton is closing down. We will not be re-opening. The Ministry of Education has decided that asking children to come back here after the violence they experienced would be wrong, it is spoiled as a place of education. Added to that, whole parts of the school need to be rebuilt and that would be too costly. The children will be given a choice between other schools in the area. It is a very sad time for all of us.'

He didn't look too sad though.

They left him shaking his head and went down the corridor to the canteen but found it was blocked off. The caretaker was nailing some wood across the doors.

'What's happened?'

He recognised Gloria. 'They say the building is not safe ma. No-one supposed to go inside now.'

'I hear it's closing down, what will happen to the place?' Caretakers always knew more than everyone else, but he just stared at the ground.

'I don't know, no-one knows.'

'Maybe that's what your principal is discussing with the teachers, shouldn't you pop along and listen in.' She tried smiling at him.

The caretaker looked up again. 'No teachers here today ma. Most of them are off looking for new jobs.'

'Oh, I thought they were teachers in with Mr Sawyer.'

'No ma, that's just his friends, they are always here, talking, talking, and talking.' He clearly wasn't impressed with all the talking when the school was in a mess, even if it was being closed down. 'He could have saved the school but he just wants to retire, so when the Ministry people came he made the place look really bad.'

Gloria's Polo was blisteringly hot when they got back in.

'So old Sawyer has seen his chance to make some money out of this trouble and get early retirement. He is no fool.'

'I don't know Lawrence, there's something about him that gives me a bad feeling. I understand the school is in a terrible state, and with people moving back up country there are plenty of schools in town now. But I don't understand him. We saw him a few days ago and he appeared to have been badly beaten but now he's sitting there chatting away. And his story has changed as well. The first time I talked to him he told me the students had been in his office complaining about the quality of the food in the canteen, now he tells us it was something to do with exams. We only have his word for what happened and he's not willing to let us talk to the students or the teachers. And the other thing is his eyes. The way he looks at us, it's as if he is always weighing us up, even laughing at us.'

'Come on Gloria, he's an old man who can't even remember what stories he's told us and is probably still in shock from having his school attacked and his students kidnapped and killed.'

'Well, that's the other thing, he didn't even mention the two boys, two of his students who have been murdered. Now that is very strange.'

'Ah Gloria, it would be strange for you but he's an old man, talking about death, crying in public, he's not going to do any of those things. I just don't see how he's connected except as a victim. And don't start talking about his eyes and those feelings you get. We have done enough in this case on the flimsiest of evidence, the raid on Clay Ashland and on the Towehs. Let's just stick to the evidence?'

Gloria didn't say any more but the feeling was like an itch she kept wanting to scratch. 'I want to call in at the clinic and then meet Ambrose.'

Lawrence shrugged. The heat inside the car was driving him crazy.

'You could bake bread in this car, Gloria. Well, *you* couldn't bake bread, but you know what I mean.'

Gloria shrugged. Insults about her cooking skills were the least of her worries.

'You are right. Let's go back and get one of your escort cars. There's going to be a lot of driving today – for you – and I can't stand you moaning all day.'

Lawrence gave a small salute and tipped his cap. 'Yes ma'am, anything you say ma'am.' But as they were slowing down outside the clinic Gloria was already getting out the car.

'Just wait for me here, I don't want any of those boys breaking my mirrors.'

As if they would dare, thought Lawrence.

The clinic was busy as usual and she had to fight her way upstairs. She went first to see the young doctor. He looked harassed, surrounded by a large woman in very tight jeans and a Lone Star football jersey who was demanding to know why the patients' food was so terrible, a nurse in improbably high heels who needed him to sign for some drugs and Monrovia's famous blind beggar and his child guide who were asking for ten dollars for food. Gloria took pity on him. She called the blind man over and gave him five dollars and he went away happy with a 'thank you Inspector' that always left her wondering if he really was very intuitive or just pretending to be blind. She then showed her badge and told the other two to wait outside.

'Thank you Inspector, every day the complaints and the demands get more and more.'

'You need a proper administrator, doctor.'

'I have had three administrators already Inspector. They either sleep all day or allow their family to get free treatment or disappear on errands which take all afternoon. It's impossible.'

'No, I mean a proper administrator who will deal with all the nonsense, one who knows when something is serious, who can control your staff and generally let you get on with being a doctor. If Franklin the blind man thinks he can get right in here and ask you for money, he will be up every day.'

'Do you know of such a person Inspector? They would be a life-saver.'

Gloria had already thought of Ma Anderson. She was looking for work and was one of the most organised and efficient people Gloria knew. Plus she would be strict with the staff and kind to all the really sick people.

'I will get back to you today doctor. How is Alex anyway?'

The doctor's face clouded over. She could see he really cared about his patients. 'I can't get him stabilised, Inspector. I think he is too far gone and his whole system is breaking down. I am just treating all the symptoms as they occur.'

'So there's no way for him to be discharged.'

'At the moment, no. He is still in crisis and I don't know if he will come out of it. I'm sorry Inspector, the ending was always going to be hard but I thought he would have some time left.'

Gloria just felt empty. She went down the corridor to Alex's room. He was lying very still with his eyes open. He managed a grin when he saw her.

'Eh old ma, you finish catching all the rogues now?'

She smiled back at him.

'No, not yet Alex, and not all of them. If I catch them all I will have no job either so…'

He rolled his eyes at her.

'In this place? Rogues can't finish, you know that old ma. You will always get plenty work.'

'How are you?'

'I'm trying ma, but this sickness is really giving me hard time. I don't know if I will make it.' His voice was faint and he looked exhausted.

Gloria was stuck for words. Alex was tough, but he was also a child and whose job was it anyway to tell a child he was dying. She felt a hand on her shoulder and turned to see Mrs Anderson.

'How are you Gloria?'

As always, Mrs Anderson looked calm and untroubled. Saved from talking to Alex about his sickness she instead told Mrs Anderson about the administrator job.

'If you want it, I will tell that doctor right now. He will be very happy to get someone he can trust.'

She was delighted. Even with her husband working, life was still hard, the extra money would be useful plus she liked to be busy and she enjoyed responsibility. Having spent hours with Alex in the clinic she already had a pretty good idea of the things that needed to be changed.

'Thanks Gloria, I do need the job and it's one I will enjoy, plus I will be near Alex.' Her tone told Gloria she knew Alex was most likely not going to get out of the clinic.

Grateful for something practical to do Gloria went to tell the young doctor about Mrs Anderson and then, promising Alex to see him soon, she left.

Her car was surrounded by street boys when she got back to it and Lawrence, leaning on the driver's door, was in his element, talking, joking, laughing – and collecting information no doubt. Gloria wondered how many more of these children were already infected with AIDS, or some other disease which was eating away at them even as they laughed and joked.

They greeted her exuberantly and it was five minutes and several promises later before they could get away.

'How is he?'

'Not good.' Was all she could get out and Lawrence didn't press her.

'I want to get back and speak to Barnyou. We have only today and tomorrow to finish this and we are still wandering in the dark.' She banged the dashboard making Lawrence jump.

'And I can't wait any longer for the Varleys to do something. We surely have enough evidence to move on them. Nessee is convinced we will find human remains if we dig up the floor of the new cinema room they installed.'

'They have a cinema –'

'Human remains Lawrence, concentrate. Nessee is sure that's where the bodies are because no-one will ever find them. So we have to get digging, today. Call Barnyou and tell him to meet us at that restaurant he likes, without Paul.'

'It's a hell of a risk Gloria. You will need a warrant and even if you accomplish that miracle you've no guarantees of finding anything and Africanus Varley will destroy you.'

'Yeah yeah I know, he's big and scary and powerful. That just makes me madder. Is every case we deal with going to have some evil genius at the bottom of it? Because if so then we better get used to dealing with them.'

Lawrence confirmed the meeting with Barnyou and then Gloria added 'Oh, before we get to that eating place I need to see a judge about something. Pull over into the Capitol Building.'

Lawrence did as she asked. She was in no mood for any more needless questions but he was beginning to feel as if they were on a slippery slope to disaster. He finally brought himself to ask who they were going to see.

'Judge Dorothy Weah.'

Lawrence stared at her. 'Is this the right time to be confronting her about Richard Varley's case, she's only making noise, you know that.'

'This is not about Richard's case, it's about a warrant to dig up the Varley home cinema.'

They were out of the car by this time and Gloria was racing towards the grand entrance.

'You better stay in the car Lawrence. If it doesn't work out there's no sense in both our careers going up in flames.'

'Oh no you don't, if your attempts at blackmailing a judge don't work I'm finished anyway. I may as well be there to see it for myself.'

Gloria stopped.

'I'm not blackmailing anyone, I'm just going to put some points to her and see if she wants to cooperate.'

'Yes whatever, let's just do it.'

They raced up the stairs and showed their badges to get through the armed security at the corridor entrance.

'How did you know her office was here?'

'Another snippet of information I received from Nessee when she was encouraging me to do exactly what I'm going to do. Honestly, that woman knows more than our security people.' She stopped outside a heavy wooden door at the end of the corridor and knocked while opening the door at the same time.'

'Welcome to my world,' she heard Lawrence mutter as they took in the gleaming white carpet, imported furniture, fresh flowers and the smell of real coffee. They both shivered, partly from the blast of cold air which hit them and partly at the thought of what they were about to do.

Gloria had that fixed expression on her face that said nothing was going to stop her now. She walked over to the large desk where a beautifully perfumed young girl was staring at a sleek computer screen. She looked up but before she could wrinkle her nose at their crumpled uniforms Gloria leaned over her desk and whispered. 'If you call security, I guarantee you that I, or my friends, will come looking for you. Do you understand? Yes or no?'

The girl managed a weak 'Yes' as Gloria walked around her and straight into Judge Weah's private office.

Like a scene from a movie Judge Weah was stretched out on a long couch, one hand in a box of chocolates by her side and the other holding her phone. It took her a moment to understand who had entered her office, but before she could begin to make a noise Gloria silenced her by slapping her hand onto the carved wooden desk.

'We have no time your honour…'

'You have no time! You have no career Inspector, I don't know what you think you are doing but –' she had got up from the couch.

'Well, I think you had better listen just for a few minutes –'

'I don't have to listen to you, you, you… ' she was actually spluttering with rage.

'It's about adoption papers.'

The silence came suddenly, like a physical thing and for a little while the only noise was the hum of the air conditioner.

Dorothy Weah sat back down on the couch. She had regained her composure sufficiently to speak to the security guard who appeared at her door. In some ways Gloria was pleased that she hadn't been threatening enough to stop the girl calling for help. She sat down too and heard the judge tell the security guard there was no need for him to stay.

'Now Inspector, I hope you have had time to think carefully about what you are going to say to me.'

Gloria looked at her, this survivor of civil war and political instability. She would not want to lose her position now.

'I will try to be clear your honour. I have it on good authority that you personally signed the certificates which gave certain people leave to take many hundreds of children out of this country into a diamond mine slave camp in Sierra Leone, where many of them died and all of them were abused. By good authority' – she pressed on aware that she was beyond the point of no return now and sure that if she stopped her voice would seize up – 'I mean I have the papers which prove it. I intend to open an investigation into this and charge you with a variety of crimes against children.'

Dorothy Weah was a survivor and a pragmatist and had obviously decided that this was no time for bluster or denials.

'You have these papers or you have seen these papers Inspector? I was told all the papers had been collected and sealed under the national security provision.'

'Not all your honour, the copies we used to establish what had happened at the border have been sent to my captain who is in the States along with copies of several people's handwriting. The tests prove conclusively that it is your signature.' This didn't even sound that plausible to Gloria, but she was relying on the fact that Judge Weah had an awful lot to lose if it was true.'

'If you knew all this why are you only confronting me, and why are you not arresting me on the spot. I sense you have some other matters you wish to discuss.'

The judge had a cunning look in her eyes, as if Gloria had revealed the price of her silence. Everyone had a price, in some ways it was a comforting thought.

Gloria paused. As soon as she started speaking again she knew she would effectively be guilty of blackmail but she was trapped.

'The case of Richard Varley. It is a non-case and you know it. I want you to agree with the Attorney General that there is no case to answer and let the boy go.' She saw relief on the judge's face. That would be easy.

'That's the easy part.' The judge stiffened again 'When you have done that then of course the case is wide open again. I have good reason to believe that the real responsibility for the death of Titus and other people lies with Africanus Varley. I need a warrant to search their house and garden where I believe the bodies of at least three people are buried.'

Judge Weah looked horrified.

'And I need the warrant today, right now in fact.'

'But Inspector I can't just issue warrants like this against the Varleys, they are –'

'I know, very influential people. I will take full responsibility if I am wrong and I will give you credit for being brave and resourceful if, as I am sure I will, we find the remains.'

Judge Weah said nothing.

'You really have no choice your honour.'

Lawrence had seldom seen anyone do something so unwillingly, but after ten minutes they had a general warrant to search 'in any way thought necessary, the home, grounds and person of Africanus Varley and his household.' It was done.

They left knowing they were leaving behind a dangerous enemy but Gloria was still on fire.

'Thanks Lawrence, I was not at all sure she would give in.'

'She's as guilty as hell isn't she, that's why she did it. She got off lightly considering she made huge amounts of money from selling children. You don't have any copies of those papers though do you? And you certainly have not sent anything for testing in America.'

'Of course I don't, but she couldn't take the risk of challenging me. And who says she got off lightly?'

'Well, you said you will credit her if we find those bodies, or bones.'

'Oh I will do, and I'm sure we will find them. But I didn't say I wouldn't also come back and charge her in connection with the trafficking of hundreds of children into a slave camp, which I will also do as soon as this is sorted.'

It was only five minutes later that they met up with Barnyou. 'Please tell me you have some good news for me Gloria.' It was a heartfelt plea.

'I need some of your men so we can move on the Varleys.'

'The Varleys. Have you gone completely mad? We have one full day left to find the President's grandson before war breaks out again and your answer is to attack Monrovia's most influential family.'

'I am still working on the case but all I need is a few men, oh and some machinery, to do a search of the Varley house. It will not detract from the investigation but it has to be done now as there could be another life at stake.'

'Even if I agreed Gloria you will never get…' Gloria put the search warrant on the table.

'Judge Weah signed a search warrant.' He looked incredulous.

'It's genuine, you don't have to know how. Will you get me some men and some digging equipment? I can't waste any more time.'

Barnyou shrugged. 'You can have some people if you are sure, if you are really sure.'

'Thanks. How is the investigation going into Gwedu?'

'We are following it up. We are still reviewing all the security clearances for everyone working at the Mansion and we have teams out combing all ocean-facing properties with a tower. It's a bit desperate but it's all we have.'

'And Toweh?'

'Mmm, he's back at work but I don't think he will be calling me to go eat with him for a long time!'

'What has he threatened?'

'At the moment nothing, he is preoccupied with the Mansion security checks and the President's new personal security detail.'

'New?'

'Yes, since he can't find out how someone got into the Mansion to leave a body, he has redeployed the security and appointed new ones. All ones he says he can personally vouch for.'

'That's quite a claim. I wouldn't personally vouch for many people at the moment.'

Lawrence raised an eyebrow.

'I said *many* Lawrence. And anyway, why are you not part of this security scramble?'

Barnyou jumped in. 'The President has moved her family into the Mansion, all of them, so there will be no motorcades. She is working from the fifth floor.'

'I hadn't realised it was getting so serious.'

'Gloria, there are two helicopters on the roof of the Mansion waiting to ferry the President and her family out if everything breaks down. Tonight the army will be deployed around the city and put on full alert in all bases throughout the country. Embassies are sending non-essential staff out and foreigners are being advised to stay indoors tomorrow. This is very serious.'

Gloria and Lawrence exchanged looks. How had they missed all this?

'I just didn't see it developing like this.'

'Look, we all know the President depends on her personal popularity. All this security stuff, including the army, is a smokescreen. So if she cancels the elections as they have told her to do, then everyone will say she is not in control, she has put her family interests ahead of the country, and she is not fit to be President. If she doesn't cancel and they kill the grandson, which I believe they will do, they will say she is a ruthless, power-hungry monster, still not able to control the country but also bang goes her image as mother of the nation. Either way, it will add fuel to the situation we have at the moment. Did you hear that three taxis were set on fire in Gardnersville today?'

Gloria shook her head.

'One driver was killed and the other two injured. Another group has occupied the City Hall and a gang of young people has looted the Ministry of Youth and Sport and then tried to get into the Ministry of Finance. Whatever the president does there will be uproar and we have reports that, along with Gwedu, there are other politicians out there stirring unrest, and giving out money and rice, to ensure there will be widespread disorder whatever happens. She can't win.'

Gloria was stunned. Was it all going to end like this, another war?

'Well, if that's the way it's going let me at least have the Varleys behind bars when it does. No point in stopping now. Get me the excavator then erm…' she looked at Barnyou, 'I'm sorry I don't know your first name and I can't keep calling you Inspector when you call me Gloria.'

Barnyou laughed out loud for the first time that Gloria could remember.

'My name is Abraham. I'm glad we have established that before all hell breaks loose again. I will get you the excavator.'

'Just the machine will do, I'll take my own team. You sound as if you need every person you can get.'

Barnyou called a number and told her the excavator would be at the Varley house in an hour's time. 'Good luck Gloria, let me know how it goes.'

'I could have told you his first name, Gloria.'

'You knew it?'

'Of course I did, you should have asked.'

'Call the team and… what…'

Lawrence had that look on his face.

'Gloria I am here to protect you, I am not your deputy or your assistant. You call your team.'

Gloria got out her phone muttering that it was bit late in the day for Lawrence to start getting so fussy. 'Alfred? Call the team, yes everyone.'

'Except Christian.' Lawrence hissed at her.

'Oh that's right, except Christian. I want to meet all the others outside the Varley residence in one hour's time. Twelve o'clock sharp.'

'See how easy it is when you try.'

Gloria just frowned in response.

Chapter Twenty-one

As instructed, the entire team with the exception of Christian and Paul were gathered around Gloria's car outside the Varley house within the hour. Gloria explained what was going to happen. She told them the work Ambrose had been doing and the conclusions they had reached. They were going in to look for the remains of Kwame and Fanta and then arrest the Varleys. She saw Izena eyeing the excavator.

'We have been told that Kwame, and possibly other unknown victims, are most likely under the foundations of the new addition they built on to the house fairly recently. We have no idea where Fanta's body might be. So we will be doing some digging. Izena, Old Alfred and Lamine will search the house. Ambrose, Alfred, Lawrence and I will be in the grounds making sure no-one tries to escape. We have to be thorough but we also have to be quick. I want everything completed before dark given the tension around town.' They nodded. 'So the sooner we start...'

She rang the bell and through the intercom announced their arrival. It was quite a strange sight she had to admit when she saw Lawrence taking some photographs. A red Polo, a mini excavator and a police escort car – it wasn't exactly the arrival of the SWAT team but it was all they had.

The doors were opened not by the steward but by Africanus Varley himself. He looked genuinely amazed and then started laughing. It was a full belly laugh and it went on for some time.

'Inspector Sirleaf, this looks like a circus troupe. Have you come to entertain us?'

Gloria didn't respond, instead she just presented him with the warrant. His laugh died away as he read it. He couldn't believe it. She hoped it was only the first shock he would be getting that day.

'I'll need to check this, I will have to make some calls so...'

'You make any calls you like sir but we have to get on with the search. My officers will start in the house and we,' she glanced at the excavator, 'will start in the grounds.'

'I would appreciate it if you would wait until I speak with my lawyer and with the judge.'

Gloria raised an eyebrow. 'Unfortunately, due to the security situation in the town we will not be able to wait. I'm sure your lawyer will be here as soon as you call and as for the judge, I doubt if you will be able to get through to her today. I have a feeling she is very busy.'

Africanus Varley had stopped smiling. 'I think you are making a big mistake here but I can see there is no point in talking to you and your team.'

He then disappeared into the house and Gloria indicated to Izena and the others to follow him and start their search.

'Ambrose, you know these people the best. I want you to stay at the gate. No-one leaves and only the lawyer gets in.' He nodded.

Gloria made a show of poking around the undergrowth and in the flowerbeds at least until Izena was able to report that they had found nothing much upstairs. They had been in the grounds for almost an hour now and Gloria thought Africanus was beginning to look relaxed again. His son, Richard's father, did not look relaxed. The man looked a wreck, shuffling from foot to foot and nervously tapping the side of his face. He was most definitely terrified of his father, keeping an eye on him all the time, only speaking when he had received permission from him and then bursting into a stream of abuse aimed at Gloria and the team.

The grounds at the back of the house were not spacious. There was a walled-in yard which she knew was accessible only from the kitchen and which had no entrance into the gardens. The remainder, in contrast with the lawns, flowerbeds and fountain at the front, was very utilitarian. On one side there was a small paved area with a very old palaver hut with a bar and chairs and tables and on the other, a recent addition to the house, a long brick building with tall windows, dominated the rest of the space. Gloria had watched Africanus during the search and seen his anger turn to anxiety and then smug arrogance. He had them beaten apparently.

'As the initial search has revealed nothing sir we need to move on to the next phase.'

Gloria's words met with a blank look from Africanus.

'This building here,' she pointed to the new extension, 'I believe it has gone up very recently and may therefore be covering the scene of a crime. I am sorry but we will have to excavate underneath. We will give you half an hour to remove the equipment, I'm sure your staff can get it done quickly.'

What followed this announcement was a scene Gloria and her team would not forget in a hurry. Daniel Varley became quite hysterical, ranting about criminal damage, looting, rebels and other things but it was his father's performance that took their breath away. Africanus Varley, solemn patriarch and dignified elder statesman bellowed – there really was no other word for it – he put his head back and let out a roar. He lifted his cane and advanced towards Gloria who remained stock still. She was immediately surrounded by Lawrence and Alfred but she elbowed them out of the way to face this bull of a man. Africanus Varley stopped in front of her and lowered his cane but he was furious, so furious he could not speak and Gloria wondered if he was going to say anything at all or just continue staring at her. This was not simply about having his property damaged, he could have it all fixed in a matter of days. Here, in front of his eyes, his cherished beliefs were being dismantled. He had genuinely believed himself to be above and beyond the law, now he had these people tramping through his house and property but more than that, the leader of this team was a woman and he had made his contempt for women quite clear.

He raised the cane above his head again and brought it down on his leg with a ferocious cry breaking it in half. 'I am Chief Africanus Varley and –'

And you look as if you are going to have stroke, thought Gloria before butting in. She hadn't flinched.

'Yeah, we know all that Mr Varley,' she knew he was no chief either, 'but you still have half an hour to get that room cleared before the excavator starts working. I will write you a receipt and you can make any claims you like. Perhaps you better see to your son first though.'

With a last glare Varley strode over to where his son was rolling on the ground, literally frothing at the mouth with rage. He kicked him hard in the ribs and told him to get up and they both disappeared inside.

'Follow them Alfred, and just observe.'

Gloria had surprised herself. Usually at this point she would be shaking with relief having faced down such aggression but she felt nothing except the cold fury that had been growing inside her since the visit to the clinic.

'Wow Gloria, that was quite a performance.' She realised Lawrence was still next to her, ready to take the blow or to restrain Varley if need be. She smiled at him.

'We finally have him rattled Lawrence, so let's see what secrets he's got buried under his fancy cinema room.'

'There had better be something there Gloria, or we are in big big trouble.'

'Well, I don't see all his powerful friends rushing to help him Lawrence, even the lawyer is not here yet. That tells us something.'

'There are already army checkpoints going up around town. Movement is restricted so there may be no-one rushing here.' Gloria nodded.

'Well, we better get on with this.' She went over to speak to the driver of the excavator who looked delighted at the prospect of knocking a new building down rather than just digging holes.

'I want the main floor area dug up so I take it you will have to knock the building down.'

The driver looked in the large glass windows where Varley's people were hurriedly packing away electronic equipment and dragging out cane furniture.

'It's mostly glass, which is a strange choice for a cinema room. It doesn't even have air conditioning. A few nudges with the old lady here,' he patted the excavator affectionately, 'will bring the walls down and then I can lift the roof and leave the floor space free for digging.'

'Great, well they have ten minutes left so let them finish first.'

Alfred had come out the building to re-join them.

'Nothing of interest in the room Alfred?'

'No ma'am, in fact when we searched it the first time we noticed that although it looks fancy it's all quite cheap. They had one large TV and a few chairs and nothing else – no sound system, no DVD equipment, really nothing that would make it a cinema room. It's just a large porch and I got the impression it was hardly used at all.'

Gloria nodded. 'That's good to know.'

Her phone was ringing and she could see it was the Chief calling her from headquarters. She ignored it. After three tries it went silent and then Lawrence's phone started ringing. Gloria gestured to him that she was not available and heard him stammer out something about going to look for her. She signalled the driver and he immediately drove the excavator into the now empty extension. It wasn't a loud crash. There was the tinkling of glass as the large windows shattered but the low brick support wall just fell away and the roof sagged. Gloria gestured that she would talk to the Chief now and Lawrence brought the phone over.

'Inspector what are you doing. Have you gone completely mad?'

'I do have a warrant sir and good reason to believe that several murders have been committed here.'

'I have spoken to Africanus Varley's lawyer. He tells me you are going to knock some building down. You can't do that, do you understand?'

Gloria looked at the excavator which had demolished two of the walls and had removed most of the roof.

'I'm afraid you're too late sir. The building is already down.'

There was silence.

'You may have gone too far this time Gloria, even for you. I will not be able to help you with this.'

'Understood sir, I will report back later.'

She handed the phone back to Lawrence.

'Trouble Gloria?'

'Yes, that's my name.'

Lawrence laughed, he was enjoying himself.

'No I mean –'

'I know, it was just the Chief giving me the belated order not to touch any of the buildings. He's not too happy. But I think we can start digging up the floor now.'

Two hours later there was a huge pile of rubble and dirt and a very large space where the floor used to be, but nothing else, not a bone, not a piece of cloth nothing. Africanus had drifted back after an hour and settled himself in one of the cane chairs. He said nothing but his smirk said it all for him. He was convinced he had her now.

'Are we in trouble Gloria?' said Lawrence. They were both sweating along with everyone else. Gloria looked around at the team. Izena was sitting down but Alfred, Lamine and Ambrose were still frantically sifting through the rocks and the dirt. She was convinced there had to be something there. Well, she hoped for her sake there was something there.

'Look Lawrence, Varley's little display, and his son's, was surely an indication that we are on the right track. It's just the lack of time, we can't dig up the whole yard tonight and that's all the time we have.'

She looked around the yard again. This fancy extension was the clue, a cinema room that wasn't a cinema room. She looked at it again. The walls had collapsed easily, the floor had been a thin layer of concrete easily dug up. There was nothing else, except the thin foundation where the brick wall had rested on. Gloria went over and gave it a kick, it didn't move. She tried harder but still nothing. She called Alfred to try with his pickaxe. It was solid concrete but he eventually managed to crack it.

'Right everyone, forget the floor area. I want everyone to concentrate on the wall foundations, get down as far as you can. I know you are tired but let's give this a go. Come on, everyone.' She clapped her hands and the team, re-energised, got to work. It was then she noticed that Africanus had disappeared.

'Ambrose, find the Varleys and bring them back here and make sure none of them and none of the staff leave the property.'

It was Lamine who made the first discovery. He was digging with enormous energy in the far corner and after pulling up a huge piece of cement he held up a long piece of coloured material. Gloria was over in a second and together with Lawrence they started gently scraping away dirt from the body in the ditch. The body still had clothes and some hair and was easily identifiable as a young girl. Gloria stood up and looked at the Varleys who were standing in silence in a corner of the garden. Daniel was shaking and looking at his father while Africanus was trying to look surprised. She said nothing but called the team over.

'So we have a result, and I'm sure there will be more bodies unfortunately. I want us to dig up the rest of the foundation if we can. But take your time and do it carefully, any remains will be easily damaged.'

She looked at her watch. 'It's already going to three. If we can at least uncover them before dark, then we can cover the site to preserve it until it can be carefully examined. Remember, all of this is evidence but these remains are also victims.'

She went over to the Varleys and officially charged them with kidnap, murder and attempted murder. Africanus was impassive, his face set like one of the polished wooden masks hanging in their library. Daniel looked more and more as if he was on the edge of some kind of breakdown but his father ignored him completely. Gloria told Ambrose to watch them until they were able to get them to the station. She called the Chief and Barnyou and explained what they had found and that she had charged the Varleys. Barnyou was delighted and the Chief was cautious.

'It is going to be tense tonight Gloria. You will have to do what you can before dark and then leave some officers there until we see what happens after tomorrow.'

'Inspector Barnyou is sending two officers down to guard the site tonight. I will be bringing the Varleys down to the station. It might be good if we had some extra officers there tonight just in case…' The Chief agreed but was clearly preoccupied with the national security situation.

'I need you back on the President's case, though Gloria. We have one day left and not much hope so we need to throw everything at this or we are all finished.'

She rang off and went back to the team. They had already discovered two more sets of bones. Izena and Alfred were lifting them out while Lawrence tried to tag them but it was hard to tell which bones belonged where. Lamine was engrossed with digging up the rest of the wall foundation, sweat pouring off him. It was then that Lawrence's phone started ringing again.

Lawrence's first thought was to ignore it until he saw it was his mother's number. As soon as he pressed the green button his mother started talking. She was calm but obviously very tense.

'Lawrence, is Gloria with you? Lawrence, I need to speak to Gloria.'

'She's here ma, what's the problem? Is it something to with Richard?'

'That woman is here, the mother and she says she is taking him away but Christian is saying no. I tried to talk to her but she has a gun and he has a gun and neither of them looks very stable to me.'

'Right mum, we are just down the road, we'll be there in a few minutes.'

Gloria had got the gist of the conversation. This was turning into a full scale nightmare.

'We'll have to take these characters with us,' she indicated the Varleys, 'I can't leave them here. Ambrose,' she called over to him, 'put the Varleys in the car and then get in. Keep your eyes on them at all times. Alfred, we have to go but you three stay here and recover as much of the remains as you can, but then you have to get home as soon as the CID officers get here. The city is tense so make sure you are home before dark. Your uniform Alfred,' she had caught his frown, 'will not protect you, and you have to make sure Izena is home safely.'

It was as they were rather clumsily bundling the Varleys into the car that Lawrence pointed out that they were carrying Africanus Varley right into the path of the woman he had almost killed, and right into the place where they were keeping his grandson.

'Of course.' Gloria frowned, how could she have been so stupid. She paused for a moment then went back and called Lamine. 'Ambrose, you and Lamine will take the Varleys to the police station so we can charge them. Lamine, you are to keep your eyes on them at all times. Have you got that?' Lamine nodded. 'I will call Inspector Barnyou to make sure he is there to receive them and do the paperwork. They must be kept in there, make sure of that.'

They both nodded, but at the same time knowing that the chances of keeping someone as powerful as Africanus Varley in overnight were almost nil.

As they raced up the hill towards Lawrence's house she called Barnyou and explained, 'But if I book them that means the case will sit with CID and it's your team who have done all the work.'

'I don't care, and if we don't get a breakthrough tomorrow none of that will matter.'

They were almost at Lawrence's gate when Gloria took out her pistol and gave it to Lawrence.

'If we have to use this here then we will have lost this one.'

Lawrence took it. Although Traffic police did not routinely carry guns, Lawrence was an excellent shot and it was his mother and sister who were in danger here.

The yard was quiet but out of the open front door they could hear an urgent exchange going on. As there was no way to sneak up on anyone Gloria headed straight for the door and went in. It was like a scene from a black and white movie, the kind they used to show on TV before the war. Nessee was standing with her back to the kitchen and with her pistol trained on Christian. He was also standing but his pistol was by his side and he was just watching Nessee out of half-closed eyes. Between them were Richard sitting on the floor with his head down and a group of women with Edith in the middle of them and open copies of Camara Laye's *African Child* on their laps. Her first thought was that if they had continued their discussion on the book they could probably have sent both Christian and Nessee to sleep, and solved the problem like that. Her second thought was that none of the women looked even remotely concerned. Edith spoke first.

'Ah, Gloria you are here, maybe you can sort this out. Nessee arrived this afternoon and announced she was taking Richard with her. I explained to her that couldn't happen and when she discovered that Christian is actually a police officer and not my son, she pulled out her gun. That's as far as we have got I think. Ladies?' Edith sounded as if she was reading out the notices at the end of the Women's Guild meeting.

The group of women murmured their agreement and then sat back to watch.

'There's only one person here with a gun out Nessee and that's you. As I take it you don't want to harm these old ladie...' she caught herself just in time, 'the book club members or your son, maybe you should put the gun down first and we can talk.'

'I said it all last night Inspector. You know my story and you know the circumstances, there's nothing more to talk about. I want my son and then we are going to disappear.'

'Based partly on what you told me last night we have arrested Africanus and Daniel Varley.'

Nessee looked shocked.

'You arrested them? You arrested Africanus Varley?'

'We dug up the grounds and part of the house and what we found backs up your story.'

'You found Kwame?'

'We found more than one set of bones. Apart from anything else we will need your help in identifying the remains and we will also need you to give evidence. This is what you wanted. Help us with this and you will get Richard back in the best way possible.'

Nessee looked uncertain and then shook her head.

'No, sorry Inspector. Even with them in custody and all those remains there is no way you will ever get Africanus Varley to trial. No, I wish you all the best but I am going to take my chances on my own with my son.'

She looked over at Richard whose head had come up at the news that his grandfather had been arrested.

'So, Richard you come over to me and then we will leave. I don't think either of your officers wants to start a shooting match inside a house Inspector. And I am his mother, I'm not doing anything illegal.'

Gloria didn't bother responding to that.

'Come on Richard, come over to me.' His mother was half ordering and half pleading with him. 'We are going to go somewhere safe. I promise you.'

Richard stood up slowly, looked at her and started to walk but instead of going to his mother he stopped next to Edith. He was shaking but when he spoke Gloria could see he was angry, not afraid.

'My mother...' his voice was cold, his words clear, 'my mother who ran away and left me with those wicked people.'

For the first time Gloria saw Nessee hesitate. Of all the responses she had anticipated this was clearly not one of them.

'But Richard I had to, otherwise they would have killed me too.'

'Fine, so you saved yourself. But you left me with *them*.' He spat out the last word. 'Do you know what they did to me? Do you?'

He was shouting now and crying.

'The beatings, the punishments, over and over…'

He had gone to another place inside himself, a place full of dark memories.

'You went away but you never came back. So, who took care of me? Not you, not my father, not my *grandfather*,' he shuddered, 'only Titus. Titus talked to me, advised me and protected me. He even stood up to that wicked old man. So they killed him. Titus and this old ma here,' he was squeezing Edith's shoulder and she gently patted his hand, 'they are the people who took care of me and now you come here with a gun and say I should go with you. You're no different from them and no, I not goin no place with you.' He shouted this last sentence, wiping at his tears.

There was a silence. The book club members were absolutely rapt, their heads turning from Richard to Nessee like spectators at a tennis match. The only sound came from Mrs Gray, the bishop's mother, who was furiously fanning herself with a rolled-up copy of that morning's Spectator newspaper. Live drama was so much more interesting than any book club discussion.

Nessee looked at Richard but her expression didn't change and the gun stayed pointed at Christian. There was no time, no words to explain why she had done what she had thought was for the best. The silence stretched on but Gloria knew it wouldn't last long. In a room full of Liberians someone was going to say something. It was just as she was thinking this that Mrs Kromah fainted, dropping rather dramatically to the floor. Instinctively they all moved towards her and by the time Gloria looked up Nessee had gone.

'Lawrence, you and Christian go after her. But no guns, I don't think she really intended to shoot anyone.'

Edith stood up tutting and straightening her dress and then with her arm tightly round Richard's shoulders announced she was going to get them all some drinks. She hugged him wordlessly before giving him a tray and setting out glasses and cartons of juice. Enough had been said for one day. Behind her she heard Mrs Kromah, now recovering on the couch, tell the rest of them that, during the afternoon's drama it had occurred to her that maybe they should write their own book instead of reading other people's.

'Come on Richard, let's get these old ladies a drink and then maybe they will go home. I think I have heard enough for one day.'

Lawrence and Christian were back in ten minutes. Nessee had disappeared completely.

Gloria wasn't surprised but there was something about the kind of information she had and the way she seemed able to come and go at will – and handle a gun – that made Gloria very suspicious. This was more than a frightened woman on the run from an abusive relationship. No wonder Richard was so confused, although he hadn't been confused when he spoke to his mother.

'I don't think she'll be back, especially seeing Richard's reaction but I'll leave Christian here if that's ok Lawrence. I don't think tonight is a night for taking risks.'

To her surprise Lawrence agreed immediately and Christian nodded.

'Are you going home now?'

Gloria hesitated. It was almost curfew time now and getting through checkpoints would be tricky but it didn't feel right to her to just go home and wait.

'Gloria, I'm asking you.'

She nodded.

'Yes I'm going home. I'll just check on Izena and Alfred first.'

'You have done well today, you took a huge risk and it paid off.'

Gloria shrugged. 'But we never found Fanta, we couldn't save her and we can't even find her body.'

'You won't find anything else tonight.'

Gloria agreed. There was just never enough time or the right resources for doing things.

One call was all it took. Barnyou's officers had arrived at the Varleys' house and the site had been covered. Everything they had dug up had been bagged and tagged and was now at headquarters under lock and key and with an officer on guard for the night. Varley senior and junior had been booked and because of the late hour and the curfew, that news would not leak out until tomorrow.

It was getting dark by the time she left to drive down the hill to her apartment with Mrs Gray and Mrs Kromah to drop off en route. In that way that could still catch her by surprise, the night seemed to drop on them like a blanket and by the time she reached the main road she needed her lights to negotiate the hill. The lights picked up the wooden pole across the road just in time for her to brake and narrowly avoid crashing into the checkpoint. It was lit by two kerosene lanterns and as she stopped two tall soldiers came over to her. Gloria was expecting the usual banter and perhaps even a request for a few dollars but the first soldier touched his helmet in a kind of half salute when he saw her uniform. The other one shone a torch into the back seat onto the two old ladies and muttered a half apology as they blinked in the glare.

'Are you going home ma?'

Their nervousness was obvious.

'Yes, I'm just dropping these two home first.'

She pointed to the side road straight after the checkpoint.

'To the bishop's house?'

There was only one compound down that road.

'Yes my son, I am the bishop's mother and this is my friend.'

Everyone sounded nervous now.

'Well bishop has already gone through ma so you better go.'

He straightened up.

'And then I would advise you go home too, Inspector. We don't know what is going to happen tonight.'

Gloria nodded and drove through the opened checkpoint and off down the rocky track that led to the bishop's residence. At Mrs Gray's insistence she dropped them outside and turned around immediately to go back. Her headlights swung around and for a few seconds lit up the community well where some small children were still pumping water. They froze in the light staring back into the dazzling brightness and something clicked inside Gloria's head. They were using buckets to fill a large blue water barrel which they would then roll down to their house. It was one of the commonest sights in Monrovia where water was still a problem for many people, but in that instant it also told Gloria where she would find the body of that young girl, Fanta, the girl they had failed to protect.

When they were searching the Varley's house and the grounds she remembered glancing up at a blue barrel on the small roof over the back door. A common sight, many houses used the barrels to collect rainwater, so she had looked and then been distracted by the call from the Chief. But the details of it had stayed on the edges of her memory. The Varleys had a huge water tank on the roof and several barrels in the yard to collect the run-off water, so why would they need another barrel on the porch roof? And they clearly had a thing for those barrels. She remembered Nessee's description of Kwame being suspended over one when she had discovered them and how Titus's body had been stuffed into one for the cook to find – and knew in that instant that Fanta's body was in the barrel, right under their noses and they had missed it. Because Varley had not been hiding the body, he had been displaying his power in having it right there in front of them. Yes, he would have loved that.

Gloria drove slowly back up to the checkpoint. She knew she should go home but decided she would not get any peace until she had checked that water barrel. The Varleys' house was not far but she couldn't drive there alone and she was not going to call Lawrence again. He would be furious but she would just have to deal with that later. She stopped at the checkpoint and the tall soldier came over to her again. Under the security light of a nearby compound she could see he was very young. He must be one of the new recruits she thought.

'What is your name?'

'Jonathan, ma.'

'Right Jonathan, I need you to do something for me. I need you to come with me to a house down the hill here. It's very important.'

His eyes widened. It was bad enough being on full alert but now he was being asked to break the rules. He stammered, not knowing what to say. In theory he couldn't take orders from a police officer, even if she was an inspector, but she hadn't ordered, she had just asked for help and everyone knew this old ma here, she was famous. Gloria was looking at him. His partner had sauntered over by this time.

'What's up?'

Jonathan explained what he had been asked to do and his partner just shrugged.

'Go help the old ma, nothing's going to happen here tonight with all these people around.'

He looked around at the lights from the American Embassy, the EU delegation and other consulates. 'If there's trouble, it will be in town.'

He carried on chewing.

Gloria opened the passenger door and Jonathan the soldier folded himself into the Polo, his gun sticking out the window. It wasn't a look Gloria usually went for but it might be useful tonight.

They drove down the hill towards the Varleys' house. It was eerie. All the bars and restaurants were closed and silent. You could actually hear the hum of the generators and the quiet 'whoosh' of the incoming tide.

'It's like the war,' she volunteered but Jonathan had decided that if he was along as security then he was going to act like one. He stared out the window intently as if looking for ambushes and Gloria didn't try any more conversation.

There were no further checkpoints along the beach road and they got to the Varley house in ten minutes. It took another ten minutes to rouse the officers and persuade them to let her in. Everyone was nervous tonight. They had to check with Barnyou first which meant everyone would now know where she was. But eventually the gates opened and she drove to the front doors. The two officers had made themselves at home judging by the food and drinks spread out on the table in the palaver hut at the back. Gloria ignored that and simply explained she needed the water barrel down from the porch roof. It was Jonathan who eventually climbed onto the porch and then hauled Gloria up. She explained briefly what she expected to find and then got him to cut off the tape and open the lid. The beam of her torch bounced back from the opened lifeless eyes of the young girl she had spoken to only a few days previously and, despite the fact this was exactly what she had expected to find, a shudder of nausea and anger shook her. Jonathan had looked once and then turned away.

'Is it who you've been looking for?'

'Yes it's her, someone else we have let down.'

She banged the lid back on. Now what were they going to do? They couldn't leave the barrel here now they knew there was a body inside it and there was no point in taking it to headquarters. The only place with facilities for storing it at least until it could be formally identified and examined was the Catholic Hospital. She groaned to herself imagining the number of checkpoints that would involve. Jonathan was staring at her.

'You need to take this somewhere now don't you?'

He sounded more resigned than anything else.

'I do, but I think it's going to take more than you, me and my small Polo for this one, and if we get searched at a checkpoint and they find a body in a barrel, I will have a lot of explaining to do. And you will probably be court-martialled for deserting your post.'

Her phone started ringing then. It was Barnyou.

'Gloria, what are doing there that couldn't wait until morning.'

She told him.

'Wait for me.' Was all he said and then rang off.

She called Abu while she waited and he was fine. He and Rahul along with Morris were writing a proposal for a football tournament. He assured her she would love the idea and although she doubted that, she was happy he was ok. Now for Lawrence. She knew if she waited until morning Lawrence would be seriously offended, so better to tell him what was going on now. He answered on the first ring.

'Are you all right?'

'I am fine Lawrence but there have been some developments.'

She told him quickly what had happened and then paused.

'So do you want me to come down there?'

'No, that's not necessary. I think Barnyou is arranging to get us through the checkpoints.'

Lawrence was very cool. 'Okay then, let me know when you are back.'

She rang off just as Barnyou arrived in a jeep with a flashing light and siren. When he pulled alongside her he was grinning. 'So what do you think?' He patted the door as if he was stroking his favourite horse. 'I think this will get us through, or if it doesn't at least we'll have the consolation of knowing nothing else would have!'

'You're very cheery Inspector.' She was genuinely surprised.

'You know it has all got so bad that it's almost a relief being able to do something and solving several murders is very satisfying.'

Gloria couldn't see it quite like that, not yet.

'We need to drop this soldier back to his post first. Let's get the barrel in the car.'

Barnyou delegated that task to his two officers and then ordered them to clear away their food and drink and to call him every half hour for the rest of the night.

'So now only one of them can sleep at a time,' he said to Gloria.

They were already up the hill and Jonathan told them he would walk the rest of the way back to his checkpoint so they could get on with their trip.

As they were driving past the police headquarters Barnyou told her what had happened earlier that evening.

'Your officers delivered the two Varleys but by the time we got them to an interview room Daniel Varley had confessed to everything. Apparently he is responsible for all the killings, he runs the group involved in the rituals, he is the mastermind.' Gloria stared at him.

'Daniel Varley a mastermi –'

'I know. I doubt if he even has a functioning mind much less a mastermind. But his father played the part of bewildered old man brilliantly, claiming he knew nothing of all this. He has total control over his family, and his son is more afraid of him than of anything else.'

'Just like they did to that pekin.' She told him how they had persuaded Richard to confess to killing his cousin. 'He is a bad bad man.'

'Maybe so, but he's a bad bad man who is very rich and has a lot of powerful friends.'

He hesitated, trying to gauge her reaction.

'With Daniel confessing to everything, and no physical evidence and no witnesses linking him to any of the murders, they would have to let him go but I told him the streets were not safe and we could not get him back home so he is sleeping in a cell tonight. But he will be free in the morning.'

They had arrived at the City Hall checkpoint which prevented Gloria from saying anything but it was only a brief stop. The soldiers had a word with Barnyou and then waved them through without another word.

'We can't let him go. He is the main one. Africanus Varley is a murderer, the rest of them are just pawns. He's the one responsible for the deaths of those young people. And if he escapes all of this, the killing will continue and we will have a serious enemy on our hands, well, mostly me I think. That's if we survive tomorrow of course.'

She added this last as they were approaching another checkpoint at Vamoma House. There were at least a dozen soldiers on this one and they swarmed around the jeep. They ignored Barnyou's papers and told him to get out of the vehicle.

Checkpoint etiquette, whether in the middle of a war or during a security alert, was the same. If you got out of your vehicle there was a good chance you would not get back into it again. You might lose your life, you would almost definitely lose your car. In their case, being found with a body in a barrel at night in this atmosphere of high tension, they would almost certainly lose both.

The soldier at the window shouted again for them to get out the car. Gloria looked at Barnyou but his expression was angry not afraid.

'Are you stoopid? Eh, I asking you,' Barnyou was tapping the side of his head, 'answer me.'

Gloria watched as Barnyou continued to insult the soldiers who were momentarily reduced to silence. It was a risky strategy, to say the least. Out of the darkness she could see more soldiers coming to the jeep, attracted by the shouting. Barnyou didn't seem to notice them, or if he did he didn't care.

'You see two inspectors in an official vehicle at night with all the correct papers,' he waved the paper in the man's face, 'and you tell us to get down. You soldier people really are stoopid.'

Calling someone stupid in Liberia had always been one of the greatest insults, liable to get you into a fight or into court. Gloria thought Barnyou might be slightly overdoing the angry inspector routine. The soldier backed off a little but his colleagues pressed in. One of them banged the side of the door, another hit the roof with his weapon. These young soldiers were already jittery and itching for some action. This was getting out of hand.

'We have some people in the back,' he indicated the blacked out windows behind him, 'go check them.' Gloria wondered where he was going with this. The soldiers moved a little and she heard Barnyou add, 'they are suffering from cholera so be careful.' The soldiers stopped. Cholera was much feared and was believed to be caught on contact with another sufferer. Barnyou tapped the paper again. Gloria wondered what was really written on it. 'No-one can get out of the hospital to collect these people but they can't be left in their own community or the disease will spread so the inspector and myself were asked to carry them to hospital. That's why you see two inspectors carrying sick people, no-one else would do it.'

The soldiers had moved back from the jeep as if they might catch cholera from leaning in the window.

'Inspector sir.' The man's attitude had changed. 'But you were too rude. We also doing our duty here and it is dangerous for us. You not supposed to speak to us like that.'

Barnyou changed his tone in that conciliatory way people did with children and upset adults.

'I know, but the longer we stay with these people the more chance there is that the inspector and myself will catch the cholera too. And if we stay here too long you all will catch it too. That what make me to talk so. Please, I beg you, for all our sakes let us go through.'

The soldiers, placated now, and their self respect restored by Barnyou's explanation, nodded and sprang into action. The gate was opened and they went through waving, driving into the darkness.

Gloria clapped slowly and then they both laughed. 'Cholera! It used to be lepers or AIDS victims we would tell the rebels we were carrying.'

'It was the first thing that came into my head.'

'When we finally get well-trained educated soldiers we're going to have to think of better stories though!'

'I think we have a few years yet, Gloria.'

The road past the airfield was surprisingly empty and they arrived at Catholic Hospital without further incident. All the lights were on and they drove straight around to the morgue at the back. Gloria had phoned ahead and the same morgue attendant she had met the last time was waiting for them. She wondered if he slept there. He received the barrel without comment, told Gloria he would cut it open and then put Fanta's remains in cold storage until tomorrow. He looked insulted when Gloria asked if he needed any help.

'The only thing I need Inspector is for you to sign the papers so I know who will be paying for all this, otherwise I will be in trouble.'

She signed everything and then left him to his work.

'Well, that was all over very quickly.' She looked at her watch and saw that it was after midnight. 'And we have to get back.'

'And there's tomorrow to get through.' Barnyou looked defeated. He had just phoned his officers again and all his excitement and energy had left him.

'We have so many pieces of the jigsaw but no time to put it all together. By the way I forgot to tell you that I spoke to my sister, the one who used to be in that cultural dance troupe.' Gloria nodded, only half listening. 'She says the troupe is still together but she's not a part of it any more. Some big person gives them money but my sister didn't like what they were being asked to do. She said there was too much talk of power and animal spirits and how their dancing was to get in contact with these spirits and use that power etc. My sister just likes to dance, eat and have fun, that was all too serious for her.'

Gloria couldn't see that it was any help. It just confirmed their suspicions that there was such a group. Besides, even if there was a connection she didn't think she would make it tonight. She was beyond tired and the sadness that often hit her after a case was creeping up on her, she could feel it like the waves lapping at her feet. She knew why. All they were doing was playing catch up, they weren't protecting anyone and tomorrow another child would die.

'We are going to detain Senator Gwedu tomorrow, officially it will be for his own safety but he's our one remaining suspect although we don't have much on him actually. We have investigated him and I think we have enough evidence to hold him on public order issues but no connections with kidnapping. It's a long shot really.'

Gloria agreed but couldn't add much more.

'Let's just go.'

They got in the jeep and set off back across town. The checkpoints opened up for them like magic and they drove through the silent town and out towards the beach. There had been no trouble tonight but tomorrow might be different.

Barnyou dropped her off and she called Lawrence just to tell her she was alright and then dragged herself up the stairs. Abu was sitting up waiting for her.

'Abu, you should be sleeping.'

'No aunt Glo, not till you got back. How are the roads?'

Gloria was too tired to argue and rather than talk about Fanta she told Abu a comic version of the incident at the checkpoint while she ate the jollof rice he had made. Abu listened but shook his head.

'It's too dangerous aunt Glo, anything can happen.'

But he could see she was tired and Gloria found herself being hustled off to her room.

Chapter Twenty-two

'It's the last day,' was Gloria's first thought when she woke, any small triumph of yesterday already drained from her. It was all death and killing and today would likely see another one. The death of another child followed by, if the politicians could be believed, more death and destruction. This last thought spurred her on. She needed to make sure Abu did not go to school today although she had heard that many schools had closed due to the heightened security situation. She dressed and went out to find Abu and Morris eating bread while listening to the radio.

'Hello Morris, did you finish your proposal last night?' Morris laughed and pointed to a pile of papers on the table. It certainly looked impressive. 'Are you applying to the World Bank then!' Abu shook his head seriously. 'No aunt Glo, we are sending it to the UN people.'

'Impressive.'

'And the government, Global Vision, St Luke's...' he continued naming organisations while Gloria made some coffee. 'It's a child protection football tournament in honour of Titus. They will love it.'

Gloria wasn't so sure they would love it but said nothing more about it. 'So you people are not going to school right?'

'No ma, no school today.'

'Well don't go walkabout then, stay close to the house, if you're staying here,' she added, looking at Morris.

Lawrence's arrival interrupted any further discussion and Gloria left with him. She told him about the previous night's events as they got into his car. Today was no day for her Polo which was, in any case, still parked at the Varley's house.

They were half way down the hill when Lawrence asked where they were heading. Gloria stopped, realising she hadn't really thought about it. They looked at each other.

'For a moment there I wasn't sure, Lawrence. We are going to headquarters. There's still all the Varley stuff to follow up on, the rest of the remains to recover from their house and a case to make against Africanus Varley. He is not going to get off so lightly. I also want to know what happens with Gwedu and then by midday we will know our fate.'

'Hmm, so we will just keep busy until the fighting starts again.'

'I am still thinking Lawrence, but what more can we do?' They had reached the bottom of Randall Street and Gloria wanted to visit Alex before going anywhere else. The streets were deserted. The checkpoints from last night were all empty although there were soldiers sitting in small groups along the road. All the shops were closed, shuttered and, in some cases, boarded up. There were no vehicles on the road, eight thirty in the morning and the roads were silent. Gloria could feel the prickling fear in the bottom of her stomach. The car felt stifling even with the air conditioning on. She remembered those days and nights during the war when all they could do was wait. Wait for the ECOMOG to arrive in town in 1991, for the rebels to arrive in 1992 and 1996, for the trouble to spread from the Capitol building in 1998, for the different rebels to arrive in town in 2001, and on and on. The same nameless fear, because you couldn't allow yourself to think about what might happen when they did arrive, the same feeling of helplessness. The whole town was once more holding its breath.

They passed the convent and she saw its gates were open as usual although she knew the school was closed. She had taken refuge there during the war and she imagined Sr Margaret was even now in her element marshalling her troops, nuns and volunteers, to set up an emergency clinic, feeding point and sleeping quarters. If anyone could be ready for social breakdown it was her.

The clinic was quiet when they arrived. The reception area was empty and Gloria wandered down the corridor. It was obvious any patient who could do so had gone home. Bitter experience had taught them that in the heat of war no place was safe.

In Alex's room she found Mrs Anderson and Pascal sitting by his bed and Alex half sitting up.

'Eh, the old ma is here auntie. Maybe she want to arrest me.' Gloria and Mrs Anderson smiled.

'No arrest yet pekin, not enough evidence. I have tried to beat a confession out of your friend here but no way, no-one is saying anything. All of them must be scared of you.' Alex laughed and then in seconds had closed his eyes and drifted off again.

'Where is everyone?'

'There is only one other patient left here, an old man who will probably die today anyway. The doctor is with him. Everyone else has gone. Scared.' Mrs Anderson looked at her. She was obviously torn between staying with Alex and being with her family. It wasn't a choice she should have to make. Gloria thought.

She found Dr Lee sitting with the old man whose laborious breathing was the surest sign he was quietly fading away.

'What are your plans doctor?'

'My plans? More importantly, what are yours? The clinic will not be safe if there is trouble. Our friendly soldiers will probably be the first to loot the place. Can't you take the child somewhere safe?'

Gloria looked at Lawrence who shrugged and said tentatively, 'The convent?'

It was what Gloria had been thinking. It was nearby, at least one of the nuns was a nurse and Sr Margaret was probably more effective in fending off looters than any soldiers.

'Ok, but we have to be quick. Dr Lee can you get him ready and give us any drugs he might need?' He nodded.

She phoned Margaret who immediately said yes. In ten minutes Lawrence had carried Alex to the car wrapped in a blanket. Gloria insisted that Mrs Anderson and Pascal go back home.

'It should only be for today, go and be with your children, and you too Pascal, the old ma will need you today. Unless you want to sit in the convent all day with the nuns?' He didn't. They both hugged Alex and then hurried off, Mrs Anderson insisting they would make it back home by themselves.

Another ten minutes saw Alex installed in a small quiet room at the back of the convent. He woke for a few minutes and then, heavily drugged for the short trip, he fell asleep again. Gloria thanked Margaret who was in full command mode – and in full multi-coloured battle dress. She refused a coffee and they were back in the car and heading up the hill.

'Was that fresh bread I could smell?' Lawrence asked.

'Delicious eh!'

'The whole town is on the brink of war and they are baking bread!'

'And we are reporting to the office. We can't just sit about wringing our hands. Some of those nuns have been through this war eight or nine times. Baking bread is probably the only thing that's kept some of them sane.'

'I'm not sure 'sane' is the right word Gloria, did you see what Margaret was wearing?' Sr Margaret had been in one of her very loud trouser suits.

Gloria laughed. 'The first time I saw her in one of them I wasn't sure if she was going to bed or to some new religious event. Anyway, maybe it helps scare away the looters.'

They drove in silence the rest of the way to headquarters where in contrast to the hush of the city centre there was a kind of feverish activity. The main reception was not as crowded as usual. She supposed most normal police activity had been suspended, although she could see auntie Fata and her colleagues were still selling food. Before they could cross to the stairs the familiar voice of Rufus Sarpoh reached her.

'Inspector, Inspector.'

She stopped, feeling vaguely guilty. She couldn't remember if she had promised him information or something. She didn't think so.

'Inspector,' he ignored Lawrence, 'what's the story with the Varleys? I hear you've got them locked up.'

'Rufus, this is really not a good day for investigations. We have about two hours before the President makes her speech and whatever happens after that we are all going to be busy.'

'Yes, but the Varleys getting arrested, that's a story I have wanted to report for a long time.'

'Well don't hold your breath Rufus, they are very slippery. We have them at the moment but I don't know for how long.' She could see by Lawrence's face he was wondering what had happened to the agreement they would keep the story out of the papers. It was a bit too late for that.

'Come on Inspector, just give me the information you have. You need to talk to me anyway, remember we are doing a piece on your brave attempt to stop the siege at that school.'

That all felt like a very long time ago to Gloria.

'My attempt, that's right. We managed, let's see, to... oh yes, we managed to not rescue any of the children, or stop those riot police from smashing the place up so badly it has now been closed. Yes, that was a big success Rufus.' But Rufus did not give up easily.

'It would have been a lot worse if you hadn't gone there Inspector, who knows how many more children would have been killed. And that school was falling down even before the war. Old man Sawyer has invested nothing in the buildings for years. The old hall at the back, the toilet block and the tower have all been out of use since before the war started so don't blame yourself for everything. And anyway it is about –'

But Gloria had frozen. She heard Lawrence's voice repeat the word as if from very far away, the word she had heard but found it hard to get out. 'The tower?'

They had all three of them stopped now, obstructing the flow of people up and down the main stairs. Rufus looked confused.

'There's a tower at GW Horton School?'

'Yes, it was a bell tower,' Rufus had a photographic memory, 'but it hasn't been used for that for years. There was a very nasty incident in the tower in July 1972 during a storm. Three boys were killed there, supposedly struck by lightning. It was declared unsafe after that, closed for repairs and never reopened.'

'Come on.' Gloria was running up the stairs practically pulling Lawrence with her. Rufus, for once, was lost for words and stood staring at them.

'I thought you said you went to that school, didn't you know about the tower?'

'I said a school like that, I didn't know any of them had towers.'

'We have to get Barnyou, I bet he doesn't know about it either.' They said nothing more but their instant reaction said it all. Sawyer's lack of consistency in his accounts of the riots and his unwillingness to allow them to talk to the children, the strange group of friends the caretaker had told them was always visiting, including the very tall one Gloria remembered who had scowled at her.

Barnyou looked bewildered when Gloria almost physically dragged him out of the interview room where Senator Gwedu was being held for his own 'safety'.

'When you searched all those towers did you look at the one at GW Horton?'

Barnyou was baffled. 'Tower? Horton? What are you talking about Gloria?'

'Just think for a minute. Did you search the tower at GW Horton School?'

'No,' he was thinking now, 'no, there were no schools on the list apart from Holy Redeemer. We searched the Law Library, the two cathedrals, the Mansion of course, the army barracks on Camp Johnson Road and even the apartment blocks around the beach. Why?'

Gloria explained briefly their suspicions about Sawyer and the revelation there was a disused tower at the school.

'He's been playing a part, his story doesn't hold up. And I don't know why but I'm sure he is involved. Unless Gwedu has admitted to everything?'

'What? No, he has been playing games of course, he's admitted to that. He's been stirring things up, making speeches and even talking with the election monitors, waiting to take advantage of the President's trouble but he's got nothing to do with this.'

'Then leave him, get your men and let's go. We have only one hour before the President goes on air. Do we have any idea what decision she has made?'

'No, no-one has any idea what she is going to say except Dr Fofana, but the rumour is she will cancel the elections.'

It took another twenty minutes to assemble a joint team. The tension was palpable. With time so short they agreed a head-on attack was the only option. Barnyou and his team would arrest Sawyer and secure the building while Gloria and her team would then take the tower and search for Prince.

It was another silent drive to GW Horton. The streets were even emptier than they had been earlier that morning. It was simple. They were either on the right track or they weren't. They would either save the child, and possibly the nation, or they wouldn't. There wasn't much else to add.

They had all agreed on the need to be discreet, to get control of the tower before any alarm could be raised. The school entrance was deserted when they arrived and Barnyou's men impressed Gloria by their swift professional deployment. Two of them took up position at the gates as they went through, two more at the school entrance while the others covered the back exits, and in seconds the rest of them were walking quietly down to Sawyer's office. The look on Sawyer's face when they burst in was enough for Gloria: shock, anger and a touch of fear. The small office was full of men but they were taken by surprise and Barnyou's officers had them on the ground without any resistance. As soon as she knew they were secure Gloria and Lawrence headed back out to get to the tower. They had been told the entrance to the tower was from a small room off the canteen hall. When they got there they were met with the same blank walls they remembered from their previous visits.

'Check the room, come on.'

They moved around tapping the walls as they went but the answer was a lot simpler than that. The large cupboards they had seen on their first visit were not fixed to the wall as they had first thought. They were free standing and some pushing and shoving revealed that they were blocking a wooden door. It wasn't locked. Behind the door a set of stone steps led up into the darkness.

'I will go first with Lawrence and Lamine, and Alfred will follow. Izena will stay here with Ambrose to cover us.' Her tone brooked no argument. They nodded. 'Now, quietly, let's go.'

Those stone steps seemed to go on forever and the musty smell and the damp heat were so thick it felt as if they were walking through a physical barrier. Their initial silent charge slowed to a walk and then to a crawl. The darkness was absolute and they almost fell onto the small landing at the top of the stairs. A few moments of gathering their breath also gave time for their eyes to adjust and take in the outline of another wooden door from the faint light seeping out from around the frame. It was then that the high pitched squeal of Gloria's phone made them jump, the noise sounded incredibly loud in the enclosed space and before they lost the element of surprise completely Gloria turned the handle and pushed on the door.

A tall man was turning from the window as they entered. Gloria recognised him as the man who had glared at her in Sawyer's office on her last visit. She couldn't see his expression now but she could see the gun in his hand. It was pointed straight at her and as she struggled to raise her own gun, she heard two sharp cracks, not a deafening roar but still enough to kill her she thought as she fell to the floor and the room exploded in noise.

It was Lawrence's hand on her shoulder that she felt first and it took her a just a few moments to realise she had not been shot. The tall man was lying sprawled out in front of her with two neat holes in his chest and a spreading pattern of blood covering his white t-shirt. Lawrence, his pistol in his hand, was looking a bit shaken. Violence did not come naturally to him.

'Get up Gloria. Are you all right? I think you tripped over the rope.'

Feeling a little foolish Gloria stood up shaking his hand off her.

'I'm fine. Where's the child?'

Lawrence just pointed to a small figure in a chair. Lamine was untying the ropes and even from here Gloria could see he was alive. She looked at her watch. It was now eleven forty. They had twenty minutes before the President went on air. She crossed to the boy who was rubbing his hands and ankles, staring at them with apprehension.

'Prince, I am Inspector Gloria Sirleaf and I need to get you to your family as quickly as possible.' He was very thin and obviously weak but his eyes were bright and he managed a smile before nodding, but when he tried to stand his legs couldn't hold him. It was Lamine who caught him and then scooped him up as easily as if he was a baby.

'Be careful with him, let's get to the car. Lawrence, call the Mansion and tell the President we have her grandson. Alfred you and the others stay and clear up.'

Their relief was short-lived. Joining Barnyou downstairs they called all the numbers they had, including the President's own mobile but nothing was going through. The car radios were the same. The Mansion had been cut off, and they now had ten minutes to get through any number of checkpoints and deliver Prince to his grandmother before she went on air. Gloria's heart sank. They couldn't fail now surely.

'My car!' was all Barnyou said and she and Lawrence, who now had Prince in his arms, climbed in.

Gloria stared miserably out the window wondering if all her major cases were going to end with a death-defying dash in a car. But Barnyou surprised her. He turned left and headed for the beach. They bumped onto the sand and by keeping to the firm areas Barnyou had covered the distance to the Barracks in five minutes. The checkpoints at the Barracks and the back road to the Mansion were manned by police who recognised them and swung them open with no explanation needed. Gloria wasn't sure if this really counted as tight security but she was relieved nonetheless. They careered through the back entrance to the Mansion where they had found the body of Tony Kamara and were dashing through the empty kitchens with Prince when Amos Toweh appeared. He took a look at them and at Prince and without requiring any further explanation set off at a run down the long corridors.

Through the Mansion's intercom system they could hear the sound of the national anthem fading and a slight pause before the President, in grave tones, started speaking. For the first time in her life Gloria was thankful that there was no such thing as a short speech in Liberia, the long-winded introduction might just give them the extra moments they needed to reach the President.

Toweh led them past astonished security guards, none of whom attempted to stop them, and without knocking he ran into the President's office with all of them following behind. The President looked up and paused, thinking, as she admitted afterwards, that the coup had started already. They stood panting and sweating with Lawrence lifting Prince so the President could see him. Prince smiled and waved at her. She smiled back and then moved the papers she had in front of her away from the microphone and continued speaking, without notes, to a weary nation.

'I will keep my speech short today as I know many people are anxious about what is going to happen. I am very happy to announce that our elections will go ahead as planned and absolutely on schedule. I am even more happy to announce that thanks to the wonderful efforts of the national police, my grandson Prince is now safe and back with his family.' There were faint whoops of delight from some distant part of the Mansion. 'And those responsible for his kidnapping and for the terrible deaths of Anthony Keimouth and Tony Kamara are now,' she looked over at Gloria and Barnyou with a raised eyebrow and they both nodded vigorously, 'in custody. This has been a terrible time for many people, especially for the families of these children but we cannot allow anything to obstruct our path to rebuilding our country. As our country's motto says 'The Love of Liberty Brought Us Here' – I know some people object to it but this motto doesn't refer just to our forefathers coming from America, it's for all of us. The love and defence of liberty has brought all of us Liberians to this time and this place and it is that, and only that, that we should fight for. This is a time for unity. Let us look to the future as one nation, one people, and show the world that our war is over and we are healing, forgiving and re-building. God bless the republic.'

There was silence and then a noise like a distant rumble of thunder. Gloria felt the hairs on the back of her neck stand up as she realised that what they were listening to was the sound of Monrovia and its citizens clapping and cheering their President. Round and round the noise reverberated before dying away again to be replaced by the sound of the same citizens pouring back onto the streets to resume the daily struggle to earn enough money for food, clothes and school.

The President had taken Prince from Lawrence and was hugging him tightly. Gloria nudged Lawrence and Barnyou who were staring at the President, mouths open.

'Ok guys, happy ending over and we have an awful lot of clearing up to do I think.' Both Lawrence and Barnyou looked a little wistful, as if they wanted to stay and enjoy the moment for a bit longer but they followed her out.

Her phone rang again as they were leaving and Lawrence tutted loudly. 'That ring almost got us killed Gloria. Don't you have a mute button?'

'Don't *you* have a mute button?' muttered Gloria as she pulled it out.

She saw several missed calls from Sr Margaret and her heart sank. 'I need to make a call,' she said and stepped into an alcove off the long corridor. Margaret answered immediately.

'Gloria, sorry to keep calling but I'm afraid it's bad news. Alex died an hour ago. He never really regained consciousness. I am very sorry.'

Although it wasn't unexpected, the news still hurt. Just for a moment the light and the noise around her dimmed and she could think of nothing to say.

'Thanks Margaret, I hope it doesn't make things difficult for you.'

Margaret assured her they would take care of everything until Gloria could get to them.

She told Lawrence as they were driving back to headquarters and he wisely avoided any hugging or hand holding. He said he would go and collect Pascal and Mrs Anderson and they would go to the convent.

'You will probably have to make all the arrangements, Gloria. Will your uncle Hilary be able to organise the funeral?'

Gloria's uncle was the only funeral director in town who never seemed to be busy for reasons Gloria couldn't work out, but he had helped her out in the past.

'Yes, he will. I will talk to him tonight.'

Chapter Twenty-three

It was only the next day that Gloria realised the uneasy feeling she had had for many days had not left her. Sawyer and his group were all now in custody and the lengthy interrogation had started. Sawyer had already admitted to organising the elaborate plot to destabilise the government. It hadn't taken long to establish his connections with a network of illegal businesses, former rebels and foreign mercenaries who all needed an unstable Liberia to conduct their various activities, or to give them the protection from prosecution they needed. The tall man Lawrence had shot turned out to be a renegade army commander from Burkina Faso, and the one giving Sawyer his instructions. But they were all small fry, people who could dress as riot police, kidnap children, threaten and intimidate, they were not the leaders and Sawyer would say only that he was responsible. It was this that made Gloria feel uneasy. Sawyer was definitely responsible for much of the organisation but he was no more a mastermind than Daniel Varley was. He was obeying orders.

'Gloria, we have broken this ring, saved the country from war again, rescued the President's grandson and found the people responsible for killing the children. That's enough, don't you think?' Barnyou paused. 'I know the big people are still out there but with our resources I think we have done as much as we can. It's going to take us weeks to get all this sorted out as it is. Let it go, otherwise you will go crazy.'

'Look Barnyou, I know what you are saying is true but I can't just let it go. There's a piece of this terrible puzzle that is right in front of us and we are missing it. All these links with the Mansion, Sawyer wouldn't be able to kill a child and place the body inside the Mansion grounds would he?'

Barnyou shrugged. He couldn't see it, and he had enough to deal with.

'Anyway, we have to be at the Mansion this afternoon don't forget. The President is launching her 'Each One Teach One' education campaign and apparently we have to be present. She is insisting that everything goes ahead as planned. The Head of Protocol has sent a message to say we all have to be seated half an hour before it starts.'

'Oh, the famous Matilda. She will be there with her stop watch I suppose, we better not be late then.'

Once back in her office, Gloria called Ambrose. 'Those children, the ones who were kidnapped and then released, I hope you are bringing them to the event at the Mansion today?'

Ambrose looked surprised. 'I hadn't thought ma'am, I wasn't invited myself.'

'Well, they should be there. Can you get them here by one o'clock and I will take them?' He agreed and by one sharp the two boys, Abel and Kollie, were sitting on a bench outside her office. She was pleased to see they looked excited rather than fearful and their mothers or guardians had obviously scrubbed them for the occasion.

'Great. Ambrose, you can come too in case the children get scared.'

'I think they are fine ma'am.'

'I wasn't asking Ambrose.' Dragging small children to events was not Gloria's idea of fun but she felt it was important for them to be there, and Ambrose was good with children.

The main parlour of the Mansion was already filling up when they arrived and Gloria headed straight for seats near the front. She was stopped by Matilda Wesley, clipboard in hand, who didn't look at all happy to see her extra visitors.

'Inspector, who are these people?'

'They are my guests Matilda.'

'Your guests? What do you think this is, a village meeting or something? Only the President can invite people and *your* guests are not on my list. They will have to leave.'

Ambrose was already turning towards the exit when Gloria tapped him.

'Those seats near the front will be fine for us.'

Matilda Wesley was momentarily struck dumb.

'Are you mad?' she was hissing through clenched teeth 'Did you not hear what I said? Get these people out of here now.'

Gloria remained very calm. 'I don't think so Matilda. Now why don't you take your pencil and add their names to your list like a good girl eh?'

'How dare you, you nothing! How dare you talk to me like that!' Her composure had dropped completely and heads were turning as her raised voice and harsh tone pierced the low hum of conversation. Her voice cut through the room.

'Get them out of here or you will be sorry.'

Gloria glanced at the two children beside her who were now clinging to Ambrose with a terrified expression on their faces.

'Sorry to put you through this boys,' she patted Abel, 'but you have been a big help.'

'Matilda Wesley, I am arresting you for the kidnap and murder of Tony Cole and Anthony Keimouth, for conspiracy to overthrow the government and for...' she hadn't thought this part through, 'other things connected with public disorder.'

Matilda Wesley looked around the parlour but apart from Barnyou and his men posted at all the exits, she was in a room full of the great and good of Liberian society. In a final gesture of helplessness she let the clipboard fall to the floor and allowed herself to be taken away.

There was no time for any further discussion as the President, who had been forewarned, sent a message that she was going to start the launch. There was just time to send Ambrose out with Abel and Kollie to go buy them ice cream, calm them down and then take them home before the speeches started. It was, Gloria felt in her bones, going to be a long afternoon.

'There were too many gaps in our case,' Gloria was explaining to the Chief the afternoon's events. It was five o'clock and they were sitting around the Chief's desk.

'We knew Sawyer was involved but I couldn't get rid of that feeling,' she looked at Barnyou and Lawrence but they didn't react, 'that there had to be someone else, right here who was controlling him. Someone who had access to the Mansion and knew all the President's plans – and someone who was a woman. The children talked about being terrorised by a tall woman and all Sawyer's people were men. So I figured this woman must be the real organiser. When Barnyou reminded me about attending the launch this afternoon, I remembered Matilda. Tall, efficient, and the only woman with complete access to the President and the Mansion grounds, and surely the most organised person in the city. I needed the children to identify the 'voice' they had heard threatening them, and to do that I had to make her annoyed enough to drop that calm exterior of hers.'

'Well, you certainly have a talent for annoying people Gloria. Thank goodness you put it to good use this time.'

'Thank you sir.' Gloria grinned.

He went on. 'She has admitted nothing but her address book makes interesting reading. Look, in her job she met everyone who came to the Mansion, and she used her position to build up her own network of corrupt business people, disgruntled military, freelance mercenaries, the mad and the bad actually. All people who needed an unstable Liberia to conduct their business. But why, is what I keep asking myself, what's in it for Matilda? If it was money, why couldn't she just take a few bribes like a lot of people do?'

'Well, it wasn't about money sir was it? Not for her anyway.' Gloria sat back in the chair. 'For her and the rest of her family it was about power surely. They wanted to bring down the government, that's what they were trying to do, so they could step in. Who knows, maybe she even saw herself as the next president. But whatever their long term plans, she was prepared to do anything – even torture and kill children – to make them happen. That kind of ruthlessness is hard to understand. And she has shown no remorse for anything.'

Gloria shrugged, exhausted.

'All that killing and madness to run a country where we can't even keep the air conditioning on during the President's speech, I really don't get it.'

The Chief made one of his non-committal faces. He had just been confirmed in his post as Police Director and was taking it very seriously.

'Now we just have to get Africanus Varley and I can get some sleep.'

The Chief groaned. 'It's not going to happen Gloria. He has the best lawyers in town, his son has confessed to everything and has taken sole responsibility for all the killings there and your mysterious source, Nessee, has disappeared. We are not going to get him. You will just have to live with that I'm afraid.'

Gloria neither shook her head nor agreed. 'I need to go now anyway sir. We still have a lot to do.'

'You need to slow down Gloria, at least for a day or two.'

'As Amos Toweh said to me sir, "if you slow down it just gives your enemies a chance to catch up with you," and we all know how many enemies I have now. I really think it's better if I just keep moving.'